The Thief of Love

Bengali Tales from Court and Village

TRANSLATED BY

EDWARD C. DIMOCK, Jr.

THE UNIVERSITY OF CHICAGO PRESS

This work was developed pursuant to a contract
between the University of Chicago and
the United States Office of Education,
Department of Health, Education, and Welfare.

ISBN: 0-226-15235-9 (clothbound); 0-226-15236-7 (paperbound)
Library of Congress Catalog Card Number: 63–11396

THE UNIVERSITY OF CHICAGO PRESS, CHICAGO 60637
THE UNIVERSITY OF CHICAGO PRESS, LTD., LONDON

Published 1963. Second Impression 1975. Composed and printed in the United States of America

The Thief of Love

FOR LORAINE

Preface

IT HAS NOT BEEN very long since the discovery by the West of the value of studying the so-called "vernacular languages" of South Asia. We have of course a long and rich tradition of the study of the classical languages of that area —Sanskrit, Persian, and Pali, but with the exception of a few isolated nineteenth-century scholars such as William Carey of the Fort William College at Calcutta and Sir George Grierson, Western scholars have until recently neglected the modern languages. The historical reasons for this are clear enough. The founders of Sanskrit study in the West were concerned with their discovery of the closeness of the relationship between Sanskrit and the classical languages of the West, Latin and Greek; but Western scholarship in Sanskrit has been outstanding, not only in the grammar of that language, but also in its immense literature and in the culture which that literature embodies.

More recently, the attention of Western scholars has been called to the fact that the languages descended from Sanskrit are also worthy of study, not only as languages, but for their literatures and the cultures, not always the same as that represented by Sanskrit, transmitted by these literatures. In the United States, the reasons for this new direction are two.

The first is that studies by anthropologists, both Indian and American, have shown us that there are many varieties of the culture of South Asia—that the "great tradition" represented by Sanskrit is only one in a complex of traditions. For a long time, to scholars in both South Asia and the West, Sanskrit literature and thought towered so high that it hid all else in its shadow. In India itself the literature and thought of the regional languages has long been referred to with apology, and this has been reflected by the West, not in contempt for the regional languages and literatures, but by ignoring them. Modern anthropologists and linguists feel that all languages and cultures are subjects for study and this approach to South Asian languages and cultures has uncovered a wealth of literary and historical data. We are becoming aware of why some scholars, like Sukumar Sen in Bengali, have given so much of their lives to the study of regional traditions.

The second reason for this rediscovery of India is a more practical one, and is itself two-fold. In the first place, more and more young scholars of history, anthropology, political science, etc., are going to South Asia to work. Not only they, but the departments of their universities, are becoming increasingly aware of the necessity that scholars in these and other fields should be able to deal with both the written and spoken regional languages. The attitudes of scholarship are changing. It is becoming clear that a historian of nineteenth-century India, for example, must know at least one regional language. Familiarity with a regional language, far from being restrictive, allows a scholar not only to gain knowledge of a single area, but also insight into all the other areas of South Asia; it helps him to learn other languages of the same family with greater ease.

In the second place, recognition of the significance of regional languages has been shown in the financial support which has been generously forthcoming from a number of sources, both for students working in these languages and for research. For support for the work represented by this volume, for example, I am most grateful to the Ford Foundation through the University of Chicago Committee on Southern Asian Studies, and to the United States Government Department of Health, Education, and Welfare, in contract with whom a large part of the work has been done.

The purposes of this volume are several. First, I have wanted to show that there is a good deal of enjoyment as well as enlightenment to be had from study of the regional literatures of South Asia. Secondly, the "medieval" period of India—that period from the thirteenth through the eighteenth centuries—is one which has been largely unknown to the West except through the chronicles of the Muslim courts and the records of the British, French, Portuguese, and occasional Western travelers of other nationalities. Material in regional languages for the study of this period is there, not only in the relatively few texts which have been printed, but in the incredible number of manuscripts in libraries and in private possession, which have never been examined by scholars, much less printed. Finally, this volume has come from a need made clear in course work at the University of Chicago: there are precious few translations from the literature of the medieval period of any South Asian language.

Those who look for deep scholarship in the translations will be disappointed; and I should be distressed if I thought that they were being judged as such. I have often taken liberties with the Bengali which careful scholarship would not allow; I have avoided as much as possible explanatory notes and other apparatus which so often hinders reading pleasure. When I did the translations, I had in mind my students' needs; I did them also for my own enjoyment. If the reader gets from them but half the fun I had in doing them, I shall be more than satisfied.

For help in preparing and typing the manuscript, I owe a debt of gratitude to Miss Judith Aronson, Administrative Assistant of the South Asian Languages Program of this University. My thanks also go to Dr. Somdev Bhattacharji of the University of Chicago, for his invaluable assistance in checking the translation of the *Vidyā-Sundara,* to Mr. Samir Ghosh, of the South Asian Languages Program of this University, for his help with some of the problems of the *Manasā-maṅgal* text, to Miss Naomi Loefer, for her help in preparing the glossary, to Dr. John W. Spellman, for his very helpful suggestions, and to various colleagues for their critical comments on the translations themselves. For her general encouragement of translation from Asian languages, and in particular for her optimism regarding this book, I want to thank Mrs. Bonnie R. Crown, Publications Director of the Asia Society. I wish also to acknowledge a debt of long standing, to Dr. Sukumar Sen, of the University of Calcutta, who has both in correspondence and in person given me unsparingly of his time and great knowledge.

Contents

Introduction

1. INDIA AND BENGAL

It is becoming increasingly clear that it is as difficult to speak of "India" as it is to speak of "Europe." As one does not attempt to deal with the literature, let us say, of France, Poland, and Italy in the same breath, so one should not attempt to deal with that of Kerala, Kashmir, and Bengal. To be sure, India as a unity is a political fact, and to a certain extent an anthropological fact: caste, Brahmanical ritual, certain types of legends and beliefs are found throughout the sub-continent. And India as a unity is again to a certain extent a historical fact: the great Sanskritic tradition lies beneath ritual, philosophy, and parts of the literature, even in those Dravidian lands whose languages and cultures come from a non-Sanskritic stock.

When we considered India at all, most people of my generation, growing up in the thirties and forties, thought of it in terms of the British Empire.[1] A few of us had a nodding acquaintance with Indian thought through the New England Transcendentalists; a few read Schopenhauer; a very few had read the work of the philologists who were concerned with the Sanskrit language, and thus with Sanskrit texts, through studies of Indo-European linguistics. But for most, India was a British land, and her culture, represented to us in movie versions of Kipling stories, was that of Britain, re-enacted in a tropical and foreign land.

Then, the story goes, here as elsewhere, came the war. Many whom we now know as scholars of modern India were among the Americans stationed in that country. Through them the picture of India changed from one characterized by heroic charges on the Northwest Frontier, Maharajas, tigers, and ruby-eyed idols, to that of a culture of far greater complexity than that conceived by Schopenhauer, the Transcendentalists, or the philologists (with the possible exception of Sir George Grierson and a few others). The "Indian language" is not Sanskrit—a word synonymous with "esoteric" to many of us in school—but is, in fact, a number of languages, some descended from Sanskrit, some not. "Indian religion," it appeared, is neither that so sympathetically followed by robed cultists in California nor the worship of jewel-eyed idols, suggesting mysteries too dark to be thought upon, but a complex of monotheistic Islam, Zoroastrianism, even Judaism and Christianity, all of

[1] See the data gathered by Harold Isaacs in his excellent book *Scratches on Our Minds* (New York, 1958).

these in various combinations with Hinduism, itself a complex of myth and exceedingly intricate and refined theology. Nor is "Indian philosophy" the monolithic "towering Vedanta," the monistic theory which we had been led to believe representative, but a complex of philosophies and theologies, including systems of dualism and devotion so close to Christian views that enthusiastic Christians have been reluctant to believe them really Indian. Finally, "Indian literature," as well as the delightful stories and lovely poetry which had been introduced to the West by Sanskrit scholars, comprises a complex of literatures of considerable antiquity in each of the regional languages. In short, it began to be realized that the culture of the Indian sub-continent, far from being either British or monolithic, is one of overwhelming complexity, not to be comprehended in its entirety by any single individual. Not only is there the Sanskritic culture, itself rich and varied, but also within the sub-continent many sub-cultures, each of them equal or almost equal to the Sanskritic one in richness and variety.

It is, to say the least, unlikely that large bodies of Westerners will begin to learn all fourteen major languages of the sub-continent, together with Sanskrit and Persian. If this assumption is correct, perhaps it will not be amiss to suggest that there are three ways in which India can be approached, each of the three yielding different and complementary results. The first way is to study the classical culture of India, through Sanskrit; the second, is to study India through one of the regional languages—for insofar as India is a unity, each regional culture is a microcosm;

and the third way, is to study the regional culture for its own sake. As I have tried to suggest, none of these studies will be without its satisfactions.

There is another dimension to all this. When, in the tenth century or so, the Indo-Aryan regional languages became far enough removed from their great ancestor Sanskrit[2] to begin to be languages in their own right, the two types of forces which can currently be seen at work on India's view of herself began to be objectivized. One can see from Jawaharlal Nehru's *The Discovery of India* that modern pride of nationhood is at least partly based on the view of India as ancient, great, and unified. The other force is most obviously represented by the recent separatist movements based on regional culture as defined by language: the demand for linguistic states. The distinction between these two forces is not as clear, however, as is at first apparent. For, while there is jealousy and conflict of loyalties, scholars and critics seem to be far more ready to recognize the debt of modern thinkers and writers to the Sanskritic tradition, to the Upanishads, to great classical writers such as Kālidāsa, than they do to recognize the debt of these thinkers and writers to their regional traditions. Yet such a debt is clearly there. I am sure that the fact of belonging to Bengal connects such early writers as those

[2] There are three major language families (excluding Tibeto-Burman) in South Asia. The languages of the Indo-Aryan family, descended through Sanskrit, are Bengali, Hindi, Gujarati, Sindhi, Assamese, Oriya, Panjabi, Nepali, Singhalese, Marathi, and Kashmiri. The other language families are Dravidian (Tamil, Telegu, Kannada, and Malayalam), and Munda (tribal languages). The tenth century is a very rough estimate indeed for the beginnings of the development of the "New Indo-Aryan."

represented in this volume with the Bengali moderns at least as much as the classical tradition connects writers and thinkers of modern Bengal with their counterparts from other areas of India.[3]

2. TYPES OF MEDIEVAL LITERATURE

BENGALI LITERATURE, like that of other Indo-Aryan languages of India, dates from about the tenth century A.D. The language is a direct descendant, through an eastern branch, of Sanskrit, and stands in relation to that great classical language much as Italian in relationship to Latin. Bengali today is spoken by about seventy-five million people in India and Pakistan, and its literature, many people feel, is the most vigorous and extensive of all the languages of modern South Asia. The literary tradition is unbroken, from the ninth or tenth century Buddhist esoteric texts called *caryā-padas,* to the present. It is somewhat surprising that little is known in the West about a literature so old and so rich.

Some scholars have concerned themselves with the ancient literature, and many with the modern. But only a few have dipped into what lies between. Perhaps the reason for this is that suggested above—that both within Bengal and without, the hold of Sanskrit has been too strong on all except a few. Even that part of Bengali literature which

[3] I have tried to point out that the roots of Rabindranath Tagore lie at least as deeply in older Bengali tradition as in non-Bengali tradition in an article "Rabindranath Tagore—Greatest of the Bāuls" (*Journal of Asian Studies,* 1959).

was non-Sanskritic was measured, not against itself, but against Sanskrit literary and esthetic values.[4] A nineteenth-century writer, forced to write in Bengali because of his position as teacher at the Fort William College in Calcutta, justified his doing so by stating that of all the regional languages of India Bengali was, after all, "the closest to Sanskrit." The result of this attitude, which still persists in some quarters and is the basis for not a little literary "criticism," is not only that a great oral literature is still largely unknown, but also that only a minute proportion of the manuscript material in the language has ever seen the light of day. Manuscripts lie unread in libraries, in temples, in village houses, in boxes in family storage places; they lie decaying, eaten by insects, to be washed away in floods. I have said that the literature of what I shall call the "medieval period" (thirteenth to late eighteenth centuries) is rich. In fact, no one knows how rich it really is.

Medieval Bengali literature falls more or less naturally into three broad categories. The first is the literature of the main religious stream, that of Vaiṣṇavism; this we shall treat in the present volume only in passing. The second, which we might call "village poetry," is represented by the last selection, the Behulā episode from the *Manasā-maṅgal* poem of Ketakā-dāsa. And the third is court poetry, which fashions itself largely on the Sanskrit *Kāvya* of the classical period. An example of such court poetry is the *Vidyā-Sundara* poem of Bhāratchandra, the first selection in the volume. A remark or two on classical court poetry may

[4] Just as some critics tend to measure modern Bengali literature against that in English. See J. C. Ghosh, *Bengali Literature* (Oxford, 1949).

serve to put into focus both the closeness of this type of Bengali poetry to its Sanskrit progenitor, and the differences between the style of the court and that of the village.

3. SOME ASPECTS OF COURT POETRY

The Sanskrit word for "literature," which appears in many of the regional languages as well, is *sāhitya,* "a joining" of word and sense. This statement—that in order to express a meaning you have to express a word—is not as completely obvious as it might seem.

There is a school of thought which believes that in a particular place in a particular poem there is only one word which fits. In this sense, true meaning is carried by the word. But this is also no simple matter, for words can have several levels of symbolic value. "There is a lamb in the field"—means that a four-legged woolly animal is standing in the field eating grass. "You are a lamb"—means that, in the opinion of the speaker, the person addressed possesses certain qualities of the lamb. Or one can say, quoting Blake,

> Alas, the time will come when a man's
> worst enemies
> Shall be those of his own house and
> family, in a Religion
> Of Generation to destroy, by Sin and
> Atonement, happy Jerusalem,
> The Bride and Wife of the Lamb.

The estheticians say that of these various levels of meaning, the third is the best, the most poetic, because it is the most suggestive. The second one is of some poetic value, being the base of such figures as metaphor. The first is, for poetry, useless.

The second concept to be borne in mind is that called *rasa,* a difficult word and a difficult concept to translate. It might best be illustrated by this example, of which the estheticians are particularly fond, taken from the drama.

On the stage, actors are playing a sad or painful scene such as the abduction of Sītā in the *Rāmāyaṇa.* The player is depicting the emotion which Sītā, assumedly, felt; but clearly, the anguish which the player is showing is not the same as that which the woman herself felt while undergoing the experience. The audience, furthermore, is yet another step removed from the passion felt by the original Sītā. If the audience were not so removed, say the estheticians, people could not witness such a scene and afterwards say, "I enjoyed it." The esthetic experience, then, is dissociated from personal pleasure and pain, dissociated from personal interest and involvement. It is a condition of depersonalized pleasure. This is *rasa.* We shall see, in the *Vidyā-Sundara* poem, that the poet, even in his *bhaṇitās*—the signature lines in which he makes remarks to his characters—stands apart from them; he inserts nothing, not even himself, which might disturb the crystal-like unity of the *rasa* which he is trying to communicate to us. For that which would involve us personally in any way would shatter the effect.

Each work of poetry or drama has a *rasa* which is dominant, and it is toward causing his audience to appreciate and experience this *rasa* that the poet directs his whole art. His subject matter, his words, his images, his linguistic devices—all these are combined by the poet's skill to bring the *rasa* to the audience, and all must be entirely appropriate to the *rasa* which the poet treats; no image must carry a suggestion which would jar this unity.[5]

This type of court poetry is particularly difficult to translate, for the audience has as much responsibility for its success as the poet. It was written for the *sahṛdaya,* "the man with heart," the man of cultured taste; it assumes a knowledge and a background such that a single image can arouse a whole series of associations. This might best be seen by a couple of examples. The first, in the erotic *rasa,* is from the Sanskrit *Gīta-govinda* of Jayadeva, court poet to the Emperor Lakṣmaṇa Sena, who ruled Bengal toward the end of the twelfth century. Krishna's cause is being pleaded to Rādhā by one of her companions:

> The *malaya* [i.e., sandal-bearing] wind blows, bearing love; the flowers burst into bloom, piercing the heart of him who is separated from you; in this separation, O my friend, Vanamāli [i.e., Krishna] pines away.
>
> The moon-beams burn him; he is as a dead man. Love's arrow strikes him and he weeps, his despondency increased. Separated from you, O my friend, Vanamāli pines away.

About the figure "sandal-bearing wind" two things should be known. There are certain times of year appropriate for lovers. One is the approach of the rainy season, when the

[5] Types of imagery, like other categories in poetics, are exhaustively listed by the poeticians. For example, there are twenty-one types of the figure called "comparison": "your face is like the moon," "your moon-face," "the moon seems stained, next to your face," "the *cakora* birds are delighted when they see your face (thinking it the moon)," etc. See S. K. De, *Sanskrit Poetics* (Calcutta, 1961). Bhāratchandra treats two types of *rasas-hāsya,* the humorous, and *śṛṅgāra,* the erotic.

clouds begin to gather and the air is heavy with rain and with perfume—"bearing love." The wind then, scented with sandal-wood, is blowing from the south. It is the time when lovers should be together. It is more poignant that they are apart. The next two images are based on paradox: the natural qualities of things and the change of these qualities under certain conditions. But there is here not only the natural softness of flowers and their cruel sharpness for lovers in separation, but interwoven also is the image of Kāma, god of love, the arrows of whose bow are made of flowers. These flower-sharp arrows enter the lover's heart through eyes and nose, and pierce it. And, finally, "moonbeams burn." The moon is cool. The image is an old one: the moon is cool as camphor, and as refreshing.

Let us look briefly at another, this one from Kālidāsa's *Kumārasambhava* (3.48):

Like a rain-bearing cloud without the violence of the rain, like a waveless lake of waters, like a lamp-flame, sheltered from the wind and steady, [he sat, for] his internal-moving breaths [winds —*mārutam*] had been restrained.

The images themselves are clear. But again, the suggestions might be less so.

The passage comes from that part of Kālidāsa's poem called "The Destruction of Kāma," in which the god of love attempts to entice Śiva from his austere meditation, and Śiva, in anger, burns Kāma with fire from his eye. The verse here is descriptive of Śiva seated in meditation. Let us look at only two of the images.

"Like a rain-bearing cloud without the violence of the rain": again there is the rain-cloud, the symbol of a glad and gentle time, a time for lovers. But there is no rain: the cloud does not fulfil its promise. The earth, the goddess in love with Śiva does not receive fulfilment. There is no violence: there is only the calmness of Śiva's meditation. "Like a lamp-flame, sheltered from the wind and steady . . .": Śiva is Rūdra, the Vedic god of storms, whose servants and companions are the winds. But here, within the storm-cloud, the winds are stilled. The lamp of meditation burns unflickering. The winds, Rūdra's servants, but also the internal breaths of the cosmic Śiva, are quiet. The breath has been controlled, in Yogic discipline. Here, in the stillness, is extreme potency, controlled power, the very essence of the ascetic.

As we shall see, Bhāratchandra strives toward the same ends, in much the same way, and he was a master of his craft. His orientation was toward Sanskrit, in both the form and language of his poetry. Not only did he write in Sanskrit (a fairly extensive section of his *Vidyā-Sundara* poem is in that language, the rest being in a highly Sanskritized form of Bengali), but he used many of the classical Sanskrit meters for his Bengali poetry.[6] One of his compromises with his Bengali medium was that he rhymed his lines.

4. METER AND THE VILLAGE POETRY

MOST BENGALI POETS of the period, being less skilled and learned than Bhāratchandra, usually limited themselves to

[6] See my brief paper "Notes on the Influence of Sanskrit on Bengali Literature," in *Source Readings in Indian Civilization* (University of Chicago, Syllabus Division, 1959).

variations on two basic types of meter. The first was that old Bengali meter, familiar in oral recitation, called *payāra*. *Payāra* consists of coupled lines of fourteen or sixteen syllables each, with caesura after the first eight. The rhyme scheme was that of the couplet, i.e., aa, bb, etc. This meter, with variations obtained by increasing the number of syllables per line, was mostly used for the narrative portions of a poem; it had the virtues of simplicity and directness, if not of elegance. The other basic type of meter, a Sanskrit meter popular with Jayadeva and used by Bengali poets of both court and village, was the *tripadī* ("three-part line"). *Tripadī*, unlike *payāra*, is a form capable of considerable elegance, and was usually used for the more lyric parts of the poem. Again, variations are possible through numbers of syllables per line and here also through the rhyme scheme. Some *tripadī* rhymes are aab, ccb:[7]

kaliṅga nagare chaaṛi (a) prajaa laya ghara baaṛi (a)
  naanaa jaati biirera nagare (b)
biirera paaiyaa paana (c) baśila musulmaana (c)
  paścima dika biira dila taare (b)

Leaving the city of Kalinga, his subjects,
of many castes, took all their belongings
to Vīra's city. On the invitation of
Vīra, Muslims also settled there; Vīra
gave the westernmost part to them.

Another popular type of rhyme scheme was abc, abc, etc.[8]

[7] The verse is from the sixteenth-century *Caṇḍī-maṅgal* of Munkundarām Cakravarti.

[8] From a Vaiṣṇava *pada* attributed to the fifteenth-century poet Vidyāpati.

aaju rajanii haama (a) bhaage pohaayalu (b)
  pekhalu piya mukha candaa (c)
jibana jaubana (a) śaphala kari maanalu (b)
  daśa diśa bhela nira daṇḍaa (c)

This day the long night has ended, and fate has been kind to me; I have seen the moon-like face of my beloved. My life, my youth have been fulfilled, and all my world is bright.

For, except for the theological and historical-biographical literature of the Vaiṣṇavas, the great part of Bengali literature of the medieval period (all poetry) was meant to be chanted or sung. If you go today into the villages of Bengal, you can hear, in the evening, an old man, seated in the ring of soft light thrown by a lantern, reciting the Rāmāyaṇa story according to the great Bengali poet Kritivāsa of the fifteenth century. Or if you go to a village during the festival of Manasā, the snake goddess, you can hear in this same way the long and ancient saga of the goddess as told by Ketakā-dāsa or other poets of many centuries ago.

This is a literature quite different from that of the courts. The court poetry is designed for the intellect, and for an audience attuned to the subtleties of poetry; the poetry of the village is for listeners of simple taste but keen awareness of their surroundings. Compare with the above this image from the *Manasā-maṅgal:*

In those depths the *bodālya*-fish lived, great fish with heads and gills like blacksmiths' bellows . . . and all around the craft the crocodiles, their backs like saws, rose to the surface and sank down again.

It is simple, unadorned, not very subtle, but very vivid. There are no suggestions or innuendoes, but there is, I think, a remarkable vigor and strength.

There is another basic difference. The poets of the villages, perhaps unintentionally, mingled with their records of mythology and legend the chronicle of the rural people of Bengal. Throughout the *maṅgal* poems especially, we find information about Bengali society of older times.[9] We learn, in the *Manasā-maṅgal* episode in this volume, that the merchant Cando traded in poppy-seeds and cloth, perhaps with Southeast Asia. We learn the customs of the great Kāyastha caste. From the sixteenth-century *Caṇḍī-maṅgal* of Mukundarām, we learn the social order of the day, and so on. These poems, not being part of the great Sanskritic tradition, changed with the times; and each new poet chronicled that which he saw about him.

And, finally, the poems of the village reflect the struggle of man with nature, and the dignity of people who live close to the soil and the ever-flooding river. In neither court nor village poetry do we find that penetrating insight into the majesty or sadness of the human heart which we are accustomed to call beauty; such psychological probing is not in either tradition. We do, however, find in the village poetry an almost epic quality in man's striving against a hostile nature, for instance in Cando's defiance of the snake goddess. This struggle is a form of *hybris*; the poet has no sympathy for the man in his defiance of

[9] See the introduction to the *Manasā-maṅgal* episode translated in this volume. One of the few good studies making use of the *maṅgal* material is Phulrenu Datta, *La société bengalie au XVIIe siècle* (Paris, 1938).

the gods, but despite the poet, the man is dignified and strong. He is a man unknown to the poets of the court.[10]

[10] I have not attempted, in this brief Introduction, even to sketch the history of Bengali literature, as there are several full books on the subject available in English. I refer the interested reader to Sukumar Sen, *History of Bengali Literature* (New Delhi, 1960), Dinesh Chandra Sen, *A History of Bengali Language and Literature* (2d edition; Calcutta University, 1954), and the less scholarly but eminently readable J. C. Ghosh, *Bengali Literature* (Oxford, 1949).

The Vidyā-Sundara of Bhāratchandra

Introduction

THE POET Bhāratchandra Rāy, who was given the title "Guṇākara" ("The Incarnation of Excellence") was born in 1712. He was one of four sons of a wealthy Brahmin of the village of Pēro in the middle of the Bhursuṭ area of Burdwan.[1] Bhāratchandra was married young, and for some unknown reason left his home at an early age and settled in a village near Hooghly, where he studied Sanskrit and Persian. He returned to his father's house about 1737 and undertook, at the direction of his father, the management of the family estates, which were leaseheld from the Rājā

[1] The biographical information is drawn from the introduction to the *Bhāratcandrer granthābali*, ed. Brajendranāth Bāndyopādhyāy and Sajanikānta Dās (Calcutta: Baṅgīya sāhitya pariṣad, 1950), which edition, together with that from the Basumati Press, Calcutta, was used for the translation of the *Vidyā-Sundara,* and from Sukumar Sen, *History of Bengali Literature* (New Delhi: Sahitya Akademi, 1960).

of Burdwan. When the Rājā died in 1740, the estates were confiscated. Bhāratchandra attempted an appeal against the confiscation to the Rājā's widow, but was thrown into prison unheard. Somehow he escaped and managed to make his way to Puri in Orissa, a city sacred to those of Vaiṣṇava sects. He was there initiated into a mendicant Vaiṣṇava order. Shortly afterwards he began a pilgrimage to Vṛndāvana, the holy place of Krishna, but was discovered on the way by a relative and conducted back to his father's house in safety. But his family was destitute, and soon Bhāratchandra left his home again to find support for them. He went to Chundernagore, then a French possession, and there he found employment with an agent of the French government. This agent soon discovered Bhāratchandra's literary talents, and sent him to the Rājā Krishnachandra Rāy of Krishnagar, a famous patron of poets and scholars. Bhāratchandra became the court poet of Rājā Krishnachandra, with a good salary and grants of land. To his new home he brought his father and family. Bhāratchandra died in 1760 at the age of forty-eight.

Although Bhāratchandra had composed some minor poems during his first sojourn near Hooghly, he blossomed forth as a major poet under the patronage of the Rājā. He wrote his masterpiece, the *Annadā-maṅgal* ("Eulogy of the Food-giving Goddess"), in 1752 or 1753. The *Annadā-maṅgal* is a trilogy of independent poems in honor of the goddess Kālī and of his patron. The first poem of the trilogy is called *Annadā-maṅgal,* and tells the Puranic story of Śiva and Pārvatī, with one or two original embellishments by the poet. The second part is the *Vidyā-Sundara,* an erotic romance based upon an old theme, the only religious aspect of which is that the goddess blesses in extremely practical ways her ardent devotees. The third part of the trilogy is the *Mānsiṃha,* a historically-oriented romance about the conflict of the Emperor Jahangir with Rājā Pratāpāditya of Jessore, the traditional founder of Rājā Krishnachandra's family.

The *Vidyā-Sundara* is considered to be the best work Bhāratchandra ever wrote. The story is, in brief, that of a princess who has vowed that only he who can defeat her in debate can marry her. Her intelligence and learning are such that, though long past maturity, she remains unmarried. Finally a prince appears who defeats her both intellectually and physically, and, in various clever ways, begins to visit her nightly in her room. She becomes pregnant. The prince, in a wonderful scene, is apprehended by the guards, and is about to be executed when the goddess makes her appearance. The story, of course, ends happily, but not without some delightful and witty by-play. The theme is old. Some historians of Bengali literature, perhaps ignoring the erotic tradition of Jayadeva's *Gitā-govinda,* and unable to believe that a Hindu Bengali girl would allow herself to become involved in a situation such as the one in which the princess found herself, say that the story must have come from Persian literature. There are, however, several short Sanskrit poems, including the 54-*śloka* (couplet) *Vidyā-sundara* and the 546-*śloka Vidyā-sundara upākhyānam,* which deal with it,[2] although these are admittedly of uncertain date.

In Bengali, many poets both before and after Bhāratchandra dealt with the Vidyā-Sundara theme. Among those who

[2] See *Bhāratcandrer granthābalī, bhumikā,* pp. 9 ff.

preceded Bhāratchandra are a Muslim, Shāh Birid Khān, and several Hindus—Govinda-dāsa, Śrīdhara, and Krishnarāma. Among those who followed him, most of them from the late eighteenth century, are Rādhākānta Miśra, Nidhirām Chakravarti, Madhusūdana Chakravarti, and, somewhat surprisingly, the great Śākta devotional poet Rāmprasād Sen.[3] Bhāratchandra's version, however, is considered the best of them all.

The Vidyā-Sundara theme, being sophisticated and urbane, was a favorite one in the upper social strata of Bhāratchandra's day. But even the popularity of the theme cannot wholly account for the amazing success of Bhāratchandra's version. It was Bhāratchandra's own touch, light, witty, elaborate, and to the taste of the esthetes, which dominated the literary and sophisticated circles of Calcutta until well into the nineteenth century. For Bhāratchandra was a master of his art; and his art was by intention more decorative than profound, aimed more at the courtiers than the ascetics, at the men of culture rather than the philosophers.

The imagery which Bhāratchandra uses is largely unoriginal, though often originally phrased. It is for the most part the imagery of the Sanskrit court poetry of the high classical period, and the court tradition itself was never one of great creativity. But the refinement and grace which the Sanskrit court poetry did possess appealed very strongly to Bhāratchandra. One or two examples will indicate the extent of this influence.[4]

[3] Sen, *op. cit.*, p. 166.

[4] All but the last of the following Sanskrit examples are from L. D. Barnett's translation of a portion of the *Bṛhatkathā Mañjarī;* the last is from Jayadeva's *Gītā-govinda.* Bengali examples are all from Bhāratchandra.

Sanskrit: "The female swan of beauty was brightly displayed in the pair of her slender legs."

Bengali: "He who has never seen her thinks that a swan is graceful."

Sanskrit: "She bore hips which were rods of the plantain tree for the peacock of dalliance."

Bengali: "Her hips are like young plantain trees, more graceful than those of a deer."

Sanskrit: "She bore a line of curls like a row of bees on the lotus of her face."

Bengali: "Her brows are like black bees on the lotus-blossom."

Sanskrit: "Thy long-lashed lotus-eyes, lustrous and meek; thy nose a *tila*-bud; thy teeth like rows of *kunda*-petals. . . ."

Bengali: "Her eyes like lotus-blossoms . . . her nose is like a *tila*-flower, her teeth like *kunda*-petals. . . ."

But whatever might be said of his want of originality, it is clear that he accomplished what he set out to do—to amuse, decorate, perhaps titillate a little. Giving pleasure to the listener (or, in our case, the reader) was his purpose; profundity was not his concern. Sometimes his wit bites a little deep, especially into the more bruised and softened sides of human nature. But if he finds the core rotten he does not let on. His poetry is gay and all in fun. This is part of his charm.

Unfortunately for the translator, however, the greater part of Bhāratchandra's charm lies not in his imagery, nor even in his wit, but in his language. On the most superficial level, his language is difficult. He writes, in fact, in three languages. The poem is mostly, of course, in a highly Sanskritized form of Bengali. There are also long passages of Sanskrit, as when Sundar described the beauty of Vidyā to her father the king in fifty long Sanskrit *ślokas*. There are also passages in Brajabhāṣa, a form of Hindi, as when the messenger converses with king near the end of the poem. But it is not primarily his variety of language which makes Bhāratchandra difficult to translate. Dinesh Chandra Sen, one of the great Bengali literary historians, despite his somewhat puritan prejudice against Bhāratchandra, comments on the *Vidyā-Sundara* thus:[5]

> The niceties (of the poem) are somewhat curtailed and the absurdities often reclaimed by a sweet jingle of words which please the ear like the warbling of birds . . . without, however, conveying any clear meaning.

Such a comment is to a certain extent justified. There are many passages in which a modern critic would feel that the language has completely run away with any content. For example, this description of the goddess Kālī, near the end of the poem:

> caṇḍa-muṇḍa-muṇḍa-khaṇḍi khaṇḍa-muṇḍa-maalike //
> laṭṭa paṭṭa dirgha jaṭṭa mukta-keśa-jaalike //
> dhakka dhakka takka takka agnicandra-bhaalike //
> liha liha lolajiha lakka lakka saajike /
> srikka ḍhakka bhakka bhakka rakta-raaji-raajike //

This means, roughly,

> O cutter of the head of the demon Caṇḍa, weaver of the garland of severed heads, O thou whose matted mass of hair falls loose and long, whose luster is more dazzling [lit. "dizzy-making"] than that of fire and the moon, whose tongue lolls out, rolling and avaricious, gulping and gushing forth stream on stream of blood . . .

[5] D. C. Sen, *History of Bengali Language and Literature* (2d ed.; Calcutta University, 1954), p. 537.

The difficulties of translation, I think, will be clear even to one entirely unfamiliar with the language. Often Bhāratchandra's language is more restrained than this, though always elegant:

> aalo aamaara praana kæmana lo kare /
> ki haila aamaare /
> je kare aamaara praaṇa kahiba kaahaare //
>
> lukaaye piriti kainu kulakaalaṅkini hainu
>   aakula paraaṇa mora akula paaṭhaare /
> sujana naagara peye aagu paachu nahi ceye
>   aapani karinu priti ki dusiba taare //

which means:

> Alas, how comes this (pain) within my heart?
>   What has happened to me?
> To whom can I tell that which is in my heart?
> I loved him secretly, and have disgraced my
>   family.
> My heart drifts, alone and fearful, on a vast
>   and shoreless sea.
> I found a fine and handsome lover; but I did
>   not look before me, nor behind.
> I satisfied myself. For this shall I now
>   condemn him?

It is true that often Bhāratchandra's desire to make a pun (for which Bengali is an excellent language) or to turn a phrase obscures his meaning. From one point of view, the whole poem is a long pun. The heroine Vidyā's name also means "knowledge." Sometimes the punning comes through in this translation, more often not. The discussion of philosophical systems between Vidyā and Sundar is a wonderful one in Bengali, playing on the subtle technical points of the philosophies concerned and on the differences in meaning between Sanskrit and Bengali words. This and other similar passages it has been impossible for me to translate without long footnotes which, I am afraid, would defeat the purpose of the translation. Also impossible to translate are the intricate poetic devices used by Bhāratchandra. For example, the *ślokas* which Vidyā and Sundar exchange in order to introduce themselves to each other are Sanskrit cryptograms. Good means of rendering such in English has escaped me. I have taken the easy way out and given only the first-level meaning. So there will be passages from which the reader will not get the full flavor of Bhāratchandra's wit. My only hope is that enough of the flavor will come through to indicate to the reader something of the character of the poem.

A final difficulty of translation is that it is impossible not to suspect that some of Bhāratchandra's wit is directed at people who were around him in the Rājā Krishnachandra's court. Not enough is known about such people to allow us to interpret properly all the innuendos involved.

In the following translation, in which I have taken considerable liberty with the Bengali, some parts have been edited, and some omitted entirely; for example, I have omitted the brief lyrics with which the poet prefaces each section of his work. These lyrics, of which the one translated above is an example, have to do with episodes or sentiments in the Rādhā-Krishna story which parallel those about to occur in the story of Vidyā and Sundar. They are sometimes quite beautiful, but have been left out because they are in no way structural and would clutter rather than clarify an already overly elaborate plot. Also omitted are two rather long sections, one at the beginning and one at the end. Neither is structural to the story frame. The introductory one consists primarily of the formal obeisances to king and deities; the final passage tells in an anti-climactic fashion of how Vidyā and Sundar made their way, with much amorous carrying-on, back to Sundar's home in Kanchipur.

One final remark, best stated by the translation of a paragraph or two from that excellent Bengali essayist and critic Pramatha Caudhuri[6]:

> None of the old Bengali poets are lacking in this mood of laughter (*hāsya-rasa*). But only in the writing of Bhāratchandra is it a special characteristic; thus Bhāratchandra is not much liked by genteel and pious people. This laughter, which is found from Aristophanes to Anatole France, is not always wholly decent; it is outside the accepted norms of genteel society. It is, in fact, a subtle but heartfelt attack against the very normal sluggishness and stupidity of that society, it is the raised-eyebrowed glance of truth toward the falseness and hypocrisy of that society.
>
> That the poetry of Bhāratchandra is guilty of the sin of indecency everyone knows, and that his laughter is nasty. When Sundar is being judged before the king, genteel critics, hearing his words, say, "What kind of society is this, in which such intimacy with one's father-in-law is permissible?" I must then ask, "In what kind of society is this kind of literary criticism permissible?" It is either childishness or senility. . . .

[6] From the essay entitled Bhāratcandra, reprinted in *Sāhitya-sammuṭa*, ed. Pramathanāth Beśi and Bijitkumār Datta (Calcutta: Viśvabhārati, 1960), pp. 300–315.

To my knowledge, this is the only translation of the poem in English. I suspect that the lack of attention to the poem has been due to the fear that English readers would get a wrong idea about Bengali morality, and that Bhāratchandra's dealing in a light-hearted vein with a subject very objectionable in modern Indian society would offend the sensibilities of Indian readers also. The first objection, I think, is absurd. In regard to the second I can only say that I hope my attempt to give a delightful and in many ways representative poem a deservedly wider audience through translation will offend no one. My thanks go to Dr. Somdev Bhattacharji of the University of Chicago for his help in unraveling some of Bhāratchandra's linguistic knots.

Vidyā and Sundar

Now HEAR MY STORY carefully, O king.

Once there was in this place a king of men, Virasiṁha by name. Vidyā was his daughter, a girl of most excellent virtue. Her beauty equaled that of Lakṣmī the goddess of beauty herself, and in noble qualities she was as Sarasvatī, goddess of learning. This girl had made a vow that only he who conquered her in learned argument would become her husband. Princes therefore came from near and far, only to be beaten by the wit and knowledge of the girl. And her father the king began to despair, thinking "What now will become of my daughter? Will she ever marry?"

Now far to the south there was a country, Kāñci by name. And over this country there ruled a king, an ocean of virtue, Guṇasindhu Rāya. Sundar was his son, a beautiful and charming boy. It was he who came to conquer Knowledge herself in knowledge.

Virasiṁha, hearing of this prince, sent a messenger to the throne of Kāñci, bearing news of the princess Vidyā's vow. And the messenger duly went to the south into that land of Kāñci, and gave the news to the prince Sundar. As he listened to the words of the messenger, Sundar became sunk in thought; he took the messenger aside and said:

—Is the princess Vidyā truly so beautiful? Is she truly so learned and intelligent?

And the messenger replied:

—Sir, even if there were no limits to the power of speech, the most skilled of poets could not describe her. If one whom God has given eyes does not use his eyes to gaze upon her beauty, truly there is no meaning in his having them.

When he heard this, Sundar was filled with wonder and with longing, and a wave of delight welled up in him. The picture of Vidyā which the messenger had painted absorbed his mind; he muttered to himself, thinking on her beauty—a Knowledge-gaining discipline—and his body became a boat adrift upon a sea of bliss. And, knowing that the means of gaining knowledge is the worship of the source of knowledge, he prayed to Kālī and meditated on her in this way:

—It was due to Kālī that Rāma built a bridge to Ceylon. Kālī is my refuge and my hope. I shall ask of her a boon. If she cares for me, she will help me to go at once to Burdwan. Without her help I shall never gain this princess-jewel. I must gain her whom I desire or I shall surely shrivel and waste away.

And while he meditated thus he heard a voice from the sky say to him:

—Go, child, to Burdwan, and there gain Knowledge. Take a horse, swift as the wind in its course, and dress the horse in beautiful trappings, and dress yourself as becomes a prince. Wear a ruby in the crest of your turban, and a glittering diamond, and from your neck hang a pendant, glowing with jeweled ornaments. Hang a sword at your side, and take a shield and a gun and dagger, and in your hand a cage with a talking bird. Finally, hang a box of books from the neck of your horse. But remember, tell no one that you are going, not even your parents. Nor forget the power of flowers in your suit. So go quickly, mount your horse, and let neither fire nor flood impede your journey.

So the prince whipped his horse and rode, as steady in the saddle as Mount Sumeru, as swift as the wind or a meteor. He outsped speed itself, passing through his own and other countries. The name of Vidyā drove him on; his only companion was the parrot in his hand.

From Kāñci to Burdwan is six months' journey. But Sundar, his wishing-horse beneath him, in six days' time had reached his destination. And then he reined his horse and gazed about him. He saw the blessed land of Bengal, and the mighty river Dāmodār, and said:

—Surely he who is king of this land is the recipient of all good fortune.

The city of Burdwan lay before him extending to the horizons, surrounded all by walls. He looked with wonder at the many guards at all the gates, and heard with wonder the thunder of the cannon and the crackling of muskets, the blare of trumpets, the beating of drums, and musical instruments playing; he heard the conch-shells sounding and the trumpeting of elephants and the pounding of horses galloping in all directions; he heard the rattle of soldiers' shields and weapons; he heard the crowds shouting and wrestlers slapping their thighs with a sound like the earth cracking open. He heard these things from the distance and was afraid.

Then he saw by the river a fort, garrisoned by Negro soldiers of fearful appearance. And he thought:

—Who can pass through that fort, except by the mercy of the all-powerful goddess? The city is indeed like an island in the middle of a vast, shoreless sea.

But to enter the city he had to pass this fort, so he approached. And as he drew near, a guard said to him:

—Whence do you come? Where do you go? Tell me your caste, your rank, and your business here. If you do not tell me, you cannot pass.

Sundar replied:

—Brother, my name is Sundar, and Kāñci, to the south, is my home. I have come to this place in my desire for Knowledge.

The guard said:

—Surely this is not student's dress you wear. Students wear a single cloth, and carry only a wicker box of books. They are not mounted on well-appointed steeds, nor do they have weapons at their sides. You are a thief or robber, or some sort of spy, though your speech be high-sounding.

Then the prince laughed and said:

—Sir, the only thing which I have come to steal is Knowledge.

And he showed to the guard his box of books.

The guard said:

—Hear me, sir. I see now that you are indeed a student, though you are mounted, well-dressed, and carry arms not usual for such as you. But if I let you pass, I will be responsible. The city is full of knaves with swords and thieves in disguise. I cannot therefore let you pass. Besides, I myself am only a servant, and have no power to judge. I shall ask the commander.

Sundar replied:

—Wait. If I leave with you my horse and sword and the rest, gateman, and take only my *dhoti,* my box of books, my bird, will you then let me pass?

And the gateman said:

—I will.

So Sundar gave him his bribe—the turban-jewels and arms and horse and rich trappings, and, dismounting, went through the gate on foot. The guard stepped aside, and Sundar entered the city.

II

SUNDAR ENTERED slowly, looking about him with curiosity. He passed through the first inner fort, garrisoned with foreign mercenaries, English, Dutch, Portuguese, French,

Danish, and German—artillerymen with arms and supplies brought from far parts of the world. He passed also through the second garrison, a garrison of Muslims—Sāyeds, Sheks, Malliks, Moguls, Pāṭhāns—dressed in the garb of Turkey and Arabia and Persia, and he heard the gurgling of liquor mingling with the babble of foreign tongues. In the third fort he saw Kshatriyas, learned in the art of war, unshakable in battle. In the fourth garrison there were Rājputs, powerful fighters, the king's personal guard. In the fifth were the Rahuts, and around them were seated many Bhāṭs.[1] The sixth was the Bondelā garrison, in which were the supplies for all the city. In that fort were traders and merchants of all races, doing business with great sums of money. Seeing that he was a scholar, all these hindered Sundar not at all, and stopped him only to give him greeting. Thus he passed unharmed through all six forts, and entered the seventh without fear.

As he entered the seventh fort, he saw before him a covered square. In the middle of the square was the prison and the execution ground. And all around were thousands of robbers and thieves, chains on their legs, begging for food. In the midst of them the chief of the guards, Dhumaketu by name, was standing. The noise was like that of hell itself, with the cracking of bones and the snap of the lash and the slap of leather on human flesh. Some of the wretched prisoners were praying, some were screaming, and some moaning "Father, O father! I am dying! Save

[1] Panegyrist-soldiers, whose job it was to sing the glories of the king, and in battle to stir the soldiers on to acts of valor. They also served as messengers.

me!" And in fear of their chief, none of the guards dared show mercy. Sundar also became afraid.

Bhāratchandra says—Ah, Sundar, what do you think now? Would your happiness be worth such punishment?

III

THE PRINCE went past the prison-ground and saw before him the palace of the king. All around were people of the thirty-six castes, and people of all nations involved in their particular businesses. There were markets, with passage-ways and alleys and bazaars, with crowds surging in and out, thousands of people, and rut elephants, their trunks swinging, tied to pillars, and horses and camels and asses and mules brought from Turkey, Iraq, and Arabia. There were all the kinds of people and birds and beasts which inhabit the earth. And who could number them all? In one part was a circle of Brahmins, reciting the Vedas, expounding philosophy and rhetoric and logic and the *smṛtis*[2] and grammar. From every house came the sounds of the conch-shell and sounds of the worship of Śiva and Caṇḍī, the sounds of sacrifice and celebration. In another section there were Vaidyas, feeling pulses and purging illnesses with Ayurvedic medicine. There were businessmen of Kāyastha and other castes selling flutes and jewels and perfume and brass and gold; there were coppersmiths, makers of ornaments from conch-shells, and wood-sellers; there were cow-herds and milk-men and oilmen and weavers and flower-

[2] "That which is remembered"—the texts of law, etc., opposed to *śruti* —"that which has been heard (revealed)."

sellers and barbers and betel-sellers and blacksmiths and potters and women of the town and farmers and washermen from the country gawking, and fishermen, and how many others I cannot begin to tell.

Gazing at this teeming city, Sundar exclaimed in amazement. And then, to one side, he caught sight of a beautiful lake, with four paved *ghāṭs* and four temples of the lord Śiva. On the *ghāṭs* there were lines of ascetics with matted hair, their bodies smeared with ashes. And in another quarter, by the lake, he saw a lovely garden of flowers.

In this garden the wind was gently wafting the sweet scent of sandalwood, the nightingales were calling softly, the bees were humming. The water of the lake was lapping quietly, and on the water graceful waterbirds swam and there were white and red and blue and yellow lotuses and lilies of all kinds. Peacocks were dancing and calling in the garden, and cranes and swans. In the forest of flowers the birds, awake both day and night, sang sweetly. It was the garden of the palace of the king. Surely this was the earth's finest city, a place where the god of love himself might come to rest.

When he saw these things, Sundar was trapped in the snare of Kāma. He remembered then the name of Vidyā, and heaved a sigh. People say that water extinguishes a flame. But the sight of this beautiful lily-pond made the flame of Sundar's passion burn the harder. As in a trance, he went to the pond and bathed himself among the blooming lilies. As in a trance, he offered prayer to Śiva. With pleasure he plucked a fruit from a pomegranate tree and fed it to his bird. With great pleasure he picked a lotus, and dreamily sniffed its fragrance. The lotus was the flower-arrow of the god of love; through his nostril it went and pierced deep into his heart. Trembling, he sat at the foot of a vākula tree, which burned with fiery blossoms. Fire burned in the tree and in the heart of Sundar; each made the other burn more fiercely.

It was evening at that time, and the women of the city were coming to the pond with all their friends, to bathe and gossip and fill their pots with water. And when they saw the handsome Sundar seated there, they were struck dumb; some dropped and broke their water-jugs.

Bhārata says—Take care, O women of the city. Your saris are slipping down.

They said to one another then:

—Who is this man of matchless beauty, sitting beneath the vākula tree? Has the moon itself been charmed to earth and trapped? Has the god of love himself forgotten the beauty of his wife and left her side?

And when they saw his charm and grace, old women recalled the passionate days of their youth; by instinct they arranged their hair and ornaments and pulled their loosened saris tight over breasts and hips. They all were struck dumb, and rooted to the spot could only stare and say:

—Look at him!

And the more they looked, the deeper did the flame of passion burn its way within them. One said:

—I am dying with desire for that man. For him I would leave my family; I would worship only him. For him I would go and become a Yoginī.[3]

Another said:

—Truly he is a jewel among youths, and has stolen my

[3] A female ascetic, usually Tantric.

mind from me. I am burning in my desire to unite with him.

And yet another:

—For him would I put a garland of *campa* blossoms in my hair, and rub my body smooth with oil till it became golden as turmeric. O God of Destiny, may that youth be mine! I would serve him like a slave, that when I entered my house I could see his shadow there. My husband is old, and his family vicious and cruel. The wife of my husband's brother is a tigress. My mother-in-law is harsh and sharp of tongue; my husband's sister has the qualities of a poisonous snake. But ah!—the woman blessed with fortune of whom that one is the lord and husband would be a goddess; she would live in eternal delight and love. One kiss from him would bring eternities of pleasure. Highest joy would blossom in his love. Ah, can I control my passion?

All were of like mind; crazed by their desire the women said to one another:

—Let us take our baths and return to our homes.

But, deceiving one another, they all sneaked back again in secret to steal another look at him. They were like birds in a cage; they could not escape his charm. They gazed at Sundar, seated at the root of the vākula tree, and listened in wonder as he talked with his parrot about the *śāstras*.[4]

IV

As THE SUN went down behind the mountains and night fell, a flower-woman came alone to the pond. Her tongue

[4] Texts for law, grammar, rhetoric, politics, etc.

was as sharp as a diamond, and Hīrā (Diamond) was her name. Her teeth were beautiful and polished, her face set in a smile, and as she walked, she swung her hips excessively. Her cheek was full of betel-*pān;* she wore a garland on her neck, and in her ear a ring. Her Rāṛhi[5] speech was distorted and strange. Her hair was tied up in a bun. She wore a white sari, and on her hip she carried a basket of flowers which she took from house to house. The beauty which had been hers in youth had not quite faded; her figure had not withered. She made her living by deceiving the unwary; she knew bits and snatches of the Tantras.[6] But her major skill was the creation of discord, and she was lonely. Her neighbors did not visit her, fearing the sharpness of her tongue.

Such was she who now came slowly to the pond, as she did each evening. Her hands moved rapidly as she stooped to pick the flowers. But when she caught sight of Sundar, her heart was stolen. She whispered to herself:

—Hari, Hari. Whose son can he be? Surely he could not be Kāma, who has left the arms of his beautiful wife—but again, he could be. Never have I seen such a man in this country. He must be a foreigner. But how could a mother let such a son leave home? He has a wicker box and some books. He must be a student.

Slowly she approached him, and said:

—Who are you? Where is your home? Whither do you go?

Sundar replied:

[5] The area in the far west of Bengal is sometimes referred to as Rāṛha; her dialect was of that area.

[6] The term here probably means "magical texts," by knowledge of which occult powers could be gained.

—I am one who desires and seeks after Knowledge. I have recently arrived in this city, and have as yet found no place to stay. Yet I have faith in Kālī's name. I shall stay wherever I can find a place.

The flower-woman answered:

—I am but a poor flower-woman, but my house has walls and roof. I live there alone. Daily I furnish the flowers for the palace, and I come and go with the blessings of the king and queen. If you do not despise my poverty, though I am humble I shall gladly give you lodging in my house.

The prince said to himself:

—Surely Kālī has sent this opportunity! I shall learn of Vidyā from this flower-woman. A house and information all at once is more than I had dreamed. The old hag lives alone; she is undoubtedly a woman of the streets and probably has designs on me. But on the other hand, I might never find a better opportunity. Besides, I shall call her "aunt" and get her to call me "grandson," and that will destroy any illusions she might have.

Then he said aloud:

—It is good of you to offer me a lodging. I shall be like a son to you, and you a mother to me.

The flower woman knew that she had been tricked, and, disappointed, said:

—You are shrewd as well as handsome. You are more like my grandfather than my son.[7] But be that as it may.

So, carrying his box of books and taking Durgā's name, Sundar followed the flower-woman to her house. There was

[7] The relationship between grandfather and grandchild is proverbially a joking one.

a high wall all around the house, unbroken except for a single gate, and within the wall a forest of flowers so high they hid the sun and moon. All kinds of flowers there were, and around them the bees swarmed and settled, and nightingales called. The wind was blowing gently. It would have set throbbing the mind of the most ascetic of men.

When he saw this beauty, Sundar's heart was glad, and he entered the house. Pleased, the flower-woman arranged the southern room for him, and brought to him delicious kinds of food. He ate with pleasure what she had cooked, and when he had finished he lay down and passed the night in peaceful sleep. The cool southern wind blew, the nightingales sang, and in the morning Sundar rose refreshed, the name of Durgā on his lips. He bathed in a nearby lotus-pond, and, finishing his bath, performed his morning worship. The flower-woman picked her flowers and wove her garlands. And, when she had arranged her flower-basket, she went out to the palace of the king.

V

When Hīrā returned from the palace, Sundar said to her:
—Aunt, I have no servants. Tell me, who can do my marketing?

The flower-woman replied:
—Son, do not let this worry you. I shall go to the market for you myself. Tell me what you want, and give me the money. I shall buy and bring whatever you desire. I can get you anything for money. I can buy rice and curds, or tigers' milk. Money is a most wonderful thing. Without money,

one can have no friends. With money, old men find beautiful young girls. People give their lives for money; for money men forsake their wives and families. There is nothing greater in heaven, earth, or hell than money. So if you give me money I shall bring you back the moon, or a woman of highest birth.

The prince replied:

—Ah, you are indeed my aunt.

Hīrā said:

—I am but your slave, whom you call "aunt" in your goodness. You are Hari, who called Yashodā "mother" in his goodness.[8]

Pleased with her answer, the prince gave her ten rupees. Taking the money, which overflowed her cupped hands, the old thief smiled broadly, knowing that she now had Sundar under her control. She poured the money in a little basket and, putting on her ornaments, went out to the market.

When they saw her coming, with her restless, gesturing hands waving constantly, the shopkeepers closed their shops in panic. And when she saw this, Hīrā pounded on their doors and shouted:

—Pigs! I have money; see my money glitter!

At this some shopkeepers opened up their shops again; at those who didn't Hīrā screamed and shouted so that it seemed as if the earth was cracking open. Then she began to bargain. Honest merchants she called "thief." She threw her fake-gold bracelet on the ground, and screamed:

[8] Yashodā was the wife of the cowherd Nanda and foster-mother of Krishna (Hari).

—You bastard! You took my bracelet, which was gold, and gave me a false one in exchange!

And then she called a policeman, and said:

—That merchant has robbed me! After we had settled on a price, he gave me short measure!

After every purchase she turned her back and carefully counted her money. In this way, like a leech drawing blood, she did her marketing. Her shouting worked the whole market-place into a storm; her insults she sowed freely in all the shops. She always made sure she had correct change. Ah, in money-hunting she was indeed a paragon of virtue. And when she had finished she turned with a sly smile and started on her homeward way.

When she arrived, she told Sundar all that happened and Sundar could not help but laugh.

—Son, hear this account of your money, and then judge if your aunt has not done well. But let me say at first, for all my pains I got only insults. For know this—that six of the rupees which you gave me were counterfeit. I should have examined them in your presence . . . but no matter. I was able to change two rupees with a merchant. I did buy some sweets at the price of a *kāhan*[9] a seer, and I got some sugar. And I also bought a half seer of *sandeś*.[10] The sugar I got for the same price that other people pay for *guṛ*.[11] I have some sandalwood, too, which is very hard to get, and perfumed tobacco, and some cloves and nutmeg. The fruit I

[9] One *kāhan* = 16 *paṇas* or 1280 cowries; a rupee.
[10] *sandeś:* a sweet made from milk.
[11] *guṛ:* a particular kind of brown sugar.

saw there, though, was just not good. Ah, how much trouble I had! I searched all through the market! The price they asked I had to give. But I got some *pān* for two *paṇas* and no one else gets the type of *pān* I get. But unfortunately I had to go to the river-bank for milk—who else but me would have done that for you? For eight *paṇas* I bought eight bundles of wood, but the rogues did not give me full measure. And I looked all over for lime for the *pān,* until I was exhausted. And then found that I had run out of money, and had to beg for lime. Examine the accounts carefully, son, which I am marking on the ground with this stick. Otherwise you may think your aunt has cheated you.

The prince, seeing the exorbitant sums which she was writing on the ground, was astonished; but he could make no answer. He only said:

—How can I answer you? You told me you were shamed because of me.

So the flower-woman prepared the food which she had bought and the prince ate. When he had finished, he called to her:

—Aunt! O Aunt!

Hīrā, having stuffed herself, walked slowly to his side and sat beside him.

—What do you want?

Then, Sundar, stretching himself, began to ask her questions about the palace.

—You go every day to the court. Tell me what it is like. How old is the king? How many queens does he have? How many daughters does he have, and how many sons?

Hīrā replied:

—I will tell you all these things, my young friend, but first you must tell me about yourself. I perceive that you are of noble birth, but you might also be a rogue. Swear to me you will not tell lies.

—How can I tell you lies? For even if I lie to you, the lie will eventually be exposed. But listen. You have surely heard of a great city in the southern country called Kāñci. The king of that city is Guṇasindhu, and I am Sundar, his son. I have come here hoping to meet the princess Vidyā.

When she had heard this, the flower-woman gave a bow and said:

—Please, sir, pardon my offense. May misfortune be always far from you. Though in your graciousness you call me "aunt," I am but your slave, and you my lord. I am honored that you have chosen to stay here in my house. And now I shall tell you what you ask. Make yourself comfortable, and listen to me.

I know all about the household of the king. The king himself is middle-aged, and has one consort. They have five sons, young men, princes both by birth and nature. They also have one unmarried daughter, whose name is Vidyā. The beauty and excellence of this girl are truly wonderful to see, impossible to describe in words. She is the goddess of beauty and the goddess of wisdom in one form. The king of the gods himself could not describe her, so you will understand how inadequate are my words. Her long black braid of hair is beautiful and glossy; it shames the graceful glistening beauty of the black snake. How can I describe her . . . what is the lotus-white moon, when compared to her face? One would mistake her brows for black bees on the lotus-blossom . . . her eyes are wide in modesty and fear, like those of a captured doe . . . the very moon weeps, for it seems stained, when put beside her stainless face . . . her hips are even more graceful than those of a doe . . . she is expert with the bow of Kāma, casting in her glance his deadly arrows . . . the *tilaka* spot on her forehead is like a pearl . . . the regular row of her teeth makes the greatest pandit forget the logical line of reasonable thought . . . the *devas* and *asuras*[12] are always fighting over nectar, but here is greater nectar, in her face . . . her lotus-loins are more beautiful than is the lotus-flower itself . . . her arms are lotus-stalks, to draw one down into the depths of passion . . . her breasts are high and pointed, like peaks of Mount Meru . . . the color of her body is more beautiful than that of the *kadamba* blossom . . . her waist is delicate, like the hour-glass drum of Śiva . . . let him who says that Passion is bodiless cast one glance at the swell of her buttocks, which make Mother Earth hide her head in defeated shame . . . seeing the graceful sway of her hips as she walks one admits that the Creator's *guru* has indeed taught well; he who has not seen the grace of this girl's walk thinks the walk of an elephant or a swan is graceful . . . her color is more golden than that of a *campaka* blossom or turmeric, and at the sight of her, men burn as in a fire . . . the lightning hides in the cloud because it has not so much grace and beauty, and trembles constantly in shame . . . Ah, if there were a million gods of love, they would all melt in passion at the sight of her in her dress and

12 *Deva:* god; *asura:* demon, enemy of the gods. There is competition between the two classes of beings for the possession of nectar.

ornaments. And her voice!—she could teach the bees to hum; she could teach the sweetness of their jingling to her bangles. Such beauty as is hers I have never seen or heard. Nor can I describe in any better fashion the excellence of her qualities. But I know one thing. She has said that whoever can conquer her in argument shall marry her. Messengers have gone from country to country, carrying this news, and many princes have come here only to be beaten. It is much as was the marriage of Sītā, with her vow about the bending of the bow. The king and queen are frantic with worry, fearing that there is no one on the earth who will conquer her. Now, perhaps, you understand something of this incomparable girl. She is fifteen or sixteen years old, and has the delusion that the husband of Lakshmī and Sarasvatī himself will come to take her. But hear, O prince. You are a handsome man and have great knowledge. You could conquer her in argument. Allow me to announce your presence in the city to the king and queen tomorrow.

The prince replied:

—How, Aunt, can this be brought about? Let me first see of how much wisdom this Vidyā is possessed. What wisdom have I? I will surely be defeated, and shall become the laughing-stock of all Bengal. So here is another plan. You bring your garlands to Vidyā daily. I shall weave a garland, which you will bring to her. Within this garland I shall put a message. And from her reception of this message I shall know what my next move is to be. It is like the thief's knocking at the house's outer door, to see if the householder is awake. Then, when I am sure that her proper feelings toward me are aroused, I shall approach her in person.

When have haste and heroic gestures ever borne good fruit? Good fruit on trees grows slow and gradually.
—Well spoken. You will thread a garland-hook to catch the fish, said Hīrā with a smile.

And the day passed into night, while Sundar wove the garland.

VI

The flower-woman brought the prince her flower-basket, her basket of delight, filled with all the loveliest of the children of the forest. Now Sundar knew well the art of tying garlands, and Kālī was beside him. He wove a garland so intricate and beautiful that Kāma himself would have fallen into its trap of passion, longing, and desire. The beauty and the fragrance of it were such that it aroused desire for love in all who saw it.
—I shall make this garland a work of art. Its beauty and artistry will be such as has never been seen before, and my creation will create a new future for Vidyā. First, I shall make a frame of fragrant pine boughs, decorated with jasmine and evergreen. Within, I shall put a flower-arrow like that of Kāma, and an image, a tiny image of that god, all made of flowers. His flowing hair will be of delicate *aparājitā,* his face a lotus, his nose a *tila*-flower, his lips of reddest *bāndhulī,* his fingers *cāmpā*-buds, his beautiful eyes of lotus-blossoms, his arms of lotus-stalks. I shall fashion his body from a golden *campaka*-flower and his feet from land-lilies. And I shall make the bow of this god of love with flowers of the trumpet-vine; his two hands will be fixing an arrow to his bow. And I shall place the image in such a

way that he will be ready to discharge his flower-arrow into Vidyā's breast.

And so he wove the garland. When he had finished it, he wrote this message in the needles of the pine, to introduce himself:

> If he is possessed of the treasure of the earth, the world honors even him of humble birth. O thou with thighs like plantain-stalks, thou skilled in all delights of love, thou wilt find my name in the second and fifth syllables of this verse. If thou needest more, but ask the flower-woman.

Then, when he had hidden this within the garland-frame, he entrusted it to Hīrā, and told her of his scheme.

Hīrā saw that it was late, and was afraid. She took the flowers and rushed to the palace of the king. And there, she distributed garlands to all.

When Hīrā arrived in Vidyā's rooms, Vidyā was seated on the worship-mat. She looked at Hīrā with angry, agitated eyes.

—What is this, O flower-woman? Is it now your custom to come so late? Have you no fear in your heart of what might happen to you? It is very late, and I have not yet begun my worship, as you did not come with flowers. Further, I am dying of hunger and thirst. With whom have you been dallying? At whose caress has your breast been swelling? I shall tell my mother of this. You are an old woman; act your age. Or are you like an old bull, sensual to the last? I know. You had a lover in the night, and so arose so late. So you would take advantage of me, coming here at such an hour! What punishment would be good enough for you? I shall tell this to my father!

Hīrā, hearing this, trembled with tear; tears streaming from her eyes, she replied:

—Hear me, princess. Forgive me. The time flew by, while I wove a special garland for you. I am late because of the pains I took with this work. Ah, I cannot understand the twists of fate. I did my best, I thought I would please you. But my best was not enough. All my trouble was in vain, and what I had hoped would bring you pleasure has brought me only misery.

At Hīrā's plea, Vidyā was moved. Her anger subsided and sweetness again rose up in her heart. She said:

—I see here a wonderfully delicate garland. Surely this is not of your own making. Or has your youth suddenly returned to you? Some young woman, ripe with passion, taught you to weave a garland like that.

And Hīrā replied, tears in her eyes:

—Ah, when youth and life have gone, they do not return. This thickened waist and shrivelled breasts of mine will never again attract a lover. I have left all that behind me. If you cut a flower's roots, pouring water on its head will do no good. Love and youthful beauty are temporary things, like dikes of sand. But open the string and look within the box. Look at the garland.

So Vidyā opened the box, and as she did so she set off the trap. Her heart was pierced as with an arrow discharged from the flower-bow. Trembling, she gazed at the garland. She read the verse; she became covered with confusion; her face was flushed with passion, her body swelling with delight.

—Tell me, Hīrā—and swear an oath to me that you will

tell the truth—who made this device of flowers? Who made it, and what kind of person is he. Tell me these things, and do not lie.

So Hīrā said:

—Listen to me, then. Why do you dodge again and again the arrows of the love-god? There is no use denying it. I understand it all. This is the flaw in your great wisdom. Your beauty is great, and beauty is the burden and the blessing of youth. Yet you are still a virgin. I have thought on this long and hard—where can we find a husband for you? My heart is torn at the thought of your loneliness. "He who defeats me in debate will be my husband"—what kind of talk is this for a young girl? You will wait until someone conquers you. Do you think your youth will also wait? If you do not find love in youth, the chance that you will find it in old age is slender. You are like a tree—you burn with passion as a tree burns in the scorching sun; and sometimes, when the rainy season comes, it comes too late. I have watched you, and your longing touches my heart until I no longer care for food or drink. So I have found for you a fine and handsome man, the son of a king. I have kept him in my house for you, although to do so I have had to use all my tricks. Listen. I shall tell you about him. In a place called Kāñcipur there is a king, Guṇasindhu by name, who is a great king, a king of kings. His son is a handsome lad called Sundar, a great poet. This youth has left his parents' home and has wandered alone, conquering the world. I caught sight of him on the road and was astonished by his beauty. So I have kept him in my house, causing him to forget all other things. He calls me "Aunt" in pure affection. Now, I have told him the secret of your marriage-vow. But when he had heard me out he laughed and said with a gesture of his hand, "How can I win this maiden?" Therefore, to get to know you, he made you this device of flowers. And to make himself known to you, he passed the night away in composition of this verse. This is the reason for my lateness this morning. I have found for you a lover, but instead of thanks you give me vile abuse. Even he for whom the thief steals will call him thief.

So Hīrā carried on her argument in this way, and finally, in mock distress, made a motion as if to leave. But Vidyā seized the border of her sari and held Hīrā as if she were a rare jewel. The princess said:

—Remain here with your friend, O Hīrā! The offense was mine—forgive my harsh words. Forgive me those words as you would forgive your own granddaughter for hasty offense to you. You have kindled in my heart the fire of passion, and having brought me to this state you now would leave me. Ah, would you slay your granddaughter like this, old woman? You are more to me than my own mother or father. I cannot stand—I would fall down, for I am drunken with this passion you have fed in me . . . Come, then, sit down. I shall obey you, whatever you command. Let accepted conduct go. Tell me more about this man. That which you have already told me of him has driven me almost out of my mind.

Seeing her distress, that clever mind-thief Hīrā began to whisper in her ear:

—Ah, he is a true hero, a true lover, a man of most excellent beauty, a sea of qualities. Can there be anyone else like him? In his face one sees the stainless moon. The line of his moustache is a row of black bees alighting in curiosity and eagerness upon the blooming lotus. He is truly an incarnate Kāma. His ear is like to that of the hawk in delicacy, and in its lobe there is a radiant pearl. His brows are like the taut arch of Kāma's bow, his eye aiming along the shaft ready to release the arrow of his glance. A woman cannot draw her eyes from the redness of his lips, and seeks to taste their sweetness. Between his bright and dancing eyes, his nose is long and curved like the beak of Kāma's parrot, and his arms are long and golden and strong. His heart is the home of Kāma himself, a treasure-house of bliss. In the lotus-pool of his navel the mind of a young woman swims like a carp; the three folds of flesh on his belly would make you swoon with passion. Though I am an old woman, even I fill with desire when I see him. He calls me "Aunt," and even this seems to me the source of my salvation.

Vidyā, agitated, said:

—Tell me, what did he say? Tell me more, tell me again and again . . . I can feel that my face is flushed, my mind is restless and agitated, my body is full and trembling, my heart pounds as in fever . . .

VII

I SHALL SACRIFICE my shame, I shall discard my family honor, and I shall pray to Krishna. Take me to him, O take me. I can no longer stay here in my house . . . my heart is wild with longing. There is no more patience in my mind, and swells as of the sea roll out from it. I want to see that Syāmarāya—I shall sell myself to his reddened feet. When Bhārata thinks on this love of the Gopīs for Krishna, his mind is swollen.

Then Vidyā said:
—Hīrā, hear me. How can you bring him to me? Somehow I know that he is the one who will conquer me. Even though I were to defeat him, I should be defeated. The others who have come in the hope of gaining me were kings' sons, but are only plowmen on this prince's estate. In such could the mind of Vidyā be absorbed? The husband of Vidyā will be a slave to knowledge. But perhaps it is not this one who will conquer me—perhaps fate will not give to me this treasure—when I think of this, I think that I shall die. But I have made my vow. Perhaps my wedding is at hand. Perhaps at long last Śiva has been gracious unto me. Perhaps at long last Bhāgavatī has caused the marriage-flower to bloom.

Then she gave to Hīrā her own crown and diamond necklace, and she said:
—Now understand these things. And cause him also to understand. Tell him this; and then, O flower-woman, think on a way in which he can be brought to me. Listen. Below my window there is a chariot in the street. Bring him and stand him there. And tell me when you will bring him there, so that I can look upon him. Now, he sent to me the Kāma made of flowers. What shall I send him in return? Ah. By a similar device Kāma's consort Rati will send *rati*

(passion) to him. From his verse I have learned Sundar's name. I shall write a verse with my own:

> To the lotus of this verse you are the sun; even the gods would say that there is none who is your equal. This verse is in three parts, and in these parts there are three separate meanings. You will find my name in the second syllable and the fifth. And if you ask the flower-woman she will tell you other things.

With this she said farewell and sent the flower-woman on her way. And then she sat in great devotion at her worship. But before she began her worship, she asked a boon. And having asked this boon, she began her *pūjā*. But when she meditated upon the goddess, she saw her lover. When she brought water to wash the feet of the goddess, when she brought the articles of ritual to present them to the goddess, she imagined that she was presenting them to her bridegroom. She hung the sweet-smelling garland around the goddess' neck, but her words were these:
—This garland I put upon the neck of my husband.

When she circumambulated the goddess she was really circumambulating her bridegroom. Her *pūjā* was a *pūjā* to the god of love. She became disturbed, and could not finish. But the goddess saw her anxiety, and said to her in a voice from the sky:
—Your future bridegroom has come to the house of the flower-woman. And though you have not worshiped me, you should have no fear. I see all things, and I have received the offerings which you have made.

When she heard this voice from heaven, Vidyā knew

that she had been granted the boon which she had asked; she had sure knowledge that Kālī would fulfil her hope.

VIII

So THE FLOWER-WOMAN went to her own house, and told Sundar all that had transpired.

—Hear this, my son. She wants to see you.

And she told him of the assignation on the road. As soon as he had heard this, Sundar went quickly with the flower-woman and stood by the chariot in the road, as Vidyā had directed. And, informed by the flower-woman, Vidyā in great excitement ran to her window to look upon him. Hīrā pointed her finger at the prince, to direct the gaze of Vidyā. They stared at each other, the beautiful girl and the handsome man; they were absorbed in one another and overcome with delight. Who can say what understanding passed between them? It was as if their eyes were caught in traps, each bound tightly by the other's eyes. In their minds they exchanged the wedding garlands. Then each returned as he had come. Each took the heart of the other.

To exchange glances and then go home can only lead to trouble. Ah, Bhārata says, love is made up of all such kinds of foolishness.

IX

WHEN THE MORNING CAME, Hīrā went quickly to the palace, taking with her *kusuma* flowers. Sundar remained in the house, staring at the road, absorbed in thought, awaiting her return. Vidyā also had passed the night until the dawn, going over in various ways in her mind the beauty with which the prince had won her heart. She was whispering to herself. When Hīrā saw this she said:

—O princess, tell me. Why do you stand there whispering to yourself? If you are eager for union with this man, you have only to tell the king and queen. They will install this light in the darkness of your chamber.

But Vidyā said:

—Be still! If my father the king hears of this there will be no marriage. My father will not believe that he is the son of King Guṇasindhu. A messenger has gone to that kingdom to bring that prince, and they have not yet returned. If the son of Guṇasindhu had really come, the messenger would also have come. A prince would have arrived with pomp and ceremony. No, if my father hears of this, everything will be ruined, and Sundar will have to flee for his life into another country. Everything then will be a mockery. And what will become of me?

Then she whispered in Hīrā's ear a plan by which the union might be made, and said:

—For what Kālī does, I shall take the consequences.

But Hīrā drew back, startled.

—Hide a lover here? This could never be kept a secret! The queen's spies are everywhere, even in your own apartment. She would be as angry as a tigress! And the king would be like Śiva at the time of the destruction of the world. His chief guard Dhumaketu is the very agent of doom; he will be a scourge to all of us. He would shortly find the prince and capture him. Your honor would be destroyed, I would be killed, your companions would be in grave trouble, and the story of the scandal would quickly spread to every corner of the country. Besides, there are guards at all the doors. How could you get him in? I myself have thought about it, and can think of no way. Ah! If people found this out, I would be torn limb from limb; no one would escape wrath. Besides—listen—there is a tall girl among your attendants who, I have noticed, cannot keep her mouth shut. She would ruin the whole plan. Furthermore, she is sharp as a knife. She would reveal the scheme, only if by innuendo . . .

—What is this, Hīrā? Are you afraid of my maids? They follow my wishes; they do whatever I tell them to. Their opinions are as my own.

And the maids all said:

—Why are you afraid, Hīrā? How can slaves betray their mistress? Our lady is depressed because of separation from her lover. If you bring her royal lover to her she will again be happy; therefore, so shall we. Who among us would say a word? Instead, we shall bring sandal and perfume, and decorate the room with *kusuma* flowers, and we shall bring *pān* and betel-nut for their pleasure.

Then Vidyā said:

—So shall it be. Tell him, Hīrā, of these things, and he will find a way. Kālī will guide him, for what she wants she gets. Perhaps he will appear in my apartment as water in the coconut. He is the greatest of poets; his wit will find an entrance to my house. I shall be freed from my vow, for he will take me as Krishna took Rukminī, whose mind was always fixed on Krishna, though Śisupāla came surrounded by kings and was feasted by her father and her brother.[13] It is in just this way that my mind dwells eternally on him, though indeed I also fear my father and my mother and my brothers. I am in this also like Rukminī. "Take me, O Hari." This prayer I lay at my lover's feet.

In this way, the charming girl charged Hīrā, and Hīrā went and told Sundar all that had passed. But Sundar, pondering these things, could find no way.

—How shall I gain entrance to the room? There are strong and vicious guards at every door. A bird could not get in. What hope has a man? There is no way on earth, nor in heaven, nor in hell.

Thus he sat and wondered, at the feet of Kālī. The flower-woman brought him offerings, and he gave them to the goddess with prayer and praise. The goddess was pleased with his prayers and graciously gave him the means of accomplishing his desire. On the copper vessel used for worship she wrote *mantras*, and then from heaven dropped a pickaxe at his feet. Giving joyful thanks to Kālī, Sundar took the implement and read the *mantras* she had written.

—Aha! Kālī has shown me the way into the house! I shall cut away the earthen floor of Hīrā's house and make a tunnel; thus shall I enter the temple of Knowledge. I shall cut a tunnel through the earth, and rise up in Vidyā's presence! This is Caṇḍī's blessing, who indeed fulfils all desires.

And with these words he began to cut a tunnel from the

[13] Śisupāla was Krishna's cousin, but became Krishna's enemy when Krishna carried off Rukminī, his intended wife.

flower-woman's house to that of Vidyā; it was five hands high and two and a half hands across. And jewels, burning in the tunnel's walls, dispelled the darkness and lit his way.

X

When he had almost reached the house of Vidyā, Sundar began to glow with excitement, and with his excitement his beauty increased. He went back and put the bridegroom's lavish dress upon his handsome form. A new Kāma he became, who dulled the lustre of the old, who stole the mind of Rati from her consort; a fathomless sea of passion he became, an enjoyer of the highest pleasures. And then again, his legs heavy and his heart beating fast, trembling with desire and anticipation, he slowly went forward. Gradually he approached; his limbs were numbed. He stopped from time to time, confused, unsure, not knowing what was to happen. He suddenly saw himself as a thief, breaking into the house of the princess. He knew not how she would receive him, coming in this way.

On the other side of the wall the beautiful girl was sitting with her friends, wondering thus with troubled mind:
—How can he come here? How can he come to make this pain of separation pass away? There are many guards at all the doors. A bird could not pass by unseen. But perhaps he will come in a chariot from the sky . . . Ah, my friend Sulocanā, how will my light dawn again? If I do not see him soon, my heart will break. How can I describe my misery? The circle of the moon rains poison on the earth

instead of nectar; my *tilaka* of sandalwood becomes a spot of fire on my brow. The taste of camphor and betel leaves causes me only pain; the gentle jingling of the anklets in the dance no longer soothes my ears. My flower-garland is made of red-hot needles; my body trembles as in fever. The soft and gentle breeze makes me shudder like a thunderbolt. The nightingale's soft call and the humming of bees screech in my ears, piercing them like arrows, entering my heart. My glowing jewels burn my flesh; my limbs are scorched with their fire. My sari constricts my body, crushing me like a black snake coiled about me. My bed is a rack. My modesty has become my ruin. Ah, is it possible that life will remain in me? The night wears on, and my whole body burns as with a scorpion's sting. A moment of this night seems like a year.

In such a state she rested a moment on her couch. The next moment she was restless; she ran to the embraces of her friends. Then suddenly, with delight, she awakened her companions, saying:

—He comes! My lover comes!

In such a way the lovely girl, restless in desire, passed away the night. And suddenly, like the full moon rising from the earth, Sundar burst from his tunnel.

When they saw him, the companions of Vidyā were afraid, and Vidyā also was afraid. They drew back from him, as female swans from an advancing male.

—What is this? . . . What do I see? . . . What is that over there? . . . Is it a god or a demon? . . . How did he get here . . . the doors did not open. . . . How could he have gotten in? . . . What does it mean? . . . Truly, his form is most beautiful! But by what means . . . how? . . . He is as beautiful as Kāmadev himself!

And then they all fell silent. At a sign from Vidyā the attendant Sulocanā advanced and said:

—Who are you? How came you here? Make yourself known to us. Are you god or Gandhārva or Yaksha or Nāga or man?[14] Tell us the truth, for my lady is afraid.

Sundar replied:

—Lovely ladies, why are you afraid? I am only a man, Sundar by name, the son of King Guṇasindhu of Kāñcipur. I have come here to be at Vidyā's side. I make my home at Hīrā the flower-woman's house. A messenger came to me in Kāñcipur to tell me of the marriage-plan which Vidyā made. He told me of her beauty, and I was drawn here like a puppet on a string. Will you now consider this a crime? Even though uninvited I am still a guest; will my reception not be that of an honored man? I have come in faith. Trust me, and let me stay.

When she heard this the beautiful Vidyā gave orders for the seat of honor to be brought to him. And when he was seated, the clever Sundar said:

—Truly, I see many strange, delightful things in Vidyā's court. I see the grace of a lightning flash caught in the trap of a lady's clothing; yet a grace that hides as the stars hide when they see the full moon. In the border of the lady's sari I find a delicate lotus-scent; what other precious jewels are there contained within that clothing? And when I see

[14] The Gandhārvas are the musicians of heaven, who have a partiality for and a power over women. Yakshas are another class of supernatural beings. Nāgas are also divine beings, usually represented as semi-serpentine; they live in the lower regions.

such beauty, I am conquered. My heart is stolen by her whose loveliness is great, the nectar of whose mouth would shame even the nectar-filled moon, whose smile is yet more dazzling than the lightning flashing in the clouds. She has conquered many princes in debate, but now she seems herself conquered by shyness. If she is so easily conquered by shyness, why did she take the vow to marry him who conquered her? When I meet her in debate, then will Rati decide who will win and who will lose. But her face is lowered in modesty and embarrassment. You are witnesses to her defeat, O her companions.

Then her companions said:

—Sir, you are indeed a prince of poets. How can we answer you? The lowest of the low can never join in argument or otherwise with the highest of the high. The sharpest horns are dulled if they strike diamonds. What can we say, O prince? Our princess is modest; otherwise you would get an appropriate answer from her.

When he heard this, Sundar laughed and said:

—Speak, then, O princess. What will you give me for a reply?

Then Vidyā addressed her attendants in a low voice:

—A thief has entered this house with burglar's tools. I cannot enter into discussion with a thief, even a thief of Knowledge. What respectable modest woman discourses with a thief?

Sundar replied:

—You call me thief, but it is you who have stolen my heart. What a strange country is this, where the thief is robbed by the householder.

In this way the two bantered back and forth, each in his own mind forming plans. Just at that time, outside the room, a peacock called. And Vidyā said to her companions:

—Who called me?

When he heard this, Sundar understood the trick, and said to himself:

—It is only a pretext that she asks this of her companions. She is really asking it of me.

So he replied:

—Hear this verse, O Vidyā. And remember that the words have many meanings.

> Your birthplace is consumed in fire; the banner of your name rises in the smoke into the sky. From that smoke the clouds are born, whose rumbling strikes my ear. In a mountain cave a lonely one sits in sorrow, I hear her weeping. The peacock is the enemy of the snake, as is the moon of darkness and the gloom. The moon is now behind the cloud; the peacock calls.

I am as the peacock, on the peak of the earth-supporting mountain. You are the snake, like a snake to my peacock's ears and eyes. And so the peacock calls voraciously, that snake-devouring bird.

When she heard this verse, the princess in delight read its many meanings.

—I understand, O poet, the beauty and subtlety of your verse. But there is doubt in my mind still to be dispelled. A single action sometimes indicates there is a habit of such action. If in another situation you were called upon for such a verse, would you again speak thus? Is this your practice?

And Sundar then replied:
—Tell me, lady, what is in your mind. I answer thus: If you will give me favor, I will compose as many such verses as you like. Hear this one:

> She has a lion's eyes; and indeed, her waist is like a lion's in its grace. Her eyes are those of a deer; they are the thousand eyes of Indra, grave king of gods, in unfathomable depth like his ornaments the clouds. Your eyes, like the lightning in the clouds, strike me with a shaft of Kāma.

When she heard this verse, Vidyā's mind trembled in delight. Who can say who was defeated and who victorious in this exchange? Words passed between them as between two pandits, though these two were submerged in a sea of passion and delight. And inevitably, as in debate, a discussion of the *śāstras* rose—grammar, literature, rhetoric, drama, worship and the worshipper, and that which is to be worshipped. But beneath all these was love.

Sundar began the debate with knowledge of the self as his proposition. Vidyā could not refute his arguments. Facts were crowding and jostling in her mind, but not one of them came to her lips. Sundar spoke of the Vedānta, the Advaita, and the dualistic philosophies; he spoke of the solutions of Mīmāṁsā—but she could not follow his argument. She could not argue the Vaiśeṣika; and to Patañjali she could only make an *añjali*, hands to her head.[15] She was confused, as monism and dualism are confused in that philosophy. She could not tell the value of self-examination in

[15] *añjali:* a gesture of homage, with palms pressed together and raised to the forehead. Patañjali was the founder of a Yogic school of philosophy.

the Sāṁkhya. She could not argue from the *śruti,* for women cannot discuss the *śruti;* so Vidyā sat as if struck dumb. The prince then said:

—What then is your answer?

She tried to bring to bear an argument, but the god of love, the judge of the debate, stole it from her mind. And finally he, as judge, told her she was beaten. But at last she said:

—What the Vedānta says is true. All other *śāstras* are but forests of thorn-bush, blocking the way to truth.

Then the prince replied:

—If that is so, the truth is that all is unity. Therefore, you and I are one.

And the princess replied:

—I confess I am defeated. You are my husband, O prince. In this auspicious moment you have beaten me.

And saying thus, with gods as witnesses, she placed upon his neck her necklace, the garland of the groom.

Bhāratchandra says: Hurry. Hesitate no longer, for the night is passing by.

XI

It is said that without marriage there can be no sexual delight. With their eyes the two revealed that the Gandharva marriage had taken place within their hearts.[16] The maiden herself was the giver of the maiden, the groom the giver of the groom. The priest was Kāma, the six seasons wedding guests. The musicians for the wedding were Vidyā's ban-

[16] Gandharva marriage is love marriage, which is not arranged by family.

gles, their jingling the music. The dancer at the wedding was the ornament of her nose, the singer the *nupur*[17] around her ankle. Rati was the attendant of the maiden, Kāma of the prince. Slowly, very slowly, her companions withdrew themselves; they shrank as tinder from the fire. But with their eyes and lips and hands and hips and feet they themselves enjoyed the rapture of the happy pair, and understood their pleasure. They were glad for their beloved friend, and felt delight.

They sat together on the couch, the young bride and groom; and gazing at their loveliness, Kāma and Rati fell senseless at their feet. The hair of Vidyā spread the scent of musk-perfume. Nearby her companions placed a cup of sandal-paste and jasmine garlands in a golden bowl, and milk and sugar and sweets of many kinds, and decorated coconuts and cool soft camphor-scented Ganges water, and soft white fans of feathers and sweet *pān* and betel and lime. They arranged and decorated trays with rolls of betel-leaves, and cloves and cardamom seeds and nutmeg; all these sweet and scented things, stimulants to love, did they arrange.

It was in Baiśākh,[18] on the thirteenth night of the light fortnight. The sweet and gentle breeze was blowing, the moon was clear and spotless. The nightingales called to one another softly, mouth to mouth, drunk with the passion of the season. The bees, male and female, hummed, intoxicated with their honey. And the *cakora*[19] bird, drunk

[17] A heavy anklet of the type worn by dancers.
[18] The first month of the calendar: April–May.
[19] A fabled bird said to subsist on moonbeams.

upon the nectar of the moon, sported with his mate, brimming with the sweetness of his love.

At Vidyā's gesture, her companions began to play their instruments and to sing the gentle *rāga* and the *rāgini* of spring.[20] One played on tinkling cymbals, and one the *mṛdaṅga* drum; others played the *vīṇā* and the flute, the *tāmburā* and *rabāba* and *kapināśa,* and as they played the bells on their hands and ankles sounded. And enraptured by the music, they began to sing.

When they heard the sweet and modulated voices, the scholar-poet and his lady were transported with delight. Sundar lost himself entirely in the music, and taking up the *vīṇā,* himself began to sing. His song charmed the lovely Vidyā, and blending hers with the *vīṇā's* voice, she also began to sing. Each was delighted with the other's song and the prince embraced his lady, drunk with the nectar of love. With passion they gazed at one another. The companions, putting down their instruments, quietly withdrew. Shame was driven away by shame, fear by fear was broken, passion gave rise to the fullness of passion.

The prince, then, caught in the snare of passionate delight, loosened his garment and let it fall. He clutched the young girl to his heart, as a maddened elephant seizes a lotus; with the avidness of a *cakora*-bird he kissed her moon-like face, and took the border of her twelve-yard sari. He put his hand on her breasts like lotus-buds, but she with

[20] *Rāga:* a musical mode or system, of which six are chief; each of these is "wedded" to six *rāginis,* their union giving rise to numerous musical forms.

trembling limbs drew back. With his hand he gently tried to loose the covering of the breasts of his beloved, but Vidyā held his hand and said with trembling voice:
—Be kind, beloved. I am not in strength your equal. I know nothing of the art of love. Forgive me for today, my lord. I am in my menstrual time—but tomorrow it can surely be. You are my conqueror in both love and learning; do not torment a helpless girl. Besides, if you stay your passion now, how much more will our delight be later? When the blossom blooms slow and naturally, it will yield nectar. But does a flower give nectar when it is crushed? If you cannot contain yourself, my love, go sip the nectar of other flowers. You will crush this blossom, and the nectar will not flow. Bees do not fight with flowers. See now—your nails have scratched my breast, and the scratch is burning. O, sea of qualities, beloved, do not debase me—do not.

When he heard this, Sundar said:
—My body is aflame with Kāma's arrows lodged in my heart. You are to me as the lotus to the sun. Have no fear. Your beauty is as that of the crescent moon on Śiva's head . . . show to me that beauty . . . leave aside all sham and false pretense . . . your breasts are golden *ghaṭs,*[21] on them the blood drawn by my nails shines brilliant . . . but have no fear. Will sugar-cane give juice before it is pressed? I shall show you sweetness and joy—be gracious to me.

Thus speaking with seductive words, like the bee penetrating to the lotus' heart, he fought with her the war of

[21] *ghaṭ:* an earthen water-jar, frequently used poetically as a symbol of fertility.

love. Thus in the play of love, Sundar and his lovely mistress, trembling with the burning of Kāma's arrows, embraced; their bodies undulated, mad and drunk with passion and desire. Delirious with passion's nectar he kissed her mouth and reddened breasts like silk.

To remain in privacy, Vidyā-Rati and her lover locked the doors of the room. And then they lay together, their bodies moving, lips and teeth pressed tight, heart pressed to heart, frenzied in unruly struggle. Her bangles and her anklets tinkled. Vidyā's hair was all awry, her clothes in disarray, her cheeks were flushed; she was transported with delight, her breath was heavy, her loins and buttocks writhed. Their biting teeth drank nectar from each other's lips, their arms like strong ropes tied one to the other; two bodies paralyzed in equal bliss, trembling high on waves of sweetness and desire, quenching a thirst of many days. And the stringency of the struggle, constant and swift, satisfied the need of youth. An old, full sacrifice; and at last the fire of the sacrifice was extinguished. The god of love had poured his offering into the flame. And as the rainclouds cool the earth, when the storm-clouds loose their rain, the sky was clear again.

The nightingale sang. And then they lay, their heads together on a pillow, lazy, satisfied; they wooed each other with the glances of their eyes; both spent, their limbs and bodies senseless, slowly and at leisure they regained their minds. With a gentle smile, Vidyā went to dress. And when her companions returned, they found her gentle-faced and modest. Bhāratchandra says:

—Hear me, O Sundar. Why should you be ashamed?

XII

O MY BELOVED, the jewel of my mind is in your hands; if you love me, I shall not be afraid. I am not obliged to keep the customs of society. You come and go quietly, only here, and look upon your lover with a laden glance. You, O conqueror of Love, I say are the essence of loveliness. Do not leave my side and thus bring sinful stain upon your name. If you have love for me, of this tell no one. But Bhāratchandra says, if once I come to know of it, do not deceive me with falsehoods.

And so the handsome youth sat side by side upon the couch with his beloved, more lovely than Rati with her husband. And he anointed her body with sweet perfume and scented sandal, and gave her sweet things to eat and drink. They passed the night in talk of love, while her companions fanned their heated limbs. Then the prince said:
—I shall come again,
and prepared to bid farewell to Vidyā's house. The night-bloomed lotus closed its eyes, the moon had set. Vidyā then said to her companions:
—What shall I say? Each moment without him will be the moment of Destruction. How shall I live throughout the day, my eyes greedy *cakora*-birds starved for the nectar of his moon-like face? But if I can live through the day, though my heart burns in a fever of separation from him, I shall sip sweet nectar in the night.

Sundar said:
—I am the body, you the soul. Only in death can these be separated. Whatever word is in your mouth is also mine;

your thoughts are mine as well. Since this is so, parting can mean nothing to us.

The girl replied, her hand resting gently on his cheek, —Farewell, then. But be sure to say nothing of our meeting to the flower-woman.

XIII

As THE RISING SUN was opening the lotus blooms, the poet-prince again appeared in Hīrā's house. He went first to his morning toilet and oblations on the river bank, and having bathed and done his morning worship, he went to Hīrā. The flower-woman had picked her morning's flowers, and was weaving them into garlands. And when she had prepared her basket, she made her way to the palace.

She supplied her garlands to all the people of the palace, and having finished went like lightning to Vidyā's rooms. Vidyā, bathed and content, was seated there. Hīrā placed a garland beside her. With a gesture Vidyā told her companions to say nothing of the night's events. She thought: —Yesterday Hīrā was afraid. She would be apt to tell my mother, if she knew about these things. Hīrā would die in the present, worrying about the future. But despite her present labor pains, a woman will again sleep with her husband.

Then Vidyā said to the flower-woman:

—I shall ask you again. How shall we bring him here?

And Hīrā answered:

—To this, I have not yet found a satisfactory solution. You tell me to bring him to you, but when I hear this, fear comes to my mind. I went before, as you had asked, and told him what you said. But he answered me: "How can I go? What path can I take? Some one will see or hear me, and it will all end in disaster. I do not know what fate has in store for me." Thus he said. And you, O princess, will involve others in your scheming; I still advise you to tell your father and your mother. But do whatever you think best. God knows that I will have no further part in it.

With this Hīrā said farewell, and went back to her house. As she had previously done, she brought food from the market, and Sundar sat down to eat what she had cooked. Smiling to himself, he began to talk with Hīrā:

—Have you not yet thought of ways by which I can meet with Vidyā, Aunt? Is there any hope? Tell me how I can go to her.

And Hīrā replied:

—You are the prince; you are the possessor of all knowledge. So you tell me how to get you there. People swarm all over the palace. A thief could not get in. I have thought on the matter this way and that, and have reached this decision: Do not try it. Can a deer raid a lion's den? But if you let me tell the king and queen of you, a meeting can be brought about. Secretly it cannot be done. I could no more hide you than a pregnant woman can hide her pregnancy. Even in children's secrets dangers lurk. If you attempt this and are caught, your punishment will be severe; you will lose your head. Not only that, but I too will be punished. To help you with this job you need someone who has two heads.

So saying, the flower-woman went about her work, and the prince lay down to sleep, putting his bed over the tunnel-hole. And, as is its habit, day passed, and evening came;

and Hīrā brought the prince his evening meal. Then Sundar said to her:

—O Aunt, I am beginning to understand you. You have never intended that I meet Vidyā; yet you tricked me into weaving a beautiful garland for her. My faith and confidence in you have been misplaced. By conjuring dreams of ghosts and scorpions you try to scare me off. Ah, I should have known. She who talks much deceives much; and he who relies on a woman's promise is a fool. You have deceived me. I understand you now, O my good aunt, O nephew-deceiver. A man should trust no one, and without the gods all striving comes to naught. So hear me. Because all depends upon the gods I have dug a pit in your house; it is a way in which I worship Kālī. So do not call me in the night when I am meditating; for as long as my meditation lasts, I shall not answer you.

With these words Sundar barred his door and went happily to Vidyā's house. And you, O clever reader, now know his tricks and what a rogue he is. He even deceives his own procuress. But as cunning as he was, his mistress was the more. Only her most trusted companions served her, and their minds were stupefied with pleasure, with music and with song.

Ah, Bhāratchandra says, this thief has truly made an excellent haul. I am afraid that when they hear of this, most honest men will turn to thievery.

XIV

THEN SUNDAR EMBRACED his lovely mistress, and gently said:

—Hear, O goddess of my heart. Today, at noon, I saw most strange and wondrous things. I saw a lotus-pond in which an elephant was trapped by lotus-tendrils round his legs. Then I saw the mountain's head was hanging, and he was weeping, saying to the moon, "O lotus of the sky . . ." and the moon in bliss then lost its grip and fell tumbling to the earth. At seeing this, the *khañjana* and *cakora*-birds were laughing in delight. What a wonder all this was! What wonders more will you make me see?

Vidyā replied:

—Sir, this is not possible. You could not have seen such things.

But Sundar said:

—I saw it clearly.

The girl, then, understanding his trick, smiled and said:

—Impossible, sir—like a stone floating on the water, or a monkey singing a song. You could not have seen such things.

The prince replied:

—Listen, then. I am the elephant and you the lotus; you trap me in your lotus-stalk-like arms. I am the moon fallen to the earth in bliss, at the sight of the mountains of your breasts, glistening with nectar-sweat like tears. My eyes are like the *khañjana* birds, yours like the *cakora;* when they get their hearts' desire they, meeting, laugh with joy.

When she heard this explanation of the prince, she meditated in her heart:

—He would buy my soul and body but pay nothing. This I cannot tolerate, and should show both shame and modesty to him.

And so, aloud:

—I must acknowledge my defeat to you. A woman cannot bear a burden like a man; for you can lift a heavy load, but I cannot. This then I know: men's minds are also different, being utterly without shame. And where there is no modesty or shame, there is deception. He who taught me this has all these qualities; I know full well how much he honors womanhood. He taught me well, and what I learned has changed my fate completely. Men have no shame. Why should they have such strength and pride? But each to his own. If another were to act as you have acted, he would fail. But I must confess that nowhere could I witness such a fine performance, even on a stage. Seeing you this way, so young and idle, I wonder what will happen when you grow old. But forgive me, for the night passes vainly. Go to sleep, and I shall also. You have helped me understand many things. For one, what good can come of such as we are doing? Nothing will be gained from it. Though you are my heart's prince, you must sneak to me like any common thief. This only means you will be caught in shame, and punished. Ah, the gods, as male, have created jewels of delight, which are only pain to such young women as myself. Why should you want to change this, and take the pain upon yourself when you are caught?

The prince replied:

—Though I entreat you, I might as well be lost deep in a forest. I understand that you are shy. I also understand your modesty is designed to make my love increase, to win more passion from me. You, when we embraced, did give yourself to me. But now, may Kālī bring you fortune. Censure me no more. I came to this country with love in my heart, and now I shall go. Remember me with affection. Farewell.

Vidyā said then, laughing:

—What did you say, my jewel? That I returned your kisses and embrace? Why these adverse words, then? Your words fall in two directions, like a pumpkin split in two.

Thus Vidyā excited him with her coquettishness, and finally she fell, borne on a wave of love; her hair was loose in disarray, half-hiding her face as the cloud half-hides the moon. Her loins and buttocks swung, her waist-bells jingling with the swinging. Each clasped the other. Their faces full of passion, each drinking the nectar of the other's mouth. She with anklets tinkling, bit her husband's lip in transport of delight, and in her throat she made a nightingale-like sound. There rose a wave of passion and desire, and on this wave they floated; there was no limit to their joy. Her dark brows arched like bows of Kāma, sent darting piercing arrows of her glances. Engrossed, absorbed, on the edge of consciousness, she trembled and impatiently pressed her lips to his. Sweat stood out on all her limbs, where her clothes and jewelry touched her body. Her mouth was wet with sweat, and uttered small inarticulate cries of pleasure. Gradually, trembling with passion, she lost all control and fell inert. And when he saw her fall, her lover knelt by her side with concern, as a mother by her fallen child, and gently kissed her lips. Then, both unconscious, they sipped the nectar of each other's mouths. Seeing them thus, even Kāma, embarrassed at their intimacy, took Rati by the hand and fled away.

After a time they regained their senses and rose, limbs trembling and bodies drenched with sweat. And, when their love was satisfied, Sundar left the house. In this way they made love night after night. Thus does Bhāratchandra, himself brimming with such words of love, sing at the command of Krishnachandra.

XV

In this way did the poet embrace his mistress-wife and pass his nights in sport and sweet enjoyment. In great delight he passed away the nights, and his days were also spent in joy, in thinking of the nights to come. And every day Hīrā took his money and went to the market for shopping; he asked for no accounting when she returned. And after she had cooked and they had eaten and rested for a while, he would lock his door and go to wander in the city. He was as adept at disguise as the best of actors; he dressed himself sometimes as a mendicant *sannyāsī*[22] with a staff clutched in his hand; sometimes he was a magician gypsy, or a juggler or a doctor or a merchant or a student. And he said to himself:

—I have been successful. Now I shall go to the king, to see the court, its manners and its customs, and all its courtiers. Let me see. How shall I go? If I were dressed as a holy man, I should gain respect and honor. And what fun I could have in talk of Vidyā!

So thinking thus he put on *sannyāsī*'s dress and a wig of matted hair; he smeared ashes on his body, and in his hand

[22] *sannyāsī:* an ascetic, a wandering mendicant.

he took an earthen pot and rosary of glass beads, and Śiva's trident-emblem in his hand. He put a deerskin on his shoulders and tied a loincloth round his waist; he put a red robe on his shoulders, took in his mouth the name of Śiva, and went forth, radiating heat like that of the sun itself.[23]

Thus arrayed, he went to court. Vīrashiṁha rose and bowed to him, while Sundar muttered constantly Nārāyaṇ's name. The people of the court all bowed to the earth; he spread his deerskin on the ground and sat down. Then the courtiers said:

—O holy man, whence do you come? Where do you go? When did you come to our city?

And the king asked:

—Why are you here?

Then the *sannyāsī* said:

—My home is in the Badrika *āśrām*. I am going to the place where the Ganges meets the sea. When I reached the borders of this country I heard some news, and came to the court to verify its truth. Is not the daughter of the king the famous Vidyā? I have heard her beauty is that of Lakshmī and her intelligence that of Sarasvatī. I also heard that she has made an open vow, that who should conquer her in argument should be her husband. I have heard that many men have so far come, but none has taken her. Having heard, then, of this wonderful sport, I have come to try myself. For how shall I ever grasp true knowledge without knowing true Knowledge herself? Can this mere girl really conquer everyone? That would be disaster. If she can beat

[23] By meditation and austerity, *sannyāsīs* and other holy men generate power, which manifests itself in heat.

me in debate, I shall leave asceticism and become her servant. Once I shaved my head, according to instructions of my *guru.* If I come to honor her as *guru,* I shall once again shave these matted locks. But if I beat her in debate, I shall remain as I am. A *sannyāsī* can have no passion or desire. If then I win the wager, I shall dedicate the girl to Śiva's service. I shall put ashes on her body and a leather bag upon her shoulder. I shall put a rosary upon her throat, and glass beads in her hand. According to my vow we shall wander from land to land. If this occurs, no woman will again make such a vow as she has done.

Then the courtiers all whispered to one another:

—The girl cannot go through with this . . .

And the king said:

—A disaster has occurred! This *sannyāsī* is full of power. If he loses, he will shave his head. If he wins, I shall have to give to him my daughter, and this I cannot do. Knowledge, which was Vidyā's virtue, has become her vice.

Then the *sannyāsī* said:

—Why do you ponder about the matter? It is not necessary that you reflect upon it. She has made the vow.

The king replied:

—O *sannyāsī,* go home for today. Come tomorrow, and we shall consult together. First you must debate with all my courtiers. If you defeat them all, you will be eligible to debate with Vidyā.

With this word the king went to the inner chambers, and said to Vidyā:

—Alas, O Vidyā. You have become a curse both to yourself and to me. Your foolish vow has brought a great calamity. I brought so many noble princes here and all were sent away by you defeated. Your fortune is surely evil, that you did not marry one of them in grace. Now a *sannyāsī* comes to the court and seeks a contest with you. If he wins or if he loses, the calamity will be great.

Then Vidyā said:

—I shall not debate with him. God willing, I shall remain just as I am.

Thus did the Sundar-*sannyāsī* sport with Vidyā in the night, and in the day discourse of her with the king. He won all arguments with the courtiers, and every day demanded that she be brought to him. And every day the king, afraid of Sundar's curse, said:

—She will come tomorrow.

XVI

One day Vidyā, laughing, said to Sundar:

—There has come to the court a *sannyāsī*, a great scholar. He wants to take me, after conquering me in argument. I heard from my father's mouth that he has already defeated the whole court.

The prince replied:

—What have you said? Tell me no more! I know the man —a scholar of the greatest wisdom. When I first came here I met with him, and was beaten by him, debating the *śāstras*. There is nothing he does not know; he is perhaps the one who will steal the stolen from the thief.

Then Vidyā said:

—I shall have no part in this.

And Sundar replied:

—What will you do if the king decides to give you to him? You will gain a scholar wiser, and younger, and more handsome than myself. What harm will that do you? The injury will be mine. You will cast off the old and gain the new; and then if I return, will you even look at me?

Vidyā said:

—You are laughing at me, and taking advantage of my plight. A woman's fate is not like that of man. A man can cast away the old and take the new; a woman cannot act like that.

In this way the two bantered back and forth. How much more of it shall I describe? My book already grows too large.

So in the morning the prince once more returned to Hīrā's house, and to the river's bank to bathe and for his morning worship. And Hīrā picked her flowers and went forth to the palace. There she heard the news of the *sannyāsī;* and when she heard she quickly went to Vidyā's room and said to her:

—What is this I hear, granddaughter? What do people whisper? Is this true or false? O ill-starred girl, when I heard this, my heart wept for you, though I kept a smile upon my face, as in the palace I must always do. They told me your bridegroom has come—a *sannyāsī,* they say, whose beard is longer than your loosened hair. In the evening he gathers cow-dung from house to house. When I see him I must ask him how much tobacco, opium, marijuana, and *bhaṅg* he consumes daily. There are ashes, not sandalwood upon his body; when he stands up his matted hair falls tangled to his feet. His eyes are half-closed in his drugged or drunken trance; ah, but he will show to you Benares, Prayāg, and Mathurā. So after all this time you have found a noble husband! When I see this one, all naked, I am satisfied. He will put you on a tiger skin and smear you with ashes. He will take you on his pilgrimage to seek perfection. It will be a joke, like the marriage of Śiva and Gaurī. Ah, my heart is torn for you. As God made Rahu eat the moon, so he made that *sannyāsī* to make you waste away. Alas, not the peacock, nor the *cakora,* nor the parrot, nor the *cataka,* gets the mango; it is taken by the crow. Ah, I brought you a handsome husband, and what did you do? You lost him because you would not tell your parents. It is not in your fate that you should have him, nor are you in his. But now go, give yourself to this *sannyāsī.* Become a *sannyāsinī.* Go with him begging.

Then Vidyā said to Hīrā:

—You have said enough. You brought me a husband of highest beauty, indeed. Every day I ask you to bring him here. But you yourself are too reluctant to have him come. You will not let me go. He is my husband, you said, but when shall I have him? There are ashes on the *sannyāsī*'s head, and just as many in your mouth. You smile and call me 'granddaughter.' But you do not love me like a granddaughter. You are old, but still coquettish. Go and think on how to bring him here.

So she dismissed Hīrā, and Hīrā went home, smiling all the way, delighted with all that had occurred. Then she told the news to Sundar:

—Listen child, to what I heard in the palace. A *sannyāsī*

has come to marry Vidyā. He has defeated all the courtiers in debate, and only Vidyā now is left. I am afraid that you will after all be deprived of her. You cannot win her now. Perhaps you too should take *sannyāsa.* I told you to speak to the king and queen, but no. I cannot understand why you did not do this. Now, if the *sannyāsī* defeats her in debate, you will be left sitting and staring like a frog.

Then Sundar said:

—O Aunt, what a disaster is this! But tell me, what did Vidyā say? Tell me quickly!

Hīrā replied:

—She wants you to go to her.

And Sundar said:

—Aunt, this is a joyful thing. My hopes are all fulfilled. But how shall I go? I cannot find a way.

XVII

One day the poet desired Vidyā in the daytime, and entered her room. Vidyā had closed her door and lay asleep; seeing her thus sleeping, Sundar was filled with pleasure. Because of the night's sleeplessness, she had fallen where she had stood; her companions were asleep, outside the door. Sundar, eager for her love, was like a honeybee, uncertainly returned to drink more lotus-nectar. He had no patience, even to awaken her, but began his sacrifice to passion. He was filled with desire, and she in her deep sleep thought it was a dream; her passion began to grow. With kisses and embraces, he worshipped her with many kinds of love. And indeed, more happiness is sometimes found in sleep; in a dream much more success is had in finding what is lost, than waking. And when the play of love was finished, her sleep in joy was broken, and she awoke. Lazily, slowly, her reddened eyes opened. She woke up slowly, and saw the sun, and said:

—How can the day have come so soon?

Then she saw Sundar lying there, and anger seized her mind. She thought:

—He has seen me in the depths of sleep, and in the day. My hair is disarrayed, my clothes are all awry. Such behavior only brings humiliation to a girl. The minds of men are hard and shameful, and do not understand the proper way of things.

Thinking thus, annoyed, she hung her head in silence and in shame. She put aside her ornaments and jewels. And Sundar understood what was in her heart, what his offence had been. He thought:

—Why have I done this insane thing? It was for her happiness and mine, but it has turned to ashes. What I thought was nectar was really poison. What shall I do?

Thus the poet thought. And now the sun had sunk behind the hills, and it was evening. The moon had risen. He then made love to her with words, to soothe her mind. But can entreaty conquer anger? He said to her, deceiving her:

—When the sun comes up, the night is ineffectual, and is dispelled. So, taking its fire from your anger, that moon becomes the sun, and burns my body with its heat. The nectar of the flowers turns to poison. The nightingale screams curses in my ear, and bees answer with a war cry.

This now will spread from house to house, its messenger the gentle sandal-bearing wind. The trees are laughing at my sorrow with their perfumed and blooming flower-lips. They are all my enemies; they seek only my distress. All this because of you; if you do not, who then will save me from my misery? If I offended you, I stand ready for your punishment. Bind me with your arms. Crush my chest with the mountains of your swelling breasts. Tear me with your nails. Rip my flesh with your biting teeth. Seize me by the hair. O you, who have the power to destroy my mind, instead of being silent, give me harsh abuse. If you are angry, curse me.

In such a way did Sundar play upon her heart, til Vidyā said:

—Please stop! You press me too hard; you know too many tricks. But I shall not speak; nor need you clasp my feet.

The poet thought:

—Her honor is indeed no trifling thing. It cannot be taken lightly, or her anger would have broken at my words. She is very angry. But if I sneeze, she will surely say *jīva,*[24] and her anger and her silence will be gone.

So he put a piece of wood into his nose and sneezed. But the clever princess thought:

—If I say *jīva,* my anger will disappear. I shall not say a word. But I shall make him understand that I have said the word, though I do not speak.

And she held out her golden amulet, a charm for length of life, toward the prince. And when he saw this witty action, then he understood. He clasped her feet, and the

[24] "Long life," to be said when a person sneezes.

quarrel was over. He clasped her reddened feet, like red lotuses, to his heart, and her anklets hummed like honeybees.

Thus the crafty prince again gained union by his artfulness, and they renewed again the play of passion.

As his room in Hīrā's house or hers was always empty, there was never an impediment in their path. One day Sundar showed his tunnel to Vidyā and took her through it back to Hīrā's house. When she saw there Sundar's talking bird, she brought to it her own. The marriage of the birds brought pleasure to the lovers, and they addressed each other as "mother-in-law" and "father-in-law." When first they brought the birds together in Sundar's room they grew themselves in love, and then and there made a sacrifice to passion.

Hīrā heard the noise, and said:

—What is that I hear?

And Sundar said:

—I am giving a pomegranate to my bird.

Thus did he, first seeing that the door was tightly closed and barred, deceive the flower-woman, and sipped his nectar leisurely, a bee taking honey from the lotus. The two then went again to Vidyā's room, and in such ways played many tricks. But Vidyā was still angry about his having come to her in daylight. One day she thought of vengeance.

Sundar was asleep in his own room when Vidyā came to him. Seeing him helpless in his sleep, she gently kissed his mouth; she put vermilion and cooling sandal on his forehead and, when she had kissed his eyes, departed. When she touched him he awoke, but she was gone. His body thrilled and trembled, drunk with love. He quickly went to Vidyā's room, and there saw Vidyā, sitting on the bed, gazing at her face in a mirror. When she saw him, Vidyā laughed and said:

—Come, lord of my life. What is this I see? Who put vermilion and sandal on your forehead? And how did the betel-juice get on your eyes? Come, look here in the mirror. See if it is not so.

When he saw himself in the mirror, the poet was astonished. Then Vidyā said:

—Ah, lord of my heart, I know what this means. Hīrā's house contains your love-bed in the daytime. Hīrā has brought you new ones, perhaps. Soon you will not want to come to me at all. I am to you a faded flower, whose nectar is exhausted. Only in your words are you a vestige of him who was once my lover. What is this thing you do to me? Now you are here, then you go there. Even, I suppose, a thoughtful husband loses interest; this hurts more than shameless knavery. But even though my body burn in passion's fire for twelve years, I shall keep no company with a libertine! How can a woman give her lips to one who kisses other women? Who eats another's left-over food? He who touches such is unclean!

But Sundar said:

—O lovely one, how much more rebuke will you heap upon my head? For though you take an oath to deny it, you know that this is your vermilion and your sandal. It is the juice of your *pān* which colors my eyelids. It is because of you that my forehead is marked. However much I wash my forehead, those marks will never leave me. Your *pān* has stained my eyelids; from now on I shall see you, whether I wake or sleep. Why do you act the *khaṇḍitā*,[25] because of your own marks on my face? By such action you will only become a *kalahāntaritā*.[26] You are dressed in your finest clothes, as if to meet your lover; a woman is not at the same time eager to meet her lover and offended at his approach. Do you want to be left alone? If not, why do you reproach me thus? If I wanted to leave you for another, do you think that I would come to you like this, at risk of life?

The princess listened to his words in gladness. False anger remains no longer than water in a sieve. And with her anger gone, the two gave way to love, and the night passed in talk of tender things. In the morning the prince returned to Hīrā's house. In this way they passed their days.

XVIII

Now her companions knew that it was Vidyā's menstrual time, and she and Sundar made their second marriage then. But I cannot find it in my heart to write about all this; I know that my descriptions are not full, but my manuscript would grow too fast. So let me say just this: that the rogue Sundar went on acting in such ways, and took his constant pleasure in love's sport. But watch the whim of Kālī become manifest.

In a few short months, Vidyā became pregnant, her

[25] A term from Sanskrit poetics, one of the classes of heroine: a woman offended with her husband because of his infidelity.

[26] A term from poetics: a woman who has quarreled with her lover, but now regrets it.

child rising in her belly as the moon in the sky; the lotus closed its eyes, the menstrual flux was far away. Day by day her slender waist grew thicker; her face grew dark, her heavy breasts hung down, the nipples thick with oozing milk. When it was time, her veins began to show; her beautiful complexion, golden as the turmeric, or *campa* flower, or flash of lightning, burnt ashen pale in her body's heat. She forgot all else, and sat there moaning to herself:

—Alas, can this have happened in my womb?

And to her red *bāndhulī*-lips and lotus-mouth, over which the bees had buzzed, hoping to alight, the vomit rose. She longed continually for strange things to eat, for delicious sour foods. She told herself:

—Surely I was mad, forgetting all my modesty; how I wish I could remedy my former shamelessness.

She slept but fitfully, and often waking walked about the room, longing for sleep to come. She could not rest in her soft bed; sometimes she laid her sari on the floor and slept on it. Once she was down she could not rise again, so tired and weak was she. There was no more clarity in her mind, nor nectar in her mouth. When they saw her belly, her friends whispered:

—What will happen when her parents hear of this? Alas, why must we stay here? We have not been part of this. If we stay we all will surely die because of it. She has had her pleasure, and now she will bring destruction on us all. Hīrā said that this would happen, and it has all come true. Long ago, when arguments were made, it should have been prevented. Now secrecy is not possible. They say an evil deed can be hidden only for a time. Let us go and tell the queen the news. It will be a risk, for we may lose our heads. But then, so will we if we stay.

Ah, Bhārata says, these servant girls are models of goodness. They are faithful to one's face, but when one's back is turned they stick a knife in it.

XIX

So Vidyā's friends, with lengthened faces, went before the queen. With folded palms they bowed before her feet and humbly made this speech:

—O, queen, come and see the princess. Her belly is full, with all the signs of pregnancy, and she is ill—yet we cannot imagine that this is really so, nor how it came to be. But if you see her you will understand it all.

Hearing this, the queen was speechless with the shock, and went like lightning, her long hair flowing wild, to Vidyā's room. When she saw Vidyā's belly she was dumb; she could not say a word. And Vidyā could not give her mother greeting; she could not bow because of her belly and her shame. She covered her face with her sari's border and sat with bowed head. She said:

—Please sit down.

And the queen, her hand to her cheek, sank speechless to the earth, her face downcast. When she observed the signs, she said:

—You have done well, depraved girl, defamer of your family; perhaps a witch, perhaps some sorcerer has made you big—but the very wind is afraid to enter here. Who did this? How did he get here? Ah, he is cunning, who can make a frog to dance upon a serpent's head. Have you no money with which to buy a rope to hang yourself, or water-pot in which to drown? How could you do this to yourself and me? Your father is a king of kings, and you disgrace him! Princes came to marry you, but you, proud girl, defeated them in argument and would not have them. Now you have fallen to a thief. You bring great shame upon us all; the story of this scandal will spread to every corner of the country. A worthless thing you have become! A fine marriage bargain you have made! The princes of the world were at your feet, and still you chose a thief. The princes even now come to the palace, hearing of your vow. But will they come again? Even now there is a *sannyāsī* with the king. He comes constantly because of you. What shall I tell the king? If he gives you not to that *sannyāsī*, there will be great dishonor on our heads. Ah, the excellent Vidyā, my daughter, praised everywhere and honored most highly, possessor of all qualities, worthy of the greatest prince to be my son-in-law! I too am the daughter of a king, wife of a king. My daughter was to be wife, too, to a king, and mother of a prince. I had all these hopes; now all is gone. Scandal is my only recompense. "Vidyā's mother is the fraud," they will say; and if they say this, I swear I shall take poison. I shall throw myself into the river. I shall cut my throat, and bid the earth farewell. Ah, and your faithful companions! Indeed, they guarded well. All of you are procuresses and whores; you have heaped shame upon my head. You are her companions in this wantonness. You are lewd women—you took pleasure in this—you have deceived me—you have played me false. But let it go, let it go. Your noses will be cut off, your heads shaved.

You see, companions? Now you will lose your heads, says Bhārata.

XX

While the queen was ranting so, Vidyā stayed silent, cowering in shame and fear. Then she began to tell a story with great cunning. Weeping, she said:

—Hear me mother. You accuse me falsely of deceit. I know not of right and wrong. Only the Lord knows right and wrong, success and failure. But look—all around are guards, and with me always, my companions. I am as if a prisoner here. My life has no enjoyment. And now how falsely you blame me, O my mother. A princess, forever suffering the pangs of loneliness—who can compare with me in misery and wretchedness? My father never speaks to me, nor do I ever see my mother. To whom then can I turn? Why do I live? Perhaps because of loneliness and constant longing my belly began to grow. And now tears fill my eyes; my body has no strength. I cannot see, my head hangs in misery. Now hear me, mother, for this is all I know: every night I have a dream. And in this dream a man, a handsome god, a heavenly musician, embraces me. "Thief," I call him, and try to catch and hold him, in the depths of my sleep. And then my dream is broken, he is gone, and there is a burning inside me. As falsehood can seem truth, so this can happen to a woman in a dream. For when my dream is broken, there are signs of semen on my clothes. This is my pleasure, in a dream. I have lain with this dream husband, and because of this my belly swells.

Despite these clever words, the queen, aflame with rage, ran to tell the king.

Are you amused at Bhāratchandra's words? She would deceive her mother with a shadow!

XXI

THE QUEEN grew still more angry as she ran, her sari's border floating out behind her; her hair was all disheveled, her eyes revolving in her head like wheels, her hands beating in the air; roaring like a thundercloud she ran, and all the people of the palace stared after her.

The king was in his sleeping-room, taking his afternoon nap. His servants cooled his limbs with fans. Just then the queen burst in with angry face. Hearing the jingling of her anklets as she came, the king sat up astonished, and when he saw her said:

—What has happened? Tell me quickly.

The queen replied:

—O king, what shall I say? I am ashamed to speak . . . a scandal is to fill the country . . . in your house a virgin girl . . . whom you never see . . . whom you have not yet found a way to marry . . . you thought your happiness would come easily, that you would look upon your grandson's face . . . this even while you avoided the responsibility for her marriage. Ah, what shall I say? Alas, your daughter is a grown-up girl, who burns with passion like a fire . . . how will she marry? . . . you should go to see her at once . . . my head is hung in shame . . . her belly . . . but you will see yourself her shameless trouble. To whom can I now show my face? Proud as I once was, I am now so humbled. My pride has gone to ruin. But how can I condemn her? There is no use in anger. If she had married, she would have had many children. And how many young men could she have married? Passion burns in youth; how much can a woman endure? How long could she be satisfied with talk? You are always busy; nothing of importance touches you, though you have many men around who are capable of handling your daily work. You are like a dwindling fire, and make those around you ashes also. But how can I condemn? If only I were dead, and this were over with! Ah, he who understands himself understands in himself the sorrows of others, and he is known by all as noble.

While the queen was speaking thus, the king was waxing hot in anger. He ordered his attendants forward, and in a voice like that of doom he said:

—Bring me the captain of my guard!

When they heard this order shouted loudly, the king's attendants ran, and with them swordsmen and mace-bearers, to find the captain of the guard. They brought him, beating him with blows of fists and sticks and feet, cracking his bones so finely that their powder rose up through his skin; they threw him down before the king. When he regained his consciousness he knelt, his hands in supplication.

The king said:

—Hear me. If you catch not him who has defamed my name before this day is out, you will know the power of my vengeance. You are a treacherous rogue who eats my salt and gives me nothing in return. You have ruined my kingdom; you are nothing but a robber. You have plundered my whole country until only my own palace is left, and now you have begun on that. But I shall see you, you bastard, buried in a pit of excrement; you will know my pride for what it is. My palace was your charge. Yet a thief got into Vidyā's rooms. I am ashamed to speak of it, and my shame is not lessened by having a drunken captain of my guard.

Then Dhumaketu, the captain of the guard, spoke:

—Hear me, O great king. Spare my life and give me seven days. Within that time I shall catch and bring the thief before you.

The king gave his assent, and when they heard, the guards ran out to organize the search. Vidyā and her friends were taken from their rooms and lodged in the queen's apartment. The captain of the guard then went toward Vidyā's room and began a thorough search for the means by which the thief had come. He was saying to himself:

—What shall I do? Where shall I go? How shall I catch that thief and save my life? What kind of thief can he be? Surely he has put a curse on me. Perhaps it is a god, or some demon or Nāga. I do not understand what it all means . . . he must have come and gone in empty space. How can I catch him? My birth was taken on this earth in fruits of good or evil in my former life; who can change the course of such a destiny? Happiness is for others; only misery is written on my forehead. Ah, have pity on a poor policeman. This girl, this princess, is passionate; she is a girl of virtue, quality, and wealth. It was all right for her—she enjoyed her pleasure before disaster fell; but she has brought such sorrow on my head. Ah, how fickle fate can be . . .

And thinking thus, the captain entered Vidyā's room, depressed and sorrowful in mind, and gave the bed a pull, and looked about. And when he threw the bed aside, he saw the hole. When he saw the hole he called his aides, his brothers, and he said:

—Look, look, brothers! This is really troublesome. Perhaps her lover came from there. Indeed, this makes me ask what kind of love affair she had . . . this is probably a passageway to hell itself, through which a Nāga comes and goes. If he has come and gone through here, he probably will come today again. We can watch him come, but who among us has the heart to capture him? This is delight mingled with distress; Duryodhana's fate is visited on us.[27] If we do not seize this Nāga-snake, we oppose the orders of the king, and will be killed. If we seize him we obey the orders of the king, and will be killed. I shall have to be fast and cunning, and set a trap like the Marica-deer in Sītā's rape . . .[28]

[27] Duryodhana was the leader of the Kaurava princes in the great war of the *Mahābhārata*. When the Kaurava armies were defeated by the Pāṇḍavas, Duryodhana went and hid beneath the water; he was induced to come out and fight with Bhima, one of the Pāṇḍava brothers, with clubs. Bhima was getting the worst of it, when, unfairly, he struck Duryodhana and broke his thigh. Duryodhana was finally defeated.

[28] Marica was a Rakshasa, minister of Rāvaṇa the enemy of Rāma in the *Rāmāyaṇa*. He lured Rāma away from Sītā by assuming the shape of a golden deer, which Rāma pursued. Meanwhile, Rāvaṇa was carrying Sītā off.

And someone said:

—Quick! Call a snake-charmer here! He will catch this snake and charm him with his playing.

And others said:

—A madman speaks! Indeed, when danger comes all judgment disappears. We do not know what kind of snake lives in this hole. He may have eaten many men already, impervious to charms.

Still others said:

—Brothers, it cannot be a snake. This is the home of some spirit of the earth.

And others:

—It is certainly a jackal's hole.

Thus some, laughing, rebuked others, and others were called fools and witless. And finally Dhumaketu said:

—It seems to me it is a clever way to break into a house. Whatever you may say, I am not afraid. For we must find from whence he came. If it is indeed a black snake, we still must capture it. I myself will enter the tunnel and seize this snake, or be eaten in attempting it. For if I do not capture it, I myself will have to bear the punishment of the thief; never can I show my face again before the king; my punishment will be worse than that of the worst of thieves. What a job I have!

Saying this, Dhumaketu prepared himself to go into the hole. But his younger brother Bhimaketu was afraid, and held him, saying:

—I am anxious for your safety. Whether this be snake or god or demon, I have a plan to do away with fear. He has taken Vidyā once, and most certainly will come again in lust. Let us all then put on women's dress, and when he comes again it will be directly to our trap. If he be beast or bird or snake, or even if he flies, he shall not escape. For there are all kinds of traps: gods and demons are trapped by *tantramantra*,[29] and formless Brahma falls weeping into the body's snare. If there be fear when snakes are mentioned, bring a bird which catches snakes, and a snake-charmer for insurance, and place them near. Then, like Vidyā and her friends, we shall stand about in female dress. It is better to die than to be afraid. Besides, the thief knows nothing of our plans. If he learns that we are after him he will not come again. So what is to be done we must do at once. Let us prepare for him before we are too late.

Then Kālaketu said:

—Brother, this is an excellent plan.

And Bhārata says: O thief, you are as good as caught in the trap baited with your mistress. All prepare to catch a libertine, who has abandoned fear and shame.

XXII

So Dhumaketu gave his orders, and swiftly the brothers ran in eight directions. From the dancing-hall they brought cosmetics and other preparations, and put female dress on all. Candraketu was the youngest brother, very handsome, with a great resemblance to Vidyā; he donned her clothes, put on a blouse with blocks of wood beneath for breasts. He also wore a skirt which hung down to the floor, and underneath were blocks of wood for filling out his buttocks

[29] By the power of magical formulae the gods may be controlled.

and his stomach. The rest were dressed as Vidyā's friends.

They took up *vīṇās,* lutes, and other instruments, and played and danced with a grace that would have pleased the god of love himself; they seemed a group of charming, graceful girls. And there were also those whose skill in chants and charms against snake-bite was very great, and all put snake-repellent medicine on their heads and bodies, and antidotes for snake-bite; the fragrance of these medicines was such that even Vāsuki, the king of snakes, would flee. And thirteen snake-charmers ranged themselves about the room, guarding all the eight directions. At various stations messengers were placed, and guards and runners were alerted; they crouched in ambush by all doors; then began a restless wait, as if for the holocaust which destroys the world. At the four main city gates were four trusted *jāmādārs,* with musketeers and bowmen and swordsmen and wrestlers of the king, awful to behold; all four doors of seven forts were guarded by twenty-eight men; and all around the city great tumult arose—the military bands began to play and in the dust of marching feet the day became like night. The whole earth shook. Like beaters beating the bush to drive the tiger from his lair (though it is known that beaters never catch the prey), the king's guard marched about with much tumultuous pomp. And in the palace the queen with all her maidens, dressed in colored saris and wearing garlands of roses on their necks, vermilion on their brows, and sacrificial swords clutched in their hands, wandered from room to room looking for the thief. In every nook and cranny of the town, police spies searched, until the whole town shook with fear. Merchants, traders, mendicants, foreigners—all strangers were seized and thrown in chains. And if they saw a student with a box and books, they threw him into jail. On him whose body they saw garlands of sweet flowers, on whom were markings of sweet sandal, they heaped abuse and quick imprisonment. From all the quarters of the city a great and helpless cry arose; the city was like the prison of Jārasandha.[30]

And there were spies; here one dressed as a *sannyāsī*, a *tilaka* on his forehead, Vedic verses in his mouth, there one like a fakir; one was a barber just returned to the city, one a monk with rosary in hand, one a tanner, one a wandering magician; one here with sacred thread, one there an itinerant astrologer; one a soldier, one a merchant—in all these guises, spies swarmed about the city at the chief's command. The thief might be anywhere, in any guise. And so they wandered from place to place, and in many ways, with many tricks, they looked for news of the thief.

Meanwhile, in the palace, Vidyā thought:

—This all means mortal danger for my husband; for he, not knowing what is going on, will come again, desirous of me. O Lord! He will surely fall into the captain's trap.

And indeed, at that very time the prince, drunk with passion, was entering the tunnel to Vidyā's room. Candraketu was sitting on the bed, a trap in Vidyā's form to catch the Sundar-moon. With smiles and jokes the poet sat beside him, and Candraketu answered with a smile and

[30] "He who was joined together by [the demon] Jāra": the father of two of the wives of Kaṁsa, whom Krishna had killed, Jārasandha was a powerful warrior, whose prisons were filled with kings. On the demand of Krishna, Bhima, and Ārjuna that he release the kings, he chose to fight, and was killed by Bhima.

pulled his sari's border across his face. The poet then began to woo his mistress with words of passion and of love, and Candraketu, feigning anger, drew the veil more tightly on his face. The poet, maddened with desire, could not understand. He stroked her hands and feet, to break her pique. But Candraketu did not say a word; he made signs with his eyes. Then Sundar, in a fit of passion, seized the sari and made as if to pull it from Candraketu's face. But Suryaketu, seeing this, could keep no longer silent, and so said:

—Who is this brash and arrogant wretch? He has conquered one moon; he now wants another! God knows what he will do next.

Then Dhumaketu sounded the alarm, and there was rushing to and fro, and some pushed a huge stone into the tunnel's mouth. Then, in mortal fear, they all looked, terrified, at Sundar, wondering whether he was *deva* or Gandhārva or Yakṣa or Nāga, looking to see if his eyes were winking or if he cast a shadow on the ground[31] They knew him then to be a man, and seeing this their fear was broken. But Sundar still did not understand. Candraketu rose as if to go, and Sundar said:

—Where are you going, beloved?

And he embraced his supposed mistress, kissed his face and placed his hand upon the wooden breast. The breast fell off. But Sundar, stupefied with passion, thought it was a joke.

Bhārata says: Well done, O arrow of Kāma's bow! But why today, O Vidyā, do you seem so *sundara*, so handsome.

[31] Gods do not wink or cast shadows.

XXIII

Sundar seized his mistress in his arms and tossed her in the air. But then the companions came and seized him, and twelve more men came also. Then said the prince:
—O companions! What troubles you?

And Dhumaketu replied:
—Listen, O son-in-law of the king; I have captured you and shall not let you go, by order of the princess.

Then he put his hand upon his wooden breast and took it off. Seeing this astonishing performance, the prince was first amazed, and finally understood the meaning of it all. The guards then waved and rattled shields and swords, their swords like those of Death himself; the bowmen stood alert, the arrows on their drawn bows glistening sharp. They seized the thief, and Dhumaketu cried:
—Hari, Hari! Victory to Kālī! Good! Well done! Now I am afraid of no one. Let all instead have fear of me!

And the swordsmen leapt into the air with joy, and the whole earth trembled with their joyousness. Kettle-drums boomed out, and wrestlers, their *dhotis* drawn up tight, slapped their thighs and threatened Sundar. They took him out, and all of Burdwan was in the streets, delirious with joy. People crowded all the streets, though it was night, roused by the clamor. They shouted:
—Hey brother! Policemen! You'd better guard your heads if he escapes!

And surrounding Sundar and his guards the people came, some ahead and some behind, delighted, frolicking, delirious with joy, making noise in celebration. There was no sleep that night.

—Tie his hands and feet; beat him with sticks! Hit the lecher with your fists!

These things the people shouted through clenched teeth, and Sundar's face was full of fear; his heart was trembling. Fear lodged like a hook in his bowels. Seeing men prepared to shoot their sharp-tipped arrows, seeing their keen-edged swords, his calm was shaken. His arrogance fled. He trembled. Then Dhumaketu said:

—Throw him into prison. Tomorrow we shall take the pig before the king.

And the whole crowd, thousands strong, laughed long and loud. Sadness was dispelled and gladness came into a thousand faces; "*Jaya jaya*" was the cry, and the whole earth shook as with the tumult of a battlefield. And Sundar heard these things and shook with fear. He was surrounded by crowds of enemies, and he thought:

—Alas! A pretty situation I am in. Because of my desire I am about to die. How could I have done it? A woman has brought me to such straits, and now I am drawing my last breath. How many other bridegrooms, newly married, have fallen in such trouble? How many die like this? O God! Can I get out of this alive?

Thus he spoke, bitter and alone; his heart burning within his body.

—Tomorrow I shall be condemned. I shall have no head to bow in shame. To whom, of those in court, can I now turn? Who will there be who will protect and defend me? And if I lose my life this way, how shall I gain salvation? This deed will lead me on another round of births. And Vidyā, it would seem, wants me to suffer this affliction. If only she would come and speak with me, I would be consoled . . . she who is in every way incomparable, who was my most beloved . . . though I shall never see or hold her in my arms again, she is always in my mind. How much love I had for her! Who could be more to me than she; and who is more to her than once I was? She is the object and ideal of all my love. Shall I ever hold her in my arms again? In my own country in every place my name is celebrated. And I have wronged her; I have stained her name. I have betrayed my father, and now I burn in shame. My lust has gained me only grief. Day and night I gave unbridled freedom to my passion; and now I eat the poison distilled from that.

In such a way did thoughts come to his mind, as he sat with bowed head. He was as helpless as a snake in a basket.

XXIV

Then, in the night, with swords clutched tightly in their hands, each holding to the one before him, Kālaketu with seven men descended to explore the tunnel. The darkness was like the darkness at the bottom of a well, fearful. Some hung back in terror; some refused to go at all. The others proceeded step by step. In the tunnel's walls uncovered jewels burned like glowing lights. Then Kālaketu saw the tunnel's end and said:

—Good! Let us go, brothers, I see the end.

So step by step they went, trembling with fright, until they finally raised their heads, those heroes, in Hīrā's house.

They climbed into the house; their noise was such that Hīrā woke in fear. They all ran helter-skelter in the darkness, striking at each other and at her. Then someone lit the lamp; they seized poor Hīrā, and cursing, said:
—So this is where the thief came from!

Then some went back through the tunnel to give the news to Dhumaketu. And when he heard the news his heart was glad. He grabbed his sword and shield and with his heroes shot like an arrow into the house of Hīrā. He seized her by the hair and said:
—Tell us, who is the thief? What is his relationship to you? Where did you hide him? Whose bastard son is he? Tell me that!

Ah, the poetry of Bhārata is full of nectar; it is melodious in speech and song. It is indeed the epitome of matchlessness.

XXV

So they beat the flower-woman with their fists, until she said:
—Though you beat me to death, what will it gain you, knaves? You rain destruction on my back and head; what have I done? If you kill me it will be a sin upon your heads. You come here in the middle of the night, taking the name of the king to call it justice; do you come to rob me? I am humiliated by your beating.

Then, laughing, Dhumaketu said:
—And you are not ashamed to speak like this! Brothers,

this old woman says that she has been humiliated by me. Do you not tremble in fear when you hear this?

Then Hīrā said:

—Now hear me, you wretch! You are indeed a sea of qualities, all of them evil. Who is afraid of you? Everyone knows that you are nothing but a bandit; you seem to have forgotten that we all know this.

Then Dhumaketu said in anger:

—What do you say, you whore? You have nourished a thief in your house, and still you abuse me! You are indeed a hardened old procuress!

And Hīrā then in greater fury shouted:

—You say "procuress"! Know that I am flower-woman to the king! You say procuress! Tomorrow I shall show you. I have never kept young women in my house, nor offered the daughter of any man as a gift or bribe. He who says I have is a liar; may he be struck with leprosy! But you! You will take any man's wife or daughter; you always occupy yourself with such foul business. I know of the evil and dishonor of your house. Need I say more?

At this Dhumaketu blossomed forth in rage, and throwing Hīrā to the ground he seized her by the hair.

—Drunken, licentious old whore! I shall show you now. You and the thief will go together to the stake. Have you no fear in your heart, that you dare to speak to me this way? Do you not know that the princess is now pregnant, that you have given her her lover-thief?

When she heard these words, Hīrā became afraid, and covered her ears with both her hands.

—But I know nothing of this . . .

But Dhumaketu dragged her to the tunnel's mouth.

—Did the thief go this way?

The flower-woman replied:

—In truth, I do not know.

But she then understood the meaning of it all, and explained it in these words:

—But now I understand his tricks. He told me it was a pit for fire-sacrifice. Sundar did this thing, and you have caught him in the act. What more shall I say to you? He dug this tunnel from my house while I was sleeping . . . but who will believe me if I tell you this?

And Dhumaketu said:

—Ignore her words.

And so, whatever articles and goods that Sundar had they took. They took the box of books, the cage with both the talking birds, and all the other things, to bring to the king. And Dhumaketu, his face wreathed in smiles, hurled the terror-stricken Hīrā into the tunnel's mouth, and dragged her out to Sundar's side.

When he saw her there, the prince said, laughing:

—Hey, old aunt! This is indeed well met.

But Hīrā, burning with rage, said with a curse:

—Who are you, to call me "Aunt?" By what vile fate-line on my forehead could I be your aunt? You called me "Aunt" and took your lodging in my house—and how was I to know you were a thief? You told me you were digging pits for sacrifice, and dug away the whole night long. Ah, mother! What misery! That you could have done this to me! I shall survive this evil only by the greatest of good fortune. And if I do survive, never again shall I give shelter to a living soul. I am an old woman, of sixty years, already near death, and now have come to this! I swear that I shall never offer hospitality again. You there, young Dhumaketu! You source of merit of your mother and father, come, cut down this thief, and let me go. Build for yourself a bridge of proper action, by which to cross into the other world.

But Sundar, smiling, said:

—But you, old aunt, are the cause of all of it. It was in your flowers that she read the message which brought this all to pass.

But Hīrā did not hear, and cursed and muttered to herself:

—Libertine! Lecherous lout!

and other such things. And Dhumaketu, laughing, said:

—Surely there is blame on both the sides. Be silent, now. Tomorrow you can bring complaints before the king.

XXVI

THE NIGHT turned into morning. Her companions said to Vidyā:

—Sundar has been taken.

When she heard this, Vidyā fell down in a faint. Her companions picked her up as she lay grieving, her hair streaming down, the tears flowing from her eyes. Again and again she struck her forehead with her bracelets until the blood flowed down. She mourned:

—What has happened? What foul thing has happened? O God! How cruel you are! What has been my sin, that you have heaped such misery upon my head? For such a final sadness there is no recompense. Girls are born helpless in this world, subject to others' pleasure as well as pain. A girl is a bride in the house of others. She dies when others die. When she gives joy to another, she is glad. Her husband is a woman's heart; without him she is nothing. When the heart is torn out and stops beating, she also slowly dies. Cursed be this life! What can I say of fate? The wheel of fortune has slowly turned good into evil; the crown-jewel of my head, the treasure of my heart, the store-house of my happiness, which was given me, now is gone.

Thus weeping, Vidyā mourned, her sighs like fire, her pain a spear stuck deep into her breast; her touchstone had been stolen, her treasure house of happiness was now all empty.

—How can I bear this thing? My husband, whom I love, will be destroyed; shall I then live? My lord, my husband, lover, sea of qualities, full of bliss and beauty, rich in love and passion, incarnation of all music, dance, and song! My mother must have become a demoness, to cause this thing. The lord of my heart is called a thief! My father is a source of evil, and Dhumaketu has become the soul of doom. The heart of God is hard.

The queen, then, having heard the whispers in the inner rooms that the thief was caught, ran out to see the man. She climbed up to the roof, and, tears starting to her eyes, she looked into his upturned face. She said:

—Whose son is he? His beauty strikes me to the heart. What unimaginable grace! A well of passion! Ah, what lucky woman is his mother? And what fortune Vidyā had, to have taken him according to her choice. I also would have ruined myself for him. My daughter did not tell me. If she had, there now would be no misery. Ah, God! To think that I have had this handsome lad for son-in-law. But now the king is angry, and surely will not honor any plea from me. And if he dies, Vidyā will die also.

In such a way did all the people of the city also praise the prince, while the captain of the guard took the prisoners quickly to the king. All the people ran to follow—youths and boys and old men, and the blind and lame—all went to see the captive thief. And the pure, chaste, and virtuous women of the city looked down upon him from their windows.

—How could he be a thief? Except, perhaps, a thief of people's hearts?

—Hari, Hari! Would that I could take his misery on myself! What a chest he has! And what a face, and nose, and ears. The flashing of his eyes takes away my breath. Even when they have taken away his ornaments, and put ropes and chains upon his hands and feet, he is so handsome! How can they beat him thus with their cruel sticks upon that handsome body? Look there, the guard is beating him! It is as when Rahu eats the moon.[32] I cannot bear to see him treated as a thief—but what a thief! Even when in chains he continues to steal people's minds. He stole Vidyā; but I would steal him, if I had the chance.

And when these ladies gazed upon his beauty, they were in a trance, and could not go back to their houses. Their husbands seemed no longer pleasing to their tastes, and

[32] An eclipse is when the demon Rahu swallows the moon.

they had no more desire to be with them. They began to vilify their husbands to each other, tears streaming from their eyes. Can we now blame Vidyā, when we hear these lovely ladies abusing their own husbands thus:

—O hear of my unhappiness, my friends. My husband is deaf and dumb. In my girlhood I learned poetry, but in my wretched fate I fell in with a fool; and now my poetry is lost. I have to make things known to him by signs and gestures; it is not bad in the light, but in the darkness it is hopeless. I sleep with him because I have no other choice; I do it with reluctance. I close my eyes, as does a sick man when he takes the bitter medicine of *nim*.

Another woman said:

—O friends, she has great happiness, when you compare it to my lot. When you hear my misery, your misery will seem less. Unfortunate as I am, I have a blind man for a husband; his only forte is quarreling. Once I had a fair complexion; it has grown dark in misery. Though I am still in the fulness of my youth, I sit in empty apathy. To a blind man neither sin nor merit can be shown. He cannot see my beauty.

—Friends, hear of the diadem I wear upon my head. I am still young—still, indeed, a girl—but my husband is old. His face is drawn and sunken, his teeth fall out like boiled rice. There is little pleasure in his kiss; it brings no passion to my heart. If ever his passion is aroused, it is by a stroke of fortune. His shaking and his trembling make me also shudder. He tries to bite my lip, but his teeth break off, and then he writhes in torment with the pain. And now when I see this thief, the thunderbolt falls anew upon my head.

—At least, my friend, your old man is a husband. Listen to the misery I have to bear, and yours will be driven far away. To speak of my husband makes me want to hang my head in shame. He is very fat; his belly is huge and swollen. When I hear you others speak, indeed what little happiness I had turns to pain—for never has he kissed me or embraced me. He bends his head to kiss me on the lips, or to embrace me, but his belly pushes me away. His head begins a move but his belly stops it. Thus I am wasting, spoiling, while still a virgin.

—Do not look on this as bad. On the contrary, your happiness is relatively great. At least he tries to kiss you and embrace you, and this is joy. I have to take the initiative myself. My husband is a scrawny thing, a poor excuse for a man. Though I burn in passion, and take him in my lap, he is entirely hidden there. I fry in heat, and he cannot fulfil what I desire. His skill is small and his belly very great.

—Do not think that you have sadness. At least you take him in your lap. There is some happiness in that. My husband is a doctor, physician-courtier to the king. I see him in the house only at mealtimes, and then he only holds my hand to take my pulse. I tremble in a fever of desire, and he will say: "But you have fever. Take this mercury preparation." His medicines be damned!

—That is very good—at least he holds your hand to take your pulse. But my husband also is a courtier, a Brahmin pandit. He does not touch young women, and eats only vegetarian food. He has no enjoyment anywhere, except for chewing *pān*. And how can I describe the way he gulps his food! Even conversation between us is possible only when my menstrual period comes, when there is no longer any danger of temptation. But when the period goes, even conversation ceases.

—Let the pandit be. At least he did not deprive you from the first. A husband full of knowledge and experience is my lot; he is astrologer to the king. Consciousness of inauspicious days for love is always with him. The evil stars, bad signs, wrong timing—these things are always on his mind. They do not leave a single day to the unfortunate man. His fingers are always flipping through his almanac, while my heart bursts.

—I do not think it bad if one finds even a bare second of auspicious time for union. My husband is accountant to the king. His sole passions are his ink-pot and his pen. If I, disturbing him, cause him to make a mistake, he will rewrite all his papers over again from the beginning.

—My husband is a business man, whose temper is most foul. He always quarrels with me, even when there is no reason. He punishes me for offenses which are not mine. I must keep an account of all expenditures, and never spend an *anna* on myself. He keeps the accounts of others, with all their credits and debits, and doesn't see that I sit languishing in his house. He writes down all his foolish figures, and never looks to see his own son's face.

—But surely, your husband his fine qualities. My husband is a pleader, who pleads with me with his fists. And I, a woman, have to suffer it. He has the knack of making sin and falsehood into virtue and truth.

—My husband also has fine qualities. He is a clerk of court. He is always with his plaintiffs, sitting amidst his bundles of petitions. He sits there like a cow in a shed, moving his

arms about in gestures. I am to him one plaintiff among others; he avoids the nighttime, and lingers in his shed.
—Why, he is among the very best of husbands. My husband is a tax-collector, and among the worst of all. When people give him rupee coins, his face brightens like the golden moon. But when he has to spend, that moon seems ashen-faced in pain. And this is when he spends someone else's wealth; to get a drop of water from him if it were his own would be impossible.

Then said another vessel of bliss, her cheek stuffed full of *pān:*
—My husband is a money-changer, a lord of mercy and compassion. He holds treasures in his hands, yet it would be easier to draw his blood than to get him to spend a *pice.* When I shop and people dupe me, giving me tin and copper in change instead of silver and gold, he wreaks a fearful vengeance.
—But indeed, he is a forbearing and considerate man. The husband of this unlucky woman is a clerk with an account book. He spends the whole night working on accounts, and when he is done he wakes me up to feed him. Furthermore, he has no real knowledge of accounting, and balances his figures any old way.
—But he is truly steady and grave. A really unlucky woman is she whose husband keeps the government books. Though he is the bookkeeper, he does not know about supplies for the country. When he sees that there is excess in supply, he brings the excess back and marks it as rejected. He writes this excess then as credit in his own accounts, as he is afraid of debt. And when anyone else spends money,

though it is not even his, he has only harsh and bitter words for him.

—Why truly, his qualities are very great. My husband is a records-keeper; listen to his ways. He ponders always how to get his inventories made, because he cannot read or write. While in the market he runs his hands along the shelves, searching for hidden goods. He is also always careful to provide his inkstand for someone else's pen.

Another lady said:

—I am a Kulin girl.[33] My youth has passed by looking for a husband. And even if I marry now, much time is wasted. If I do get married, I shall be to my husband like his elder sister. When my marriage comes, the pandits will argue back and forth as to whether marriage or remarriage should come first. And he who marries me will have married sixty other girls; families in this caste are huge. He will come to me but once in several years, and when he sleeps with me will say: What service will you do me in return? And then I will sell everything and give him money; but he will only become angry and go away unsatisfied.

In this way did these lovely ladies lament their husbands, finding them fat or humpbacked or nagging—all these things and more. And finally, hearing all their miseries, one true wife finally said:

—But now you can solve my problem for me. My husband is a great poet, who knows the essence of poetics. He makes the driest words seem full of nectar and sweet beauty. But

[33] Kulin: a group of Brahmin castes, the males of which may take mates from lower castes, but the females of which may not. This results in Kulin males with large numbers of wives from groups to whose advantage it is to marry upward, as well as from Kulin families.

he puts no clothes upon my back nor good food in my belly. He sits and reads his *ślokas,* and thinks perhaps that they will thatch the roof and repair the house's walls. He knows the Kāmaśāstras[34] and all fine rhetoric, and the passion of his verses I could not possibly describe. But I have no bracelets of conch-shell or gold, nor have I crimson saris to wear. Only in his words is he the lord of love. But that one, Sundar, is a poet and a thief; he stole from Vidyā, and still she worshiped him. . . .

And when they heard these words, they all burned in their minds, and though they thought to go back home, their feet would not obey. They stayed and gazed at Sundar, and he stole their hearts as well. They watched him as his guards led him away, to take him to the king.

XXVII

WITH WHAT GRACE and grandeur came
  the Nāgara Śyāma to the court
  of Kaṁsa.
And Kaṁsa's singers play their *vīṇās,*
  and their *vīṇās* sing the beauties
  of Govinda.
Many are there who say: Let Kaṁsa
  now be slain! And wise men
  think:
Today will sin and passion be driven
  away. Let us lie in the dust
  of Krishna's feet.

Thus was King Vīrasiṁha Rāya sitting in his court, surrounded by his courtiers and friends. His servants stood

[34] The textbooks of pleasure.

with his umbrella and his fan, symbols of his royalty. And there were also scribes and minstrels, poets and pandits, teachers and scholars, *gurus* and *purohits.* And there were the king's five sons and his four brothers, his ten nephews and seven sons-in-law and sixteen nieces. And there were sons-in-law of the queen's paternal relatives, and her maternal uncles and their brothers-in-law . . . in short, friends and kinsmen of all kinds, a crowd of people, sitting in his retinue. And before him stood his soldiers, drawn up rank on rank, with shields across their chests and sharp swords in their hands. And on the great king's either side stood two tall gong-strikers, their hammers in their hands. And there were lines and lines of mace-bearers, their golden-headed clubs clasped in their hands. And before all these, clerks of the court with files and fat petitions, and panegyrists singing of the glories of the king. And all around sat parasites, whose yeas and nays came from their mouths at Rāya's order. And many others: scribes and Muslims and officers and merchants; physicians, judges, and collectors; *sitārs, vīnās,* and *tāmburās;* dancers, and singers singing songs, jesters playing pranks, and dancers spinning, and heralds shouting praises of their master. And there were huge Negroes dressed in black, and drummers, guards, and soldiers; and before them all, horse-trainers, whipping their horses, making them perform, and *mahuts* sitting on the shoulders of their elephants. And amidst all this the king himself, seated on his throne with all the majesty of Rāvaṇa.

While all this was going on, Dhumaketu brought the thief into the court. And with them guards brought the talking birds and box of books, and last of all, the flower-woman. The bailiff, then, having announced the presence of the thief, brought them forward. The ten brothers, still in women's dress, bowed low to the king, and, as the heralds called, the king acknowledged their address. He gave Dhumaketu, then, for his reward, an elephant and horse, and jeweled decorations. Then all the people, silent, looked sideways at the thief, with lowered faces, thinking:

—Surely this is a prince's son . . . see the grace and beauty of his form . . . he has all the signs of royalty . . .

And Vīrasiṁha thought:

—As suitable a one as this I would that destiny had chosen as the bridegroom of my daughter. But he has stolen; that is a crime and a vicious thing. He shall be killed. Yet how shall I do it? To wipe away the stain that he has put upon my name he must be killed. And yet the *Dharmaśāstras*[35] say that such a thing should not be done in haste. First, then, let me get the proof.

And so with angry eyes he turned to Hīrā, who stood close by.

—Who is this one? Whose whelp is he? Tell me truly and at once!

Hīrā replied:

—O king, his home, he says, is in the south. He came here to your city in a student's dress. But I do not know if ever he has spoken truth. He says that he is son to Guṇasindhu, king of Kāñci. When he came here he took lodging in my house. "I shall be a son to you," he said. "I shall love you as my aunt." He is most wise in argument, and skilled in

[35] The textbooks of law and morality.

dialectic—in truth, he does know many things. And I, deceived by him, told him of Vidyā, possessor of all knowledge, and her of him. "I want to marry her," he said. "Go and tell the king and queen," I told them. And why I do not know, but Vidyā forbade me to inform you. Instead she said: "Bring him to me secretly." But it was impossible to bring him there. I know no more than this, I swear; if I know more, may I eat my eyes, may I be damned. I swear to you, though he stayed there in my house, I did not know he was a thief. I am only a poor flower-woman. I am not depraved, and only by unhappy fate was thrown in with this deceitful wretch. He has despoiled my name. It was because of Rāvaṇa's past sins that the sea was breached. You, O king, are the incarnation of justice. If you have understood my words, do what you must.

The king felt pity at Hīrā's words, and thought to himself:

—What will I gain if I kill her? On the contrary, it will only make things worse. To kill a woman is a heinous crime.

And then he said aloud:

—Take her away and shave her head. Put lime and black stain on her face, and take her to the other side of the river.

Then the captain's brothers, pushing her along, took her away. She struggled, but was shoved along, and they departed. The king then, his doubt aroused at hearing Hīrā's words, ordered the bailiff to bring Sundar forward.

The clerk then said:

—Speak, O thief! Tell us your name. Where is your home? Whose son are you? What is your caste?

The thief replied:

—I am a son of royal family. Why do you seek to complicate the issue by demanding more? I see that you are just a clerk; why should I then answer you? From where do robbers come except from low castes? Once you know a thief's caste, what then do you know? Or perhaps, if my caste were high, I should have to have a high-caste executioner. Why do you ask about my caste? What business is it of yours?

Seeing his pride, the king asked the physician to question him.

—Hear, O thief. I am a leader of the caste of doctors. If you tell me all these things, there can be no shame attached.

The thief replied:

—I can see that you are a leader among doctors. You know all about taking pulses. Take my pulse and know my caste.

Then the king's secretary said:

—Hear, O thief. I am the secretary to the king. Leave your pride and tell me of yourself.

The thief replied:

—O honored secretary, surely you will understand: if the thief were your son-in-law, would you record that in your book?

Then the tax-collector said:

—I am the tax-collector of the king. Stop this evasion and tell me of yourself.

The thief replied:

—Ah, I have fallen into great debt. You of all people should be able to tell me that I am nothing but a thief.

Then the Brahmins and pandits tried their luck. And the thief replied:
—Now I am in real difficulty. You Brahmins see not only outward signs, but inner meanings. Judge then for yourselves. You can understand the qualities of things and castes. Why need you ask?

In this way, he evaded all their questions. And finally the king himself asked:
—Thief, I do not want to kill you, since I am inclined toward compassion. Tell me now, what is your name, your caste, your parentage, and your home. Speak truly. If you lie, you are on your way to hell.

Hearing this, Sundar said:
—Hear, then, O king. I am Kālī's servant. Therefore I have no fear. But will you believe the words of a thief? I am a king's son—if I tell you that, will you believe me? My name is Vidyā's husband, my caste is that of Vidyādhara, of Knowledge-holders, my home is in Vidyāpur. Hear me, O father-in-law. The name of my father is Vidyā's father-in-law. You are incarnate justice, yet you unjustly call me thief. Is this your kind of justice? Vidyā made a promise that her husband would be he who defeated her in argument. In that promise caste or family played no part. Look at the vows mentioned in the Purāṇas; whenever vows were made it was this way. Ask Vidyā herself if I, defeating her in argument, did not become her husband. Who I am, I am. I have conquered Vidyā, and according to her promise, I shall not abandon her. Give Vidyā to me now. You stay here and worry about my caste; I shall take her with me. Vidyā is my only caste, indeed, my heart; she is my meditation and my *mantra*, my sacrifice and worship.

In anger, then, the great king said:
—He did not tell me the truth. Take and kill him, Kālaketu.

But the thief replied:
—If I do not get Vidyā, death will be a welcome thing to me. For Vidyā I have come, abandoning my home, becoming a *sannyāsī*. For it was I who came each day into your court; it was I whom you put off with your false words. You did not present her to me, and so I cut a tunnel in the earth and went to her myself.

When they heard this all the courtiers said:
—This thief cannot be human!

And the king then cast a glance at Kālaketu, telling him to wait, and the fearless thief began to recite fifty verses in Vidyā's praise. Hearing them, the people were dumbfounded with astonishment; Bhārata will mention some of them.

XXVIII

EVEN TODAY she has the lovely golden
  color of the *campaka* blossom;
her body and the line of hair above
  her navel are like the lotus stalk,
her face the lotus bloom. Her beauty
  rouses the dormant passion of Kāma-
  deva,
and my mind is always fixed upon her.

When he heard this description of his daughter, the king in shame and wrath cried out:
—Strike him!

But Sundar said:
—Wait, O great king. Hear a little more:

Her walk is graceful as that of the *khañjana,* her breasts and hips are large and beautiful;
Madana's fire burns deep within her body, and to cool that fire I have lain with her.
If Vidyā, possessor of all mercy, gives that mercy unto me, what can you do, O best of kings?

And again:

She who is always hiding in my mind, one night in anger at my clumsiness
refused to say a word. Such was the depth of her dejection that I could not make her say a thing.
Then, in a trick, I sneezed, to make her say "Live long"—for if I live for long
it will be long that she remains a married woman, not a widow.
But she, a clever girl, saw through the trick, and took a golden earring from her ear.
Thinking of her widowhood, her body burned, but in her cleverness she said what should be said,
And never said a word.

The king replied:
—Now I understand what kind of son-in-law you are. You tell me if you die she will be a widow.

The poet then began to say:
—You, O courtiers, all are witnesses. You have heard the king call me son-in-law. Whether I am good or bad, he called me "son-in-law." Justice be witness to this thing—you have said it, and cannot take it back. For hear:

Even now the great god Śiva does not cast out the poison from his throat.
The tortoise bears upon his back the burden of the earth, the sea bears its intolerable fires.
A king protects—and the promise of a good man can never be a lie.

Ashamed, then, Vīrasiṁha sat with face averted, and all the people said again:
—This thief cannot be human.
And Vīrasiṁha thought:
—Though he has described Vidyā, by his manner of description he has praised the Goddess of Knowledge herself; he is a prince in form and qualities.

Ah, says Bhārata, if I explain all these double meanings my book will grow too long. But pandits will understand these and all the other references of the thief.

XXIX

THE KING sat there with bowed head and thought:
—What do I do now? He has not told me who he is. But I can tell from his behavior he is not low-caste. If I have him killed, how do I know what will happen at the end?
So he said aside to Kālaketu:
—Take him to the execution-ground. There frighten him, and he will tell you of himself.

In such a way the Dawn was conquered, tied, and pierced by arrows of misfortune. So the guards took Sundar to the execution ground. The poet was distressed, and thought of Kālī. But in the court were Sundar's birds, and they in words reproached the king. The *suka* and the *śari* bird were weeping, mouth to mouth, when they saw the plight of Sundar. And when he heard the *śāri's* weeping verses, the *śuka* began to tremble and to cry; and hearing it the people of the court were charmed. But then the *śuka* flapped and beat its wings and drove away the *śāri* with these words:

—Get away from me, O *śāri!* The hearts of women are cruel and cold, enticing men into the well of Kāma. For Sundar, son of Guṇasindhu, possessor of all noble qualities, jewel of goodness, dies for Vidyā. The saint is being put to death for marrying, though he was enticed with magic potion by the tyrant's daughter. She first concealed the marriage, then betrayed him, that daughter-demon of this robber-tyrant. Ah, I die, I die, O Hari! The evil, sinful girl has slain her husband. And you, O *śāri*-bird of Vidyā, have learned her qualities well. When will you take my life, as she is taking his? He is so beautiful—his grace is like the gods.

When they heard these words of the bird, the courtiers all consulted one another, whispering, and the king became obsessed with doubt. The story which the flower-woman told, the bird had also told. Perhaps the thief was son of Guṇasindhu. So he said:

—Bird, tell me again what you have said. How do you know this thief? How can we believe that he is Guṇasindhu's son? First he took my daughter like a common thief, then the captain of the guard seized him and brought him here. He did not tell the truth about himself. You are so wise—tell me why I should not cut him down, and cut you down as well. You call me tyrant?

The bird said:

—Sir, where have you heard of a prince who spoke for himself: A herald introduces a prince, as match-makers speak to families. This is the proper way for those of high estate. Sundar, O lord, will never introduce himself, and I am but a bird. Of what value are my words? But you have sent a messenger to Guṇasindhu's throne. Call him here. Let him tell all.

The king said:

—That is well. Ask the leader of the *bhāṭs* who went to Kāñcipur. Bring him here.

So an officer went, and found that Gaṅgabhāṭ had gone. The king sent Rājput soldiers to fetch the *bhāṭ*, and they brought him to the throne.

XXX HYMN TO KĀLĪ

O SLAYER OF THE DEMONS, wearer of the garlands of severed heads, shaking your unsteady mass of matted hair, loose and free, O thou of brightness like the sun and moon, dazzling light, dizzying in brightness; O thou of rolling avaricious tongue, dangling, gulping blood and gushing forth in streams, laughing madly, frightfully, rending, snatching, drinking blood. O thou who dance with awful cosmic rhythm, filled with blood in the rhythm of the song and dance, and full of lust; O thou who hold the severed head of Caṇḍa, your foot upon the breast of prostrate Śiva; O thou humbler of every demon, roaring frightful like a lion —come, come and grant our boon. O goddess with the bloody teeth, O Aparājitā, O undecaying one, younger sister, existing from eternity, existing to eternity, O eight-armed goddess, Giver of Food, Original and Self-Formed, come, fulfil our hopes! Deliver me, by your command! Fulfiller of all Wishes, Moon-Faced One, Indrānī, blue as the lotus, grant to me a sign! Goddess, I bow to you. O Goddess, Laughing One, I bow to you. O Umā, wearing serpents like the sacred thread, whose hair is long and matted, whose thighs are plantain trees, who casts away all barrenness and death, you are the form of all the seasons. O, grant to me your blessing; grant to me prosperity and hope.

XXXI

AND SO THE BRIDEGROOM-PRINCE, become a thief, was taken to the execution ground. And Kālī reddened as her anger burned within her. She called out to all her hosts:

—Prepare yourselves!

and all her Yoginīs came running, and there were peals of awful laughter, claps of thunder. The Ḍākinīs and Hākinīs, Bhūtas, Śaṁkhinīs, Petanīs and Dūtas, Brahmin-ghosts and Bhairavas and Vetalas and Piśacas, Yakshasas, Rakshasas in crowds ran to the place where Kālī was.[36] And amidst them all, the goddess—her long and matted hair flowing wildly, she laughed her long and maddened laughter, her

[36] Ḍākinī: one of Kālī's female attendants, who feed on human flesh and blood; Hākinī: the same; bhūta: spirit which haunts burning grounds and devours bodies; Śaṁkhinī: female followers of Dūrgā; Petanī: also a kind of malignant female spirit; Dūta: "messenger," also the name of one of Dūrgā's attendants; Bhairavas, "the terrible ones," names of eight terrible manifestations of Śiva; Vetala: a spirit who haunts cemeteries and burning grounds and animates dead bodies; Piśācas: the most malevolent class of being, lower than the Rakṣasas.

third eye scarlet, moving like a disc in her head, her greedy tongue protruding long and loose; she shone with brightness more vertiginous than the sun or fire; she ground her huge hard teeth, her lips drawn back, and streams of blood ran down from her lips' sides; corpses of children swung as earrings from her ears, and on her breast there hung a string of severed heads, with wild and awful faces. Her garland was the intestine of the demon, her girdle one of demons, her ornaments of bones. In lust for blood and flesh the jackals circled round her, and the earth trembled with their howling. She trampled heaven, earth, and hell, crushed them beneath her feet, preventing the cosmic dissolution; her feet were on the breast of prostrate Śiva, lying in meditation-trance with closed eyes.

In such a way she came to Burdwan in her sky-chariot, surrounded by her hosts, to banish Sundar's fear. And she called to him:

—Glory to the Mother! Who will dare to kill her son? If this comes to be, I shall allow the fearful final dissolution. I shall cause the blood to flow in rivers! I shall destroy that Vīrasiṁha and his family, and shall give you Vidyā and the kingdom. You, O lord of Knowledge, need have no fear.

The wise Sundar, and only he, could hear the voice of Kālī from the sky. He raised his face, and looked, and saw the Devī, and his whole body shook with joy. By Kālī's grace the prince gained bliss; his fetters fell away, and all the guards and soldiers were bound by Kālī's hordes. Such was the fate of Sundar, as Gaṅgabhāṭ the messenger drew near the king.

XXXII

The king said:

—Tell me, Gaṅgabhāṭ. I sent you to the throne of the great king Guṇasindhu to bring his son. Why has he not come? Explain this in detail to me; hold nothing back. I sent you there to do a task for me; or do you not remember? Have you forgotten both your duty and your king? You were the best of Bhāṭs, in poetry and wit, but you have stained your name. You have become instead a jester and a clown. You were my much beloved friend, to whom I gave fine elephants and horses as gifts, whose head I crowned; I gave you swords and shields and wealth, and taught you poetry; I gave you jewels and villages and land, and the title "Best of Poets." But all is spoiled, unless you tell me now, and keep no secrecy.

The Bhāṭ replied:

—O king, I as your Bhāṭ went to Kāñcipur, according to your will. I reached the king's court, and found the prince. I clasped my hands and bowed and gave to him your message. He listened carefully to my words, and then in private asked me more about the princess. I told him she was rare in beauty and in mind, one girl in a thousand *lakhs*. The prince, on hearing this, was gladdened in his mind; so mad with pleasure and delight was he that he ran away. He did not tell his family, for fear that they would stop his going. His mother and his father, then, not seeing him, were filled with sorrow. For five months I stayed there in this way, and then I said "I must return to Burdwan." So I came home. Perhaps you do not remember my coming to you, O king, but ask your minister if I did not.

The king then said:
—Now hear, O Bhāṭ. There is a thief now at the execution ground. Go there; see if you know him.

When he received this order from the king, the Bhāṭ ran; he cocked his head and stared a moment at the thief. And then, excited, he ran back to the king.
—O king! That man is prince of Kāñcipur. It is a stroke of luck that you have brought me here. I heard that even in your house some thief had stolen your daughter, and that for that reason you had sent him to the execution ground. Thank God you sent me there. Now you must release him.

So said the Bhāṭ. And the king, with joyful mind, heard his words. Vīrasiṁha Rāy, in great delight, rewarded him with jewels and elephants, and then went forth with all his friends and courtiers to the execution ground. When he reached that place the king saw Sundar praising Kālī with upturned face, and that the captain and his men were all in chains. But yet he could not understand who had bound them; then from out of the void the Bhutas began to shout and dance in rhythm, and all the Ḍakinīs and Yoginīs as well; and the Bhairavas in frenzied delight began to shout and dance and sing, and the darkness of the night fell on the place, though it was day. The king then knew this was divine, and so began to offer praise to Sundar in this way:
—I know that I have sinned against you; but put away your anger. I recognize your power.

Then smiling, the poet-prince embraced him as his father-in-law and said with cheerful face:
—I have become a thief, but I am not sad because of this. My only feeling is of gladness. And you, be merciful toward me in your mind.

Then King Vīrasiṁha said:
—Hear me, son. What then will happen to this captain of my guard? Will you release him from his chains? Tell me the goddess's pleasure.

Then Sundar said:
—Hear me, O King. Listen carefully to my words. Kālī is up there in the sky—all these have known her presence. Worship her, and they all will be saved, and she will bless us all.

When he heard this, Vīrasiṁha, gathering great merit in his mind, brought *gurus*, priests, and others; and having brought there gifts and articles of worship, he began his *pūjā* to the Giver of Food, the Devī, and carefully began her praise and prayer. Vīrasiṁha again then said:
—Hear me, son. I do not see her face. I must know that I am blessed by your grace.

So, laughing, Sundar touched him with his finger, and Vīrasiṁha thus gained knowledge of the divine. He saw the reddened feet of Kālī, and fell to earth in a delirium of joy. And then she disappeared, taking with her all her hosts. The captain's and the soldiers' bonds fell from their limbs. The king gained knowledge of the divine, and taking Sundar with him he went back to the palace. Then, seating Sundar on the throne, the king gave him gifts of jewels and clothes, and brought out Vidyā also as a gift. The people of the court rejoiced, and Sundar, thief become a saint, took Vidyā then and spent his life in joy and pure delight.

Mahārājā Hariśchandra

Introduction

The story of Mahārājā Hariśchandra, his degradation and release, is one of the best-known stories not only of Bengal, but of all of India. Not much can be said about its origin; it is probably a story of great antiquity. It occurs in its full form in the Sanskrit *Mārkaṇḍeya Purāṇa,* from a Bengali version of which text the present translation has been made. But the theme was very popular with the writers of the *maṅgal* poems (see below, *Manasā-Maṅgal,* introduction), especially, for reasons which will be obvious, with the writers of the *maṅgals* of the god Dharma.

The story of Hariśchandra is one of considerable power, and was treated with great skill by many writers. Take, for example, this passage from the version given in the *Rāmāyaṇa* of Kritivāsa (*Ādikāṇḍa*), who lived in the fifteenth century:

Taking his wife, the king entered the market-place. He cried out in a loud voice:

—Who will buy this woman as slave?

There was a Brahmin there, a learned and holy man, who had need of a slave-girl. This Brahmin said:

—O best of men, what is the girl's price?

The king replied:

—I know nothing of falsehood or deceit; this woman's price is four crores of golden coins.

The Brahmin agreed, and with his golden coins bought Śaibyā. He took his slave and started toward his house; but, weeping, Ruhidāsa clutched his mother's clothes. He held the border of her sari and rolled upon the earth. The Brahmin raised his stick and shouted:

—Let go!

But Śaibyā said:

—O lord, grant me this one boon. Take my son. You need pay nothing.

Hearing this, the Brahmin, mad with anger, said:

—Where shall I get rice to feed two people?

And Śaibyā said:

—I shall eat but little of the rice you give to me; I shall give the rest to him.

And the Brahmin, angry, said:

—All right. Each day you shall get one seer of rice.

And taking his slaves, he went away.

I have chosen to translate from the *Mārkaṇḍeya Purāṇa* not because that version is the best as literature, but because it is the most complete.

The legend of Hariśchandra is of interest not only as a good story, but also because it throws light on a number of salient facts and attitudes in Indian feeling and belief. It also brings up the perennial question of whether or not tragedy as we know it in the West is possible in Indian literature. The concept of *dharma* is crucial to the understanding of the story of Hariśchandra, and is crucial also to the question of tragedy in Indian literature.

Dharma (which I have translated incompletely as "righteousness") is for purposes of this story the notion that man's duty is the working out of his proper relationship to the cosmos and his self-subordination to the role decreed for him by his station in society and by his own nature. *Dharma* is a force which works against individualism (though when the individual is in harmony with the cosmic scheme, he gains rather than loses freedom). An individual's life is a role in the societal scheme, which is itself a reflection of the cosmic scheme. This is an idea not wholly unfamiliar in our own culture. In John Steinbeck's *Burning Bright,* Joe Saul feels that his own childlessness, his lack of ability to carry on his line and his profession, is somehow about to lead to the failure of the established order of things; he feels that if his line is not carried on there will be a gap which will upset the whole balance of the cosmos. This is an aspect of *dharma;* that there is an intimate relationship between man, tradition, and the scheme of things. What occurs on earth is a reflection of and reflects what occurs in heaven.

Personality, then, is to a large extent subordinated to a man's tradition, his caste, which dictates his own role in society. This is one's *dharma,* and if one transgresses it—if a wife does not abide by her role as *satī,* as a true wife who sees her husband as summation of all the gods, if one does not abide by his role as king, who is protector of his subjects and all Brahmins, then one transgresses not a human, but a cosmic law. One is cast beyond the pale. In this life he has no place in society; in the next, he is in the outer darkness.

This is not easy for us in the West to understand. Although we also play our roles, the individual who plays the role is as important as the role itself. We feel that the presence or absence of ourselves as individuals makes a difference to the role. To traditional India, the role is the important thing; the individual must above all be true to his role, and it is this truth which matters to the cosmic scheme.

A Western scholar, in commenting on Kālidāsa's great drama *Śakuntalā,* has said that "tragedy, indeed, there cannot be. Hinduism does not grant sufficient free will to man to permit of his grappling with the moral ambiguities that produce tragedy. Sadness and melancholy there may be; but the ultimate destinies are well controlled, and sunlight at last prevails."[1]

Perhaps this is a bit too simple. It is certainly true that in Indian literature there is little "probing of the dark recesses of the mind," and that man's action is rarely seen as man's immediate personal responsibility. In the story before us, the king Hariśchandra is forced, by his necessity to be true to his *dharma,* by his necessity to be true to his kingly station and the honor of his word, into misery and degradation. It is not that he has no choice. In fact, he is about to violate his *dharma* and immolate himself on his

[1] *A Treasury of Asian Literature,* ed. John D. Yohannan (New York, 1958) p. 132.

son's funeral pyre, when the god appears to him. But the choice is essentially an impossible one for a moral man. If he is to uphold his *dharma,* to honor his word to the Brahmin, misery is inevitable, for the cosmic forces are at work on him, involving him deeper and deeper in the consequences of his own error. On the other hand, to abandon *dharma* would be not only to leave himself open to frightful punishment in future lives, but in fact would be impossible for a righteous man. That he is about to abandon his *dharma* when he has been forced to the ultimate extreme of misery, when it is too late to save his wife, his son, or himself, makes his decision the more poignant.

In a sense unfortunately, the end of the story is happy. The order of the universe decrees also that those who uphold it be rewarded.

There is another element of the story which might be pointed out. I think the reader will be struck with the strange timelessness of the dream sequence in the middle of the story, as Hariśchandra, slave to the Caṇḍala, lies unconscious. The Indian consciousness of time is not that of the West. In the dream sequence, one day becomes a thousand years, one life infinite and varied lives, and there is no inconsistency. Time is cyclical. A life continues birth after birth; the world's thousand years is but a day to the gods. There is creation, dissolution, and again creation. This is all quite different from the linear concepts of the West.

Mahārājā Hariśchandra

Once, in days gone by, there lived a righteous king. Hariśchandra was his name, a man full of qualities and as graceful and gentle of mind as he was of body. In all his kingdom, in his reign, there was no hunger and no illness, nor was there fear of untimely death among his subjects, nor any unrighteousness. His people were not poor, but neither were they drunk with wealth and power; they were upright, but not proud in their uprightness. And there were no women in all his land who had reached puberty and were barren of children.

One day this king of mighty arms was in a forest, hunting deer. Suddenly he heard a woman screaming: "Save me! O save me!" The king abandoned his pursuit of deer, and shouted "Do not fear"; he thought: "What foolish man is this who harms another in my kingdom?" And he rushed toward the place from whence the cry had come.

The demon Vighnarājā, opposer of just undertakings, observed these things, thinking to himself:

—In this forest lives the ascetic hermit Viśvamitra, practicing extreme asceticism and self-mortification according to his vow. Such asceticism as his has never before been seen upon the earth. Sages of the past have tried to gain true knowledge by forgiveness, vows of silence, or control of mind, but Viśvamitra is about to gain that knowledge by his asceticism. It is Knowledge herself who is about to be taken, and thus cries out in fear. I cannot let this happen, yet what can I do? Viśvamitra is a great ascetic. He is more powerful than I, for Knowledge herself cries out in fear of him. Great pain and trouble lie ahead for me if once he gains her. But I see a way of removing this obstacle in my path. King Hariśchandra has now come. I shall enter into this king and accomplish my desire.

So thinking, the fearful demon Vighnarājā entered into the body of Hariśchandra, and the king, being moved to great anger by the demon, said to Viśvamitra:

—What evil man are you, to try to tie the lightning in the hem of your garment? I, Hariśchandra, lord of the earth, lustrous, splendid, powerful, am here! Now, O fool, you shall enter upon your last long sleep; your body will be filled with my arrows which, like the lightning, illumine the dark regions of the sky!

When the sage Viśvamitra heard the king's unholy and impertinent speech, he was consumed with fury. In his rage all the knowledge which he had gained vanished instantly.

And when the king, again himself, suddenly saw before him the great ascetic Viśvamitra, he was overcome with fear, and began to tremble like a leaf on the peepul tree. Viśvamitra in his rage addressed the king and said:

—Evil-souled man! Wretch! Stand where you are!

Then the king prostrated himself humbly and with great reverence, and said:

—Lord, I have only done my duty. Do not be angry with me. O great sage, in coming here and speaking thus to you, I have not left the path which is the righteous one for me—pray do not be angry. The duty of a righteous king, a king who knows his proper path, is giving gifts, protection of his subjects, and making war.

Viśvamitra said:

—O king, if you really live in fear of all unrighteousness, then tell me—to whom do you give gifts, whom do you protect, with whom do you wage war?

—O treasure-house of power, to those who are fulfilling vows, to Brahmins, I give gifts; to those who live in fear I give protection; and with those who are my enemies I make war, as should be done.

—O king, if you would fulfil the duties of a king, then know that I am a Brahmin, therefore to be rewarded. Give me a gift which I desire.

And when King Hariśchandra heard this speech, his heart was filled with joy. It was as if he had been born anew, redeemed from the Brahmin's wrath. He pondered in his heart, and then he said:

—Hear, O lord. I give to you my money, my gold, my son, my wife, my body, my soul, my kingdom, my city, my majesty and power—all that you desire, no matter what the cost, I give to you. Without fear or thought of me, command me. What shall I give to you? Whatever you ask, whatever is in my power to give, is as if already given.

Then Viśvamitra said:

—O king, I accept your offer. Let that now be. And then you must present to me the fee for the sacrifice which I shall make for you.

—O Brahmin, it is yours. O prince among Brahmins, tell me your pleasure; what shall be the nature of the gift which I shall give to you as Brahmin? Command me.

—O king, knower of duty, all this earth is yours, stretching to the seas, and all these villages and cities and plains and mountains, with all their chariots and horses and elephants, and a great treasury and enormous wealth. And you have also many righteous people who follow you. All these things, and whatever else you possess, give them to me! Whatever you have, excepting only your wife, your son, and your own body, give to me. Keep nothing else.

When he heard these words of the sage Viśvamitra, the king Hariśchandra, lord of men, with joyful mind and serene face, joined his palms together and said to the Brahmin:

—As you have ordered, so shall it be.

Then Viśvamitra said:

—O king, you have given me this earth, and with it all your wealth and power. Who is now lord in this kingdom?

—O Brahmin, when I gave to you this sea-girt earth, you became its sole lord. Why do you ask about such things?

—Indeed O king, you have presented this sea-girt earth to

me. Therefore take off your jewelry and ornaments, and clothe yourself in a loin-cloth made from the bark of a tree, and take your wife and son, and get you gone from my kingdom!

The king Hariśchandra assented to this command of Viśvamitra and, conscious of his duty to his word, fulfilled all that which the Brahmin had commanded. He took his wife, Śaibyā, and his little son, and went forth from the kingdom. But as he was going, he saw the sage Viśvamitra blocking his way. And Viśvamitra said to him:

—Lord of men, where are you going? You still have not given me the fee for sacrifice.

Hariśchandra said:

—O lord, my whole kingdom, filled with peace and justice, have I given you; what have I left but these three bodies?

Viśvamitra said:

—O king, though you have no wealth but these three bodies, still you must give me fee for sacrifice. If one does not give that which he promises, especially to Brahmins, he is surely lost. And have you yourself not said that giving promised gifts, and making war with enemies, and protecting the weak are your sole duties?

Then Hariśchandra said:

—Lord, according to *your* duty, be gracious unto me. I have nothing more. I shall give the fee to you by bits.

—O chief among men, how long then shall I wait? Answer me quickly, or I shall sear you with the fire of my curse.

—O twice-born sage, make no more demands upon me now. Within one month I shall give to you your fee.

Then Viśvamitra said:

—Go then, O best of kings. Observe your duty. May your way be blessed and your path free from obstacles.

Then the road was freed by Viśvamitra, and the great and wise king, ruler of the earth, departed. Behind him walked his queen Śaibyā, in the dust as ill became a queen. And all the people of the city, and their wives and children, ran to the road to see their king departing; they followed him along the way, their cries rising to the skies:

—O gracious king, you have been devoted to righteousness, a source of infinite mercy to your subjects; what evil fate now makes you leave us? O king, if you honor justice still, then take us with you. O king of kings, how long? We look now upon your lotus-face; when shall we look upon that face again? Our king, who when going forth should be preceded and followed by all the kings of the earth, goes forth now followed only by his wife, who holds her little son by the hand. Ah, he who has gone forth preceded and followed by servants all mounted on the heads of elephants now goes forth alone, afoot. O king, your handsome face is grey with dust and the grime of the road—O king! Do not leave us! Do not go! Your duty is toward us! Our wives, our sons, our wealth, our food—what pleasure will these hold for us now? For we are mere reflections of you. O lord, O great king, do not abandon us! Wherever you go, we shall go. Where you find happiness, there is our prosperity also. Where you dwell, there is our city. Where our king is, there is our heaven!

When Hariśchandra heard these cries of his people, he was overcome with grief, and he stood still for a long time in the dust of the road, looking with love toward them.

But Viśvamitra, seeing the king disturbed and moved by the people's cries, came quickly forward, his eyes rolling red in anger. And he said:

—Liar! Maker of false promises! You have given your kingdom to me. Now do you want to take it back? Vile, accursed man!

So the king Hariśchandra, cursed and goaded like a beast of burden, whispered, "I am going. I go," and reached for the hand of his beloved wife, his body trembling and shaking. But the lovely Śaibyā, her limbs as delicate as a lotus-flower, already sick with weariness, could not move. The king tried to draw her quickly by the hand. But Viśvamitra began to beat her on the back with his heavy staff. Seeing his wife beaten and goaded in this way, the king was deeply wounded in his heart. But he gave no other answer than, "We go, O lord."

II

So THE KING went slowly on his way, together with his little son and lovely queen. They reached the heavenly city of Benares, made by Śiva as the place of death, not to be possessed or enjoyed by men. Sad of heart, sunk in his sorrow, leading his wife by the hand, the king entered Benares, walking in the dust. As they entered the city, the king saw Viśvamitra standing again before him in the road. When Hariśchandra saw the sage, he joined his palms together in reverence and humility, and said:

—O lord, only my life, my wife, and son, are left to me. If you desire any of these three, it will be presented you as offering. Command me; I shall obey.

Then Viśvamitra said:

—O wise king, do you remember your promise of the payment of my fee? One month is now fulfilled. Give it to me.

—O Brahmin, today the month will be fulfilled. But half a day remains—grant me that. I shall not ask for more.

Then Viśvamitra said:

—O king, it shall be so. But I shall come again. And if you do not give my due today, my curse shall fall upon your head.

So Viśvamitra went away, and the king began to ponder how to find the money for the promised fee.

—Where can I find rich friends? Where can I get money? Ah, my promise was in vain, and I shall end in hell. There is no way. I have set upon my path, and I cannot leave it now. Even if I kill myself, if my promise is unfulfilled, I shall be a robber of Brahmins, sunk in sin, condemned eternally to hell. My next birth will be as a worm. It would be better that I sell myself, and become a slave.

The king for a long time meditated thus, his head hung down, his heart grieved and despairing. Seeing him like that, his lovely wife said to him in tear-choked voice:

—O my king, leave your meditation and despair. Fulfil your promise. A man who cultivates untruth should be shunned in every way like him who tends the burning ground. O best of men, the pandits say that duty is the preservation of one's own truth, and that it has no other form. The fire-sacrifice, the study of the scriptures, the giving of all required offerings, all these are fruitless for him who speaks untruly. The sages say in books of moral law that speaking truth is the true source of all salvation, just as falsehood brings damnation. O lord of the earth, you have performed seven horse-sacrifices and a king's sacrifice—will you now let a falsehood be the cause of your loss of heaven? O great king, I have brought forth a child . . .

And she began to sob. Then the king said to his weeping queen:

—My virtuous lady, leave your grief. Here is your son. Tell me what you want to say.

And so the queen went on:

—I have borne a son, as the wives of virtuous men bear sons. My life is complete. Therefore sell me, and with the money, give the Brahmin his fee.

When Hariśchandra heard these words he was stricken, and fell senseless to the ground. As he regained consciousness, he began to weep, burdened with the grief and anguish of his heart; he said:

—These words pain me deeply. Are the joys which you have had with me, sinner though I am, now all forgotten? O my wife, whose smile is gentle, can these foul words have come from that same mouth? How can I do this thing for which you ask?

And the king again fell to the earth, weeping in his pain. The queen Śaibyā, seeing the king lying thus on the ground, was deeply moved and filled with tenderness, and said:

—Ah, my king, what is this that has happened to us, that you should be lying on the earth—you, whose couch was covered with the soft skins of deer? You, who have gladly given great herds of cattle to Brahmins; you, my lord, the ruler of the earth, are lying on the earth. Ah, what suffering is this! Oh gods! What has he done to you, that you reduce this king, so good and virtuous, to such a state of misery?

So grieving, the queen of graceful body, unable to bear

her husband's anguish, fell beside him to the earth. And the little boy, the king's son, seeing his mother and father lying on the ground, began to cry and say:

—Father! Father! Give me something to eat. I am very hungry, and my tongue is dry.

While the king and queen were lying unconscious, Viśvamitra again appeared; he sprinkled water on Hariśchandra's face and said:

—O king! Give me now my fee! The longer your debt continues, the more your misery will grow.

The king, revived by the cold water on his face, regained his consciousness; but when he saw the sage Viśvamitra standing over him, again he fainted. At this, Viśvamitra became very angry, and said:

—O king! If you indeed have respect for righteousness, give me my fee. Know that it is truth which causes the sun to shine, and only truth which causes the firmness of the earth. Know that truth is the only righteousness, that heaven is established only by truth. If the fruit of a thousand horse-sacrifices and that of truth were placed in the balance, truth would far outweigh the sacrifice. If I were not concerned with truth, what need would there be for me to urge in this way a base and sinful, vicious-natured and false king? O king, I speak to you sincerely. Hear me well. If you give me not my fee today, before the sun sets, my curse will be upon you.

When he had spoken, Viśvamitra vanished. The king, fearing the Brahmin's curse, was deeply troubled. What could he do? Where could he turn? His mind was restless. And again his wife said to him:

—O king, do what I suggested. It is the only means left to

us; otherwise you will be seared by the fire of his curse; you will gain only death and dissolution.

In this way, she pleaded with him over and over again, and finally he said:

—O gentle wife, I have lost all shame. I shall sell you. That which the most cruel and brutal man could not bear to do, I shall do. I am indeed lost, that I can speak such bitter words as these.

Thus he spoke to his wife, wracked with bitter pain; and together they made their way into the city. When they had reached the central marketplace, Hariśchandra, his eyes filled and his voice choked with tears, called out:

—Hear, you people of the city! Hear my words! Before you ask "Who is this man," I shall tell you who I am. I am a man without a heart—nay, not even a man. I am a demon, but yet more cruel and evil than a demon. I have come to sell my most beloved wife, that my own life might be saved. If there is any among you who has need of her as slave, let him speak now; let him speak, while my breath is still in my body.

Then an aged Brahmin who was present said to him:

—I shall buy the girl as slave. Give her to me. I am rich. My wife is very delicate and unable to do the housework. Therefore give the girl to me and take this money. The money is in proportion to the skill, and youth, and beauty of your wife. Give the beautiful woman to me.

When he heard the Brahmin speak like this, Hariśchandra's heart was torn in agony; it was as if his heart was being ripped asunder. He made no answer. The Brahmin, then, thrusting money into the waistband of the king's garment, seized the queen by the hair and began to drag her away. But the boy Rohitaśva, seeing his mother being thus brutally treated, seized the hem of her garment and began to weep. Then the queen cried:

—O highborn man, loose me, that I might look upon the face of my son just once more. Please, O father—I shall not see him again! O my baby, come! Look at me well! I have become a slave! O son of a king, do not touch me! I cannot be touched by you now!

The boy, seeing his mother thus abused, could only weep; his eyes streamed with tears. Then the old Brahmin, furious with rage, began to kick the boy with his foot, to loose his hold. But the boy clung tighter, crying "Mother, mother!," and would not loose his mother's garment. The queen then cried:

—O lord, be merciful! Buy my son also. If you buy me away from him, I shall not be able to do your work. Be gracious to an unfortunate woman. Let my son come with me, as you would a calf with its mother.

The Brahmin said to Hariśchandra:

—Take this money. I buy the boy also.

And the old Brahmin, as before, put the money into a fold of the rag that covered the shoulders of the king, and bound the queen and the boy together. The king, as he watched his wife and son being dragged away by the Brahmin, was sorely grieved; he heaved a shuddering sigh and began to mourn:

—She upon whose body neither sun nor moon nor wind has ever gazed has this day become a slave. He whose birth was in a noble line, a boy with hands still soft, sold as a slave. Is there no end to the evil in me? O, my beloved! My son, my baby! What have I done? What has brought you to suffer this bitter fate? Why am I not dead?

As he was thus grieving, the old Brahmin, dragging his slaves, disappeared among the temples and the trees.

III

While the king was grieving for his wife and child, Viśvamitra appeared and, drawing near the king, demanded money. Hariśchandra gave him all he had. But Viśvamitra, seeing the tiny sum which the king had received from the sale of his wife and child, was very angry, and said to him:
—Hear me, noble! If you think that this pittance is enough for my sacrificial fee, I shall soon show you how mistaken you are. I shall soon show you the might which I have gained by my austerity, my pure Brahmin power, the terrible majesty which I have gained by my discipline and study.

When he heard these angry words, the king bowed his head and said humbly:
—Wait a little longer then, divine one; I shall get for you the sacrificial fee. But I have nothing now. See, even my wife and little son I have sold into slavery.

Viśvamitra said:
—O king, only a quarter part of the day yet remains. I shall wait until that passes, and no more.

When he had spoken these harsh, cruel words to the king, Viśvamitra took the money and departed. Then Hariśchandra, sinking in a sea of fear and pain, cast his thoughts wildly about him, hoping to find a way. Finally he determined on a course of action, and, with his eyes upon the ground, began again to speak to the people:

—Hear, you people. If there is any among you who desires me as slave, and who will give me money, let him quickly speak, before the sun goes down.

At these words of the king the god Dharma, in the form of a Caṇḍala, came forward. His body smelled foully; he was the image of a demon, his face covered with a long and matted beard, his whole aspect horrible and fearsome and revolting; his teeth were long, his color black, his belly huge, his eyes yellow and shot with blood; his speech was coarse and rough; on his neck hung garlands gleaned from corpses; in one hand he held a human skull, in the other a staff; his body was lean; he was surrounded by a pack of dogs; he muttered constantly to himself. The god Dharma came as such a Caṇḍala and said:

—I shall buy you. Tell me your price, and tell me quickly.

Staring at this half-human Caṇḍala before him, staring at his cruel, evil, and vicious face, the king then whispered:

—Who are you?

The Caṇḍala said:

—I am a Caṇḍala. I live here in this best of cities. My name is Prabi, and I am famous as executioner of the condemned and taker of the blankets and winding-sheets of the dead.

Then Hariśchandra said:

—Slavery to a Caṇḍala is the most despicable fate of all. I cannot submit to that. It would be better to be burnt in the fire of the Brahmin's curse. Never shall I be slave to a Caṇḍala!

But as the king was speaking so, Viśvamitra, powerful in

austerities, appeared, his eyes red and burning in anger. He said to the king:

—This Caṇḍala stands ready to give you wealth. Why do you not take it, and with it pay my fee?

Hariśchandra said:

—O great Viśvamitra, I am the son of a noble family. Now, out of mere desire for wealth, can I become a slave to a Caṇḍala?

And Viśvamitra said:

—If you do not give me the money at the appointed time, which is now nigh, I shall visit the fury of my curse upon you.

Then king Hariśchandra, his only thought being that of life, said:

—O divine one! Be merciful!

And his mind distracted, he knelt and embraced the feet of the Brahmin sage.

—I am your slave. I am suffering and afraid. I am your worshipper. O twice-born sage, have mercy! Being a slave to a Caṇḍala is an awful thing. O my lord, I have exhausted all my wealth—let me now be slave to you; let me do your menial work. O best of holy men, whatever you command me I shall do; I shall keep only your welfare and comfort in my mind.

Then Viśvamitra said:

—King, since you are now my slave, I sell you to this Caṇḍala. Now you are slave to him.

The king made no answer but to whisper "As you command," and the Caṇḍala, with joyful mind, gave the required sum to Viśvamitra, bound the king, and led him to his own place. Hariśchandra, grieved by the loss of wife and son, pained and confused by the blows of the Caṇḍala's staff, rose and followed him without struggle.

IV

So THE KING made his home in the place of Caṇḍalas, and morning, noon, and evening, he sang this song:
—My poor lady, as she sees her wretched son before her, thinks that when I gain wealth I shall go and ransom them from the Brahmin. But she whose eyes are gentle as a fawn's does not know my depths of degradation; she does not know that I am slave to Caṇḍalas. My kingdom is lost, my friends are far away, my wife and son in slavery, and I a Caṇḍala! Ah, misery upon misery has been heaped upon my head.

Thus did the destitute and suffering king, stripped of all possessions, pass his days at the Caṇḍala's house, remembering with anguished mind his son and the beloved wife who had absorbed his soul and his whole being. The days went by numberless, and the king Hariśchandra, subservient to the Caṇḍala, was taught to strip the garments from the corpses in the burning ground and take fees for their burning:
—You are to stay in this burning ground night and day; when a corpse comes, strip it. For each corpse you get, a sixth part of the fee goes to the king. Of the remaining five parts, three go to me, and two to you for wages.

Thus taught by the Caṇḍala, King Hariśchandra lived in the burning ground to the south of the city of Benares. It was an awful place, filled with the sounds of shrieking and lamenting, a place infested by jackals, vultures, and wild dogs, strewn with the heads of corpses, full of foul smells and heavy evil-smelling smoke, inhabited by spirits and ghastly demons; the place was littered with piles of bones, putrid smelling, filled with the wailing of the grieving relatives of the dead—"Ah, my son . . . my friend . . . my brother . . . baby . . . husband . . . wife . . . sister . . . Where have you gone? . . . Come back to me . . ." The place resounded with these grieving cries, mingled with the sound of sizzling flesh and fat and bone. The corpses burning, half-consumed, blackened, exposed rows of white teeth as if smiling with the thought "So this is the body's end." And the carrion birds, sitting on the piles of bones, shrieked as if they themselves were wailing for the dead; and the fires crackled and sputtered, and above all rose the cries of the Caṇḍalas shouting and laughing with joy, and the glad sounds of the demons and evil spirits, a fearful and horrifying wailing sound like that of the end of the world. Everywhere great piles of buffalo and cow-dung, and heaps of mingled ashes and charred bones, and offerings and ruined, rotting garlands, and lamps; everywhere the shrieks of the carrion animals and the moaning of the grieving men and women. The burning ground was like a hell itself—a hell to make the god of death himself recoil in fear.

In this place did Hariśchandra live, grieving in his distracted mind:

—My servants, my ministers, my Brahmins—where have you taken them, O god of destiny? And my wife and little son! You have abandoned me in my evil fortune—where have you gone? All is gone, consumed in the fire of Viś-vamitra's anger.

And the king, his mind wandering in this way in the burning ground, would then remember the Caṇḍala, with his filthy clothes and demon's body, covered with hair, foul-smelling, carrying a staff and club as he roamed among the funeral pyres, like the god of death himself surveying his realms, and muttering to himself:

—I have gotten such and such a price for this corpse, and a good price for that one. . . So much for me, and this for the king, and so much is due to the head Caṇḍala. . .

It was as if the king had been reborn in another life while still he lived. His clothing was of old and knotted rags. His face and arms and belly and feet were covered with the ashes of the funeral pyres; his hands and fingers were smeared with fat and marrow, and clinging bits of flesh. He satisfied his hunger by eating the boiled rice offered to the dead. His head and shoulders were adorned with rotting garlands taken from the necks of corpses. He moaned and muttered to himself. He slept neither day nor night. And in this way he spent a full twelve months dwelling in the burning ground; the twelve months seemed a hundred years.

One day Hariśchandra, exhausted, fell to the ground, overcome by sleep. And as he slept he dreamed a strange and terrifying dream. He saw that he had been able to pay the Brahmin Viśvamitra's fee, and that, after suffering for twelve years, he had been pardoned. Again, he saw that he had been reborn in the womb of a Caṇḍala woman. While he was in her womb, he thought—"When I have been born

from this womb, I shall follow the practice of giving."
He was born, and, growing, he became a Caṇḍala boy, always ready to perform his duties for the dead within the burning ground. One day, when he was seven years old, he saw the corpse of a virtuous and respected Brahmin being brought to the burning ground by his relatives. The Brahmins were so poor that they were unable to pay the cremation price, so he abused them vilely. And they answered him:
—You have done an evil, sinful thing to Viśvamitra. That is why, you evildoer, you are here performing these vile services. In a former birth you were the king Hariśchandra, and for staining the divinity of a Brahmin and destroying his merit, were caused by Viśvamitra to be reborn a Caṇḍala.

But he continued to demand the cremation price. Then the Brahmins in violent anger cursed him, saying:
—Vile creature! Go now and dwell among the horrors of hell!

As he heard the Brahmins speak these words, the king in his dream saw the messengers of Death had come, horrible in appearance, carrying nooses and clubs. Then he saw himself carried off by them, struggling and wailing in terror:
—My mother! Father! Now I have come to this!

The messengers of Death then hurled him screaming into hell, into a vat of oil. He was torn by sharp saws below him, and he stayed there in agony of mind and body, in fearful darkness, feeding on pus and blood. The king saw himself as a Caṇḍala boy, dead at seven years, burning and roasting endlessly in hell—now beaten, now torn asunder, now roasting, now frozen by ice and bitter winds. A single day was like a hundred years. Then he heard from the denizens of hell that a hundred years had passed.

The messengers of Death again put him on the earth, and he was born as a dog, feeding on filth and vomit, exposed, fatigued, and sickened by the cold. Within a month he again had left his life. Then he was born in the womb of an ass, and again as an elephant, and a monkey, a goat, a cat, a heron, a cow, a sheep, a bird, a worm, a fish, a tortoise, a boar, a deer, a cock, a parrot, a snake, and as many other kinds of creature he took birth time after time. In this way, with birth in many foul wombs, suffering much torment, a full hundred years the king passed painfully. Finally, he saw that he was born again into his own family, and that he was again become a king. But then he lost his kingdom and his wife and son in a game of dice; he wandered, alone in a forest. Then he saw a lion, accompanied by an elephant-calf, the lion approaching with open jaws to eat him. As the lion clawed and tore him, he began to cry:
—O Śaibyā! You have left me, wretched as I am! Where have you gone?

Then queen Śaibyā appeared pleading with him:
—O great king Hariśchandra! Save us, O lord! Why did you play that game of dice? O, see the state of misery to which your wife and child have been reduced.

His wife then disappeared, and Hariśchandra ran in all directions but could not catch another glimpse of her. Again he looked, and saw he was in heaven. As he was seated there, he saw his Śaibyā, naked, her hair disheveled, being taken by force, and screaming:
—O king, save me! O my great king, please save me!

He looked again, and saw the messengers of Death, at Death's command, all seated in the sky, and crying out to him:

—O king! Viśvamitra has told our master Death about you. You are to come here to this place!

He looked again, and saw that he was being bound tightly by the messengers of Death with their serpent ropes. They dragged him away; and Death was praising Viśvamitra's deed.

Despite the torment that Hariśchandra endured, no unrighteousness was established in his mind. He saw in his dream that all he had suffered was in the span of twelve years, as reckoned by men, and that at the end of twelve years he was taken forcibly by messengers before the god of Death himself. And Death said to him:

—O king! This is the fruit of the irresistible rage of Viśvamitra. What is more, the sage Viśvamitra will soon bring about the death of your son. Return now to the world of men, fulfil the remainder of your suffering. When twelve years have passed, O king, you will find relief.

When he had heard these words of Death, he felt himself again seized by Death's messengers and hurled down from the sky.

Falling, in terror, Hariśchandra started suddenly awake, and began to turn these things over in his mind.

—This is salt rubbed in my wounds. What horror have I seen in this dream—it has no end. But is it possible that the twelve years of my dream have passed?

Thinking thus, he humbly turned to those Caṇḍalas who were nearby, and asked:

—Have my twelve years yet passed?

But some said:

—No. Your twelve years have not yet passed.

And others, laughing, said:

—How can that be?

Then king Hariśchandra, when he heard these bitter words, was saddened in his mind, and prayed:

—O gods, have mercy upon me, and upon my wife and child. Praise be to thee, O Dharma, greatest of gods, and to thee, O Kṛṣṇa, creator, pure, eternal, ancient, the best of all things. O Bṛhaśpati, praise be to thee, and praise to thee, O Indra.

When he had prayed thus Hariśchandra, his memory again dimmed, began to busy himself with his Caṇḍala work, fixing the corpse price. Again he was dressed in filthy rags, his hair matted; he was black in color, and he held a club. Again he became demented. He remembered no more his wife or son. His only world was the burning ground. His kingdom and his home were no more.

Not long after, Śaibyā, the wife of Hariśchandra, came to the burning ground. She was pale and thin, covered with dust, her hair turned gray. Her mind also was distracted, as she wept "Ah, my son, my child, my baby"—for she carried her young son, dead of snake bite, to his funeral pyre. And as she came, she wailed:

—Ah, my king! Look you now, see your son, whom so often you have watched at play, who was as beautiful as an earth-bound moon. Look you now, and see your son lying dead of the bite of a snake.

The king heard the weeping woman approach, and said to himself:

—Perhaps I shall get a blanket from this one!

So saying, he went quickly toward the weeping woman. He did not recognize her as his wife, so long had they been living apart, so changed was she. Nor did Śaibyā, when she saw a man with matted, dry hair, a man as twisted as a withered tree, know him as her husband. Then the king Hariśchandra, gazing at the boy lying on the black cloth, poisoned by the snake, saw on his body signs of royal birth, and he began to think:

—This boy is surely born of royal blood. What could have happened, that he has been reduced to such a state? When I see that beautiful boy lying in his mother's lap, I cannot but think of my own boy Rohitaśva, whose eyes were like lotus-petals. If evil fate had not taken him away, indeed, I would be gazing upon my own son, who would be of like beauty, of like age.

Then the queen began to mourn:

—O my child, what sin has caused this evil to befall us and this misery come to be? O my god! My king! How can you live with peaceful mind in some far distant place, giving no hope to me, your miserable wife? Your kingdom is destroyed, your friends and relatives separated from you, your wife and son in slavery—O God! Have you destroyed all traces of my king Hariśchandra?

When the king heard these words, suddenly he knew his wife and his dead son, and he fell fainting to the earth. As he lay unconscious, she too recognized him, and herself fell in a swoon from grief. And as he came slowly back to consciousness, the king began to mourn again in anguished suffering:

—My child! When I think of your beautiful eyes and

brows and nose and the curly hair around your princely face, and when I see that beauty now so dry and dead, my heart is torn. Who will come running to me now, crying "Father" in his sweet and childish voice? Whom now shall I take up on my lap with love and call "My child"? Whose knees will soil my clothes with dust? Oh, my child, you were conceived in joy from my limbs and mind and heart, and I sold you, evil father that I am, like common goods, like chattel! The snake, my evil fate, which took my kingdom, all my means, and all my wealth, has also bitten you. When I look upon your lotus-face, lying poisoned by the serpent of fate, I too am blinded by that poison.

Thus the king, sobbing, spoke to his son and took him on his lap. The queen then said:

—I know now by his voice that I cannot be mistaken. He is indeed that best of men, that learned king, my Hariśchandra. His nose is long and arched, like that of Hariśchandra. His teeth are like the buds of flowers, like those of Hariśchandra. But why would the king come to this burning ground?

So saying, the queen, forgetting for a moment her grief for her son, stared at her husband. Emaciated, downcast, wondering, tortured and grieving for her husband and her son, she stared at her husband and saw his staff.

—I have become the wife of a Caṇḍala!

And the long-eyed queen stared in horror. Only after a long time did she come to her senses, and say:

—O vicious, vile fate! You have made this god-like king a Caṇḍala! Not only did you take his kingdom and his friends and his wife and only son, but, still unsated, you have made of him a Caṇḍala. Ah, my king! Raise me from the earth, tell me to mount to your royal couch. Why do I not see your royal umbrella and golden vase? Where is your fan? What perversity of fate is this? You, from whose path kings like servants would sweep dust with their garments; you, grieving, haunt this fearful and unholy place, alone! This place, filled with the skulls of corpses, their hair the strings of rotting garlands; this place where the dry ground is slippery with congealed fat exuded from the burning bodies; this place horrible with piles of ashes and charcoal and half-burnt bones and marrow, whence the little birds have fled in terror at the screaming of the jackals and the vultures; this place from which the sky is hidden by the palls of smoke of funeral pyres, where those who roam the night revel drunken with the taste of carrion flesh—in this place my king lives, alone!

So saying, the queen fell upon the king's neck, weeping: —Ah, my king, what is this I see? Is it a dream? Tell me it is not real! What has happened? I have lost all power to think. O righteous king, if this be real, then what means righteousness? What is the use of worshiping the gods and Brahmins, or in protecting the world? There is no righteousness! There is no truth! There is no justice! See! Righteousness and justice were your only thoughts; and you have been cast out from your kingdom!

Hearing these words of his queen, Hariśchandra heaved a sigh, and began to tell her the story of how he had become a Caṇḍala. When the queen had heard, she wept for a long time, and then related in her turn how the death of Rohitaśva had occurred. Then the king said:

—O beloved, I have no desire to suffer this misery a longer time. But I am not master of my soul. If I enter the fire myself without permission of the Caṇḍala, I shall be his slave in future births. As a filth-eating worm I shall be cast into hell, into the rivers of hell slimy with sinew and blood and fat and pus. I shall be cut to bits and burn in fire. But for those who are drowning in a sea of pain the only way to reach the other shore is the abandonment of life. I had only one son to continue my family. He too is drowned in the ocean of fate. So now the misery will be endless. It would be a sin for me to take my life. But what does a man in anguish care for sin? The suffering of hell itself cannot be worse than suffering my son's loss. I shall throw myself upon the pyre with his body. O graceful one, I ask your pardon for the way in which I have treated you. But I command you, O my wife of gentle smile, return now to the Brahmin's house. Hear my words. If you give alms and offer sacrifice and gratify your *guru,* then perhaps your merit will be such that we shall be together in another life. In this life it cannot be. By doing what is right, you shall follow me on our son's path. I smile at the thought, though the words I speak are unholy and obscene—I pray you, pardon me. Because you are a queen, do not despise that Brahmin out of pride. Rather try to please him, as you would your husband or your god.

But the queen said:

—O wise king, I cannot bear the burden of grief which you ask of me. I shall enter the fire with you and with my son this day.

Then the king prepared the funeral pyre and placed his

son upon it. He and his wife joined their hands in prayer and meditated on the gods dwelling in the inmost hearts of men, eternal, without beginning and without end.

At this time Indra and the other gods, with Dharma at their head, came quickly to that place, and said to Hariśchandra:

—O king! Now hear our words. This is Brahma manifested to your sight, and this is Dharma himself, and with them the Sādhyas and the Māruts and Lokapālas and Hagas and Siddhas and Rudra and Gandhārvas and Āśvins, and all the other gods. And here too is he who would not be your friend in the three worlds, Viśvamitra. All have come now to offer you friendship and whatever you desire.

Then Dharma said:

—O king, do not do this thing. I am Dharma. You have pleased me with your qualities of self-control, patience, and truth; I myself have come to you. With your wife and your son, you have won the greatest of rewards, that of the eternal world. That which is to other men unattainable, you by your deeds have won. Ascend now with your wife and son into heaven.

Then the lord Indra, going to the funeral pyre, showered down a death-destroying nectar. And the gods made a shower of flowers to rain down, and the sound of kettle-drums boomed out. And Rohitaśva, the princely son of the great king Hariśchandra, rose up with healthy body and clear mind. And Hariśchandra then embraced his son, and became clothed in divine garments and garlands, and became again whole and healthy in body and mind. Then the king of gods said to him again:

—With your wife and son you have gained the final bliss. Ascend to heaven as reward for your deeds.

But Hariśchandra replied:

—O divine king, I cannot ascend to heaven without permission of my lord the Caṇḍala.

Then Dharma said:

—O king, knowing that this, your suffering, was to be, by my magic power I myself became that Caṇḍala. It was I who acted in that way.

And Indra said again:

—Prepare to go to the highest place, which is prayed for by all men upon the earth; that place, O king, gained only by the most meritorious of men.

But Hariśchandra said:

—O king of gods, praise be to you. Hear the words of one filled with adoration for your heavenly countenance. In my city, the people are all filled with grief for me. How can I abandon them and go to heaven? The murder of a Brahmin or a *guru*, the killing of a cow or of a woman are not greater sins than that of leaving those dependent on and devoted to you. What joy would there be in the other world if I abandoned them? Therefore, O king of gods, if they go to heaven with me, then I shall go; otherwise I shall go to hell with them.

Indra said:

—O king, there are many different people in your city, with different sins and merits. How can they all go to heaven with you?

Hariśchandra said:

—A king is a king because of his subjects as well as because of sacrifice and birth and deeds. Whatever worthy deeds I have performed I have performed because of them. I cannot abandon them because of mere desire for heaven. Whatever merit I have gained by deeds or prayer or alms belongs to them as well as me. If the fruit of my deeds is to be long enjoyed by me, let it be instead that I enjoy it only for one day and that they enjoy it with me.

Then Dharma and Indra and Viśvamitra said: "Let it be so," and they went to the city of Ayodhya with teeming heavenly chariots and said to the people:

—Ascend you all to heaven.

And Viśvamitra, pleased with the king's speech and out of love for him, brought the prince Rohitaśva to Ayodhya and crowned him there. And all the people of Ayodhya, glad, having enthroned their king, accompanied by their servants, ascended to heaven with Hariśchandra in the heavenly chariots. And King Hariśchandra was joyful, ascending in a chariot, a figure of incomparable majesty, and was established in a heavenly city surrounded by high walls and ramparts. And Uśanas, wise in the knowledge of the sacred writings, the teacher of the Daityas, saw the majesty and grandeur of the king, and sang a hymn of praise:

> —In all the world there has been no king like Hariśchandra, nor will there ever be. Stricken with his own suffering, he listened to the sufferings of others, and he has gained the highest bliss. To him who asks for heaven, heaven is granted, and sons, to him who asks; to him who asks, a wife is granted, and he who asks, a kingdom gains. He who has patience enjoys greatness, and great are the fruits of generosity. Hariśchandra of these qualities has come to heaven, and lives a king among the gods.

Humorous Tales

Introduction

Humor is not ordinarily associated either with Bengal or with India. My suspicion is that we are inclined to look upon Indians as a rather stern and severe, somewhat arid people, absorbed in the intricacies of their philosophies and religions, taking themselves much too seriously. Actually, as a generalization, nothing could be further from the truth. Though I cannot speak for India as a whole in this or any other area, I can say that most Bengalis I have met have a wonderful feeling for the absurd, a fine sense of the ridiculous. This does not manifest itself easily, for I suspect Bengalis of wanting to put up a more serious front to the world than they do to each other. But as I think the stories to follow will show, Bengalis love to poke fun—at others, and, contrary to the belief of non-Bengalis, at themselves.

In the older times, the traditional Bengali disrespect for authority, particularly pompous authority, appeared in the form of humorous tales. No one and nothing was free from ridicule: not the gods (witness the tale of the great god Śiva, whom the sages agreed to worship on condition that he would stop seducing their wives[1]), not the scholars (witness the tale of the grammarian Pāṇini, who simply could not learn Sanskrit until he cut the appropriate line in the palm of his hand with a knife), not the princes, and certainly not the Muslim rulers who were for centuries the source of power and authority in Bengal. The picture of the fat, pompous, rich Bengali babu is one familiar to the rest of India. The babu is as much a butt in Bengal as anywhere else. Bengalis love the absurd, and what is more absurd than a man who considers himself better than other men because of money or position? This disrespect is as manifest today as ever it was in the past, though today the object of the ridicule has perhaps become the Westerner or Anglo-Indian. Some fine satire is even now being written in Bengali, by such men as "Bonaphul"[2] and "Paraśurām."[3] Although, strictly speaking, the limits of this little collection should exclude these and other modern writers, I cannot resist giving one or two modern passages. These are the opening paragraphs from Mustabha Ali's *Deśe Bideśe:*

> I had bought a pair of shorts from the Caṇḍī market. In those days there was a very fine institution, designed to carry smart Bengalis about India, called "European

[1] This story has its origin in *Skanda purāṇa, maheśvara khaṇḍa, kedāra khaṇḍa* 6, 18–19; it is still told, however, with great enthusiasm.

[2] Balai Chand Mukhopadhyay (1899———).

[3] Rajsekhar Basu (1880–1960).

Third Class." I was about to climb into such a third-class compartment at Howrah Station when an Anglo-Indian voice bellowed in my ear, "This is reserved for Europeans."

I shouted back, "There aren't any Europeans here. Come on, you and I will have it all to ourselves."

I had read in a book on Comparative Philology that if you put an *anusvāra* on the end of a Bengali word, you have Sanskrit. Just so, if you put enough stress on the first syllable of an English word, you have Sahibs' English. Accenting the first syllable of an English word is like cramming a lot of chili into poor cooking. In Bengali, which is a straightforward language, this is known as gaank-gaank English. In any case, this Anglo-Indian was a native of Taltola, and, on hearing me speak in English was so delighted that he offered to assist me in taking care of my baggage. I gladly passed the burden of cursing and haggling with the coolies to his shoulders. The coolies learned in no time that the Sahib's father, as well as uncles and aunts and cousins on both sides of his family, had high positions in the railroad. The coolies were duly impressed and humbled.

At this point the enthusiasm which I had had for my trip was just about completely deflated. I had been busy for so many days previously with the collection and preparation of clothes, passports, and such things, that I had no time to think. But as soon as the train started to move, the feeling struck me for the first time that I was alone and not very happy, and that I was a coward for feeling alone and not very happy.

The Anglo-Indian was a good man. I had lain down on my berth with a long face, and I stayed there. He saw this and said, "You seem depressed. Going far?"

I saw that he was well acquainted with English courtesy. He did not say "How far are you going?" I had learned almost all of what little etiquette I know from a parson, and understood that his "Going far?" was in the best of taste. For if I had no desire to answer at length, I could easily satisfy everyone concerned with a simple "yes" or "no." But it is impossible to avoid conversation based on "How far are you going?"

The book goes on in this vein. Secondly, here is a little story by "Bonaphul." It is called *Bidhātā*. Bidhātā is the god of destiny.

Once there was a time when tigers were ravaging the earth. They became such a plague that mankind was sorely tried. It was all right when they limited themselves to eating calves, but when men began to disappear into the tigers' maws, other men got out their sticks and spears and bows and arrows and guns and began hunting tigers. They would kill the tiger, but no sooner had they done so than another would appear to take its place. Finally, in desperation, men went to Bidhātā, and said:

—O Bidhātā, deliver us from the mouths of the tigers.

And Bidhātā said:

—All right.

But not long after, the tigers brought their suit to the court of Destiny, and said:

—Bidhātā, we live in constant fear; we have to sneak from forest to forest. The hunters give us no peace. Please save us from their hands.

And Bidhātā said:

—All right.

Now Nera's mother brought a petition to Bidhātā:

—Father, give to my Nera a healthy beautiful wife. O Creator of the World, grant my prayer and I will give you five pice worth of sugar.

And Bidhātā said:

—All right.

Harahari Bhaṭṭāchārya brought suit, and said to God:
—All my life I have worshipped you. My body is a bag of bones from fasting. Now I should like to go on a trip to see my nephew. Arrange it.

And Bidhātā said:
—All right.

Sunil tried his hand:
—O God, if you can get me a good fat scholarship, I will give you five rupees of the loot.

And Bidhātā said:
—All right.

Haren Purakāyastha wanted to be Chairman of the District Board. He went to a priest of Kālī:
—I need eleven more votes. Please speak to Him about it.

But the priest, having imbibed the fat honorarium, forgot the proper charm, and could only think enough to chant:
—Give votes, votes give, give votes . . .

And Bidhātā said:
—All right, all right!

A farmer raised his hands to heaven and prayed:
—Bidhātā, send us rain.

And Bidhātā said:
—All right.

The mother of a sick child prayed:
—He is my only son, O God. Do not take him away from me.

And Bidhātā said:
—All right.

The neighbor of the woman with the sick child prayed:
—O God of Mercy, that slut has too much pride. She always has new jewelry. She thinks the world is her doormat. Pinch the throat of her brat, O God; teach her a lesson.

And Bidhātā said:
—All right.

The philosopher said:
—I want to know you, and understand your nature.
And Bidhātā sighed:
—All right.
From China the cry rose up:
—Save us from the Japanese.
And Bidhātā said:
—All right.
From Bengal a young man's unaccustomed meditation rose:
—No editor will accept my works. If the God of Destiny would speak to the editor of *Prabāsi* about it . . .
And Bidhātā said:
—All right.
And then, incredibly, there came a moment when Bidhātā could catch his breath. He sighed and turned to Brahmā, who was relaxing comfortably next to him, and said:
—Have you any good mustard oil at your house?
And Brahmā said:
—I have.
And Bidhātā said:
—Then will you send for it?
And when the mustard oil came from Brahmās' place, the God of Destiny put it to his nostrils, drew a deep, relaxing breath, and sank slowly into sleep.
A sleep from which he has not awakened, even to this day.

This bittersweet love of the absurd runs throughout the humor of Bengal. There are motifs of form as well. The helpless king and his wily minister are found in thousands of old stories still current about Mahārājā Krishnachandra and his jester Gopāl Bhāṛ. Perhaps, as in so many other folk tales, there is some basis here in fact. There was an eighteenth-century king of Bengal, the patron of Bhāratchandra the author of the *Vidyā-Sundara*, who ruled in Krishnagar; it is perhaps to him that the legends refer. In these stories, as in those of the *dhobi* and the *zamindar*, or of Habucandra and the old cobbler, it is always the lowly man who holds his nominal superior up to ridicule.

The comparatively few humorous tales which I have gathered and translated here are, I think, representative of the thousands still current in Bengal. The stories here were all told to me by relatively sophisticated and well-educated people. Therefore they might include some details which might not be found in a version by an uneducated villager. But this to my mind does not mean that they are not folk tales. It is a difficult thing to classify folk literature. People of all types, educated and uneducated, tell and retell such stories as these; each version includes the shadings and embellishments of the teller. From this point of view the telling of a story is an act of creation. The storyteller takes liberties. In my translations I have also drawn upon the prerogative of the storyteller, and have taken more liberties with the original Bengali than would be permissible if the translations had been made from written literature.

The problem of classification also arises in the inclusion of these tales in a collection of medieval literature. An occasional hint, such as the name of Krishnachandra or Siraj-ud-dallah, occurs within the stories. But in general, here also I have taken liberties. Who can say, in regard to a story which has gone from mouth to mouth so often that it would now probably be unrecognizable to its creator, when it originated. Without worrying too much about such classifications, then, I have included these stories really because they please. That, after all, is what they are for.

The Princess and the Paṇḍit[1]

A long time ago, in India, princesses used to be married by the *svayamvara* system. By this system, a king would bring his daughter into the court, and princes would come from all over the land to compete for her affections. The princess would choose her own husband from among them, by placing a garland of flowers on his neck.

At the time when this system was in use, there lived a certain princess who had made a vow that she would choose for a husband only that man who would be able

[1] The theme of this story is the same as that of the *Vidyā-Sundara*, though treated quite differently. It is an old one in India, being that also of the famous *Nala-Damāyanti* episode of the *Mahābhārata*.

to vanquish her in logical argument. When she reached the marriageable age, the king her father announced that her *svayamvara* would be held. She was such a beautiful girl, and in addition accomplished and learned, that princes and paṇḍits, all of whom were confident of their ability to trounce this mere girl in logical argument, came from near and far. The court swelled and buzzed with their murmurings and arguments and syllogisms, until the king led in his daughter, lovely with the grace of a deer and the beauty of a goddess. Then they were silent. The king made known to all the princes and paṇḍits the vow which his daughter had made, and the princes and paṇḍits vied with one another to see who would have the first chance at argument with her, since obviously the first would be the chosen groom. Soon the controversy was settled, and the first paṇḍit stood up, and the princess stood up also, and the argument began. The suitor was confounded by the sharp reasoning of the princess, and soon found himself in an untenable position, and sat down, beaten. And so it went with the second, and the third, and with all of them. The great paṇḍits left the court, with heads bowed in shame. The king too bowed his head in sorrow, for it looked very much as if his daughter would never marry.

The paṇḍits and princes gathered outside the court. "This, a mere girl, has beaten us all. We will give up our studies forever, and go into far countries." Which they did.

But there remained one paṇḍit, whose pride was more deeply hurt than was that of the others, and he said to himself, "I will have my revenge. I cannot tolerate the pride of this female." And he pondered on how he might bring her pride to dust.

"The perfect way," he thought to himself, "would be to get her married to an utter fool. The problem is, where can I find an utter fool, and, once I have found him, how can I arrange that he beat her in debate?" Thus he thought, as he walked.

As he walked, he happened to glance up into a tree which stood by the side of the road. He saw there, in the topmost branches, a man sitting on a limb, cutting off that limb between himself and the trunk. "Here," said the paṇḍit to himself, "is a perfect fool. And I have a plan." So he called to the man to come down from the tree.

When the man reached the ground, he stood before the paṇḍit with his head bent, obviously expecting some kind of ill-treatment. The paṇḍit questioned him:

—What is your name, fellow, and where do you live?

—Sir, my name is Kālīdāsa, and I live where I am.

—Are you married, fellow?

Kālīdāsa could only look at the paṇḍit with open mouth, as he asked:

—Would you like to marry a princess?

Kālīdāsa's jaw slackened another inch, and the paṇḍit went on:

—Well, then, you will have to follow my instructions to the letter. From now on you are not to speak a word no matter what the circumstances. For, if you do, you will never marry that princess.

And Kālīdāsa consented to the condition willingly.

So the paṇḍit dressed Kālīdāsa in the very finest of

paṇḍit's clothes, circulated a rumor that a very great paṇḍit was coming to join syllogisms with the princess, and they started off for the royal court. The king received them with the honor due a paṇḍit of Kālīdāsa's rank, and, as the princess stood to question and be questioned by Kālīdāsa, the king was thinking, "Praise the gods, I hope this man has the wit to beat her. Her pride is getting unbearable. Furthermore, if such a paṇḍit as this man is reputed to be cannot take her, she will surely go unmarried for the rest of her life." At the same time, the princess was thinking, "He doesn't look very intelligent. I will vanquish him with ease, like all the others. Just the same, I rather hope he wins." And Kālīdāsa was thinking, "A princess and half a kingdom, as due a paṇḍit of my standing." And the paṇḍit was thinking, "Ha!" And, thinking thus, the paṇḍit rose to address the princess:

—My companion is observing a vow of silence for six months, of which only the third month has been seen. Therefore, princess, if you care to put any questions to him, he will answer them by signs.

So the princess rose, pointed her finger at Kālīdāsa, as was her habit in debate, and opened her mouth to speak. Now Kālīdāsa thought that when she pointed her finger at him she meant that she intended to stick it into his eye, and he, enraged at the injustice of it, immediately put up two fingers, to show her how he would retaliate. As it happened, the fallacy in the statement which she was about to make—an intentional fallacy, to see if Kālīdāsa would be able to point it out to her—could be answered by the second rule of logic. The princess was astounded, and said:

—What a paṇḍit is this! He answers my questions even before I have been able to put them!

And she confessed herself defeated, and married him, and they lived miserably ever after.

Gopāl the Star-counter

One day the Nawāb sent news to Mahārājā Krishnachandra that he wanted the whole earth measured, from side to side and from end to end, and that he would greatly appreciate it if the Mahārājā would take it upon himself to count the stars in the sky as well. Mahārājā Krishnachandra was astounded:

—I don't want to seem unco-operative, but this is an impossible thing which you have commanded me to do.

And the Nawāb said:

—But do it you will.

So the Mahārājā fell into a brown study, and wept a little, and brooded over how he might fulfil the command of the Nawāb.

It was not long before Gopāl Bhāṛ passed by, and, seeing the Mahārājā in such an attitude of despair, he tugged gently at the ends of his moustache and said:

—Mahārāj, what is this I see! If you have trouble, you need only tell your Gopāl, and lo! all will be well.

The king was not so easily consoled. He said:

—Ah, Gopāl, this is a problem which even you cannot solve. Listen. The Nawāb has commanded me to measure the earth, from side to side and from end to end. And, as if that were not enough . . . (and here a large tear dropped off the end of his nose) . . . if that were not enough, he wants me to count the stars in the sky as well.

Gopāl was not dismayed:

—Ha, Mahārāj, nothing could be easier. Appoint me as your official Earth-measurer and Star-counter, and set your mind at rest. And, when I am through, I myself will go to the Nawāb with the results. Worry no more. Only, one favor. Ask the Nawāb for one year in which to finish the job, and a million rupees for operating expenses. In one year's time, I will bring him the results.

And Mahārājā Krishnachandra, greatly pleased and relieved, since if the job was not done it would be Gopāl's head which would come off and not his own, did as Gopāl had asked.

So Gopāl passed a very pleasant year, spending a million rupees on the most delightful women and the most delectable food in the kingdom, as well as on palaces and elephants and jewels and other things of this type. He spent, in fact, such a pleasant year that at its end he went to the Mahārājā again, jingling the four annas and two pice that remained of the million rupees and assumed a worried frown:

—Mahārāj, the task is more difficult than I had anticipated. Mind, I have made an excellent start, and the results are promising. But I will need another year's time. And, incidentally, another million rupees. Operating expenses.

So the Mahārājā reluctantly petitioned the Nawāb, and the Nawāb reluctantly granted the extra year and the second million rupees. And Gopāl passed his year in activity even more pleasant than that of his first, since he now had some experience in these matters.

One year later, to the hour, Gopāl came dragging himself up the road to the Nawāb's palace. With him were fifteen bullock carts, crammed to creaking with the finest of fine thread, tangled and jumbled and pressed and matted, and five very fat and woolly sheep. He led this odd procession through the gates of the palace and into the court of the Nawāb, made a deep and graceful bow, and said:

—Excellency, it has been done as you ordered. I have measured the earth, from end to end and from side to side, and I have counted the stars in the sky.

—Excellent! And now, give me the figures. The figures.

—Figures, Majesty! Figures were not in the agreement. I have done what you have commanded. The earth is as wide as the thread in the first seven bullock carts is long, and as long as the thread in the other eight is long. There are, furthermore, just as many stars in the sky as there are hairs on these five sheep. It took me a long time to find sheep with just the right number of hairs.

And the Nawāb could only say:

—Impossible! I cannot measure that thread, or count those hairs. Still, you have lived up to your end of the bargain. Here is your reward, a million rupees.

And Gopāl lived in ease for some little time.

Gopāl and the Bull

Once the Nawāb of Bengal came to Krishnagara, the capital city of the kingdom of Mahārājā Krishnachandra, for a visit, and brought with him the whole of his army They camped just outside the city, and the Nawāb had no sooner pitched his tents than he sent word to Mahārājā Krishnachandra that he wanted food, that, in fact, the Mahārājā would be expected to supply him and his whole army with food for the length of their stay. Now it is well known that among the Muslims the favorite dish is beef. But the Mahārājā was a Hindu; how could he send beef for the Nawāb's dinner? So he decided that he would cause such huge quantities of other kinds of meat, mutton and fowl, to be prepared, that the Nawāb would never notice that beef was missing from the menu.

But, as luck would have it, as the Nawāb was sitting in his tent a magnificent bull passed by on the road, a beautiful fat bull with a glistening coat, such a bull as the Nawāb had never in all his years seen. So he sent at once for his attendants, and gave them orders to tie up the bull and, the next day, to slaughter it and prepare it for his dinner. And it was immediately done as he had ordered.

It was not long before the news of the capture of the bull reached the ears of Mahārājā Krishnachandra, and when he heard of it, he fell into a deep depression, and refused to eat, and spoke to no one at all. But it happened that Gopāl was passing by the king's chamber at about this time, and he saw the king sitting with his head in his hands, and he said:

—Mahārāj, what is the trouble? Why do you sit here with your head in your hands? Life is meant to be lived to the full, not to be spent in worry. Tell me everything, and I will help you.

The king said:
—Gopāl, I have a terrible problem. At my father's *śrāddh*[1] ceremonies I made a bull-offering, and that bull has been wandering for a year about my kingdom, eating and sleeping to his heart's content. Now, as the evilest of luck would have it, the Nawāb has captured that bull, that very bull, and is preparing at this moment to slaughter and eat it.

Gopāl replied:
—Mahārāj, you need not worry about a thing. I will arrange everything, and before the sun sets that bull will be released and will resume his wandering about the kingdom, and you and your father will not be dishonored.

So Gopāl went to the tent of the Nawāb, and he said to the guard:
—Guard, I am Gopāl, the jester to the court of Mahārājā Krishnachandra, and I am sent here by His Majesty to make the Nawāb laugh and forget the affairs of state.

The guard relayed this information to the Nawāb, and the Nawāb gave orders that Gopāl should enter, as he had need of laughter and the affairs of state were weighing heavily on his mind. So Gopāl entered the tent and went before the Nawāb, and said:
—Your excellency, I have come on behalf of the inhabitants of this city of Krishnagara to give you thanks. We will forever be in your debt for having captured that bull.

And the Nawāb said, surprised:
—What! How can this be? You give me thanks that I am going to slaughter a bull? Is this some trick?
—Trick, your Excellency? It is certainly no trick. The peo-

[1] Ceremony for dead relatives.

ple of this city have not been able to live their lives in peace, ever since that bull first began to roam the streets. It is not only that the shopkeepers have not been able to open their shops, since the moment that they do, the bull comes along and eats their wares. It is not only that. But, Excellency, this bull is a particularly evil bull. He is inordinately fond of eating human dung. Whenever one of the people of the city prepared to relieve himself in the field, as is our custom, the bull is overcome with impatience and charges the sufferer with his head down, and any unfortunate man who does not run for his life is tossed on the bull's horns. The result is that we have not been able to relieve ourselves for such a long time that we are all in the most acute kind of agony. Therefore, we offer you our most grateful thanks for your solution of our dilemma.

Hearing this, the Nawāb boiled with rage, and shouted: —To think that I was going to eat this bull for dinner tomorrow!

And he immediately gave orders that the bull should be released and driven far away from the camp. When this had been done, the Nawāb rewarded Gopāl lavishly for having saved him from a terrible mistake; Mahārājā Krishnachandra also gave him great piles of jewels and money, and Gopāl went home, chuckling quietly to himself.

The Dhobi and the Zamindar

Once upon a time there was a great zamindar who had a dhobi.[1] The zamindar would send all his clothes to that

[1] Washerman.

dhobi for washing. Now, it happened one day that the zamindar had particular need of some of the clothes that he had sent to the dhobi that morning to be washed, so he called one of his servants and said:

—Ohe! Go at once to the dhobi and tell him to bring my clothes, for I have need of them.

So the servant at once ran off toward the house of the washerman.

As he was approaching the house, a most singular sight greeted his eyes. The washerman was putting his bundles of clothes on the back of his donkey one by one, and as he was loading the donkey with clothes, he was talking to the donkey in this way:

—Gentle donkey, O most honored and respected donkey, I am afraid that I am overloading you with all these clothes. Perhaps, revered sir, I am causing you distress, and for it I ask your most gracious pardon.

And, as he talked away to his donkey, he sprinkled his conversation liberally with many a "Sir, Honored one, Respected eminence, Your honor," and "Your reverence." The zamindar's servant was naturally taken somewhat aback by this procedure, and he said to himself, "Sitārām! The dhobi has gone mad!" and immediately he turned about and ran as fast as he could to tell the zamindar.

He ran to the zamindar's room, and, bowing to the floor, said:

—Babu![2] Your dhobi has gone out of his mind; He is standing in his yard, loading his donkey with bundles of clothes, and carrying on a conversation with him all the while. And as if this were not enough, he is addressing his donkey as

[2] Form of address to a Bengali gentleman.

"Respected sir, Honorable sir, Your worship," and other such titles which belong only to persons of rank and standing, like yourself.

The zamindar was surprised and curious:

—Well, there is one thing about it. I can't very well have a madman washing my clothes, now, can I? So call him here, and we'll ask an explanation of this peculiar behavior.

So the servant went and summoned the dhobi, and the dhobi duly came and having made *pranāma*[3] stood before the zamindar with bowed head and folded hands. He acted very much like a sane dhobi might act when in the presence of a mighty zamindar. He listened as the zamindar said:

—Now, dhobi, I sent my servant to you to tell you to bring back my clothes, and he came back and told me that you were talking to your donkey. And further, that you were calling this donkey "Revered sir, Honored one" and things like that. What do you have to say for yourself? I cannot have a mad dhobi washing my clothes. So explain yourself.

And the dhobi said:

—If it please your most respected and honored eminence, I am not mad, and in fact the whole affair has a very simple explanation. I am a very low-caste man, and in our caste we do not get much opportunity to use such terms of respect and esteem as we would use to people such as your own gracious majesty. In my case, we call each other "Hey, you," or "Friend," or sometimes even "Brother," whether we are brothers or not, and other such ill-bred and familiar terms, which I could never dream of using to gentler people such as yourself. Further, since I have the honor of being your

[3] Homage, form of salutation.

worship's dhobi, I thought it wise to get accustomed to the use of such terms as "Your reverence" and "Honored sir," so that I might not slip when I have the privilege of addressing you. Thus, I practice at every opportunity. Since I cannot address my friends or family in this way, I must address my donkey.

And the zamindar was very pleased with his speech, and rewarded him heavily, and sent him on his way.

The King and the Cobbler

Once upon a time there was a king named Habuchandra. One day it suddenly occurred to him that there was dust upon his feet. So he washed them. But no sooner had he stepped from his bath onto the earth than dust clung to his feet again. So Habuchandra flew into a rage, and screamed at the top of his lungs, "Gabu!" For Gabu was the name of his chief minister. And Gabu came running, and bowed low before the king, who shouted at him:

—Gabu! Is there no law or discipline in my kingdom? My earth persists in making my feet dusty. You must take care of this immediately, or no one will be safe from my wrath!

Gabu's face became pale at the rage of the king, and his voice stuck in his throat. For a long time he sat on the ground, scratching his beard and thinking. But he could find no solution to the problem. And this, with much trembling, he told the king.

And the king said:

—Gabu, I will not tolerate this thing in my kingdom. I

will give you three days to gather together all the scientists and technicians in the land. and if they cannot solve the problem, zzzt! will go all your heads.

So Gabu went away, and called together all the scientists and technicians from all over the land, and when they had come together, the king addressed them and said:

—If you are not able to solve this problem in three days' time, zzzt! will go all your heads. I am not sure what you are worth anyhow, sitting about as you do, combing out your long tails of degrees and titles.

So the scientists sat in a meeting, and thought, and thought, and the heat of the country became intolerable with their thinking. Nineteen barrels of snuff vanished up their scientific nostrils, and finally it was settled. They purchased seventeen million brooms, and put them into the hands of seventeen million sweepers, and gave the sweepers orders to rid the land of dust.

So the sweepers began to sweep, and all over the kingdom great clouds of dust rose into the air, until finally Habuchandra choking and sobbing with the dust in his nose and his throat, gave a great shout:

—What a herd of asses you are! You clean the earth of dust, but fill the air with it! Stop this nonsense immediately, or zzzt! will go your heads!

So again the scientists sat in meeting, and this time twenty-six barrels of snuff went into their nostrils before decision was taken. But finally it was settled. Twenty-one million tubs of water were brought. "This," agreed the scientists, "will rid the king's feet of dust for good."

So the water was poured out on the ground, and it ran

in streams and brooks and finally in rivers, and the fish and other water creatures were drowned by too much water, and men and other creatures of the land began to think, "There is nothing for it but to learn to swim, For if we do not learn to swim, we will surely drown." And many creatures learned to swim, and many drowned, and those that had reached high places so that they did not have to swim or drown caught influenza because their feet were always wet. And the kingdom was filled with a great sneezing and coughing, and even the royal nose was running with cold. So the king gave a great shout, and called to Gabu:

—Gabu! My patience is running out. The cures you find are worse than the disease!

Gabu bowed low and left the king in haste, thankful that his head was still on his shoulders, and again he called the scientists together. And again they thought. They thought it would be best to inclose the king in a room made of iron, with no holes or chinks through which the dust could seep. But the wisest among them considered that the king might not like that, and besides, the kingdom would go to ruin if the king were shut up in a room of iron for the rest of his life. So they thought again. They thought that they might cover the whole kingdom with leather, so that the dust could not rise up through it. And again the wisest among them said, "But you have not considered that the rice and other things which we eat will not grow through leather." But no one paid him any heed, and they all shouted, "A fine idea!" "Cover the kingdom with leather!" and other such things, and immediately they called together all the cobblers of the land and ordered them to stitch together a piece of leather which would stretch from one border of the kingdom to the other.

The king was very pleased with this solution to his problem, and issued a formal proclamation at once, congratulating the assembly of scientists on their remarkable thinking abilities and granting them all degrees. But while the proclamation was being read throughout the kingdom, the oldest of the cobblers came to the king, who was sitting with Gabu beside him, and begged his permission to speak. The king graciously consented:

—Speak, old man, and be done with it.

So the old man said:

—O king, it is not necessary that you cover the kingdom with leather to keep the dust from your feet.

Gabu laughed and said:

—What! The greatest scientific minds in the world have thought for three days on this problem. Do you claim that your wisdom is greater?

The old cobbler uttered not a word, but knelt and put on the feet of the king a pair of sandals which he had fashioned. The king shouted for joy with this wonderful thing, and the wearing of sandals began from that time.

The Manasā-Maṅgal of Ketakā-Dāsa

BEHULĀ AND LAKHINDAR

Introduction

The Manasā-Maṅgal, of which one excerpt is given here, is representative of a type of Bengali literature called *maṅgal-kāvya.* The term *maṅgal* means something like "eulogy," and the *maṅgal* poems eulogize one or another of the gods and goddesses—Śītalā, "the cool one," goddess of smallpox; Caṇḍī, slayer of demons; and Manasā, the goddess of snakes, among others.

The legends which the *maṅgal* poems contain are old; though few of the poems themselves seem to be earlier than the fifteenth century, it is certain that they were passed down orally over many centuries before being put by a particular writer into the form in which we have them today. The dating of a particular version of the poem does not necessarily reflect the dating of the legend itself. One Bengali scholar traces aspects of the legend to the early centuries of the Christian era.

The *maṅgal* poems represent a stratum of Indian thought and literature which is not entirely within the "great tradition," the Sanskritic tradition, of India. The Śiva of the *maṅgal* poems, for example, is not the austere, ascetic Śiva of the Purāṇas, who sits in lonely meditation on Mt. Kailāsa. Rather, he is a farmer god, sweating in the fields, a bit of a rake who chases after young women, and is fond of country liquor. Manasā, the snake-goddess of the *maṅgals*, has only the most tenuous of connections with the great tradition. She is for the most part a product of Bengal villages and fields. It will, I hope, become clear in the translation, that although there are frequent references to stories of the great epics *Mahābhārata* and *Rāmāyaṇa*, these are in no way structural to the plot of the Manasā legend itself. It seems quite probable that the stories incorporated in the epics were drawn into the stream of the great tradition from folk literature like the *maṅgal* poems, and then reborrowed by the *maṅgals* and other non-Sanskrit literature.

As literature, the *maṅgal* poems differ rather widely from the Sanskrit poetic tradition. They differ as poetry, for while one will find within them many conventional Sanskritic images—"Her face was like the moon . . . her gait as graceful as that of the elephant," etc.—most of the images of the *maṅgals* are blunt, to the point, and based on the ordinary things of the world:

> As she floated on the river, she passed a man with elephantiasis sitting on the *ghāṭ* and fishing. His legs were swollen horribly, but he kept four women in his house. Since he

could not eat plain rice, he was always fishing at the *ghāṭ*. A wooden necklace hung around his neck, and from his ear dangled an earring made from a cowrie shell. He sat there, casting his hook from side to side and pulling in big fish.

They differ also in the way in which they present humanity. The people who inhabit the Manasā poems in particular are human, weak, and proud. Cāndo, for example, is afflicted like Job with all the misery the goddess can bring down upon him, but he stands and defies her, his fist in the air, shouting imprecations against her. In some of the later poems, whose authors' piety could not stand such behavior, Cāndo is unfortunately beaten at the end. This is true of the poem translated here, and it is somewhat disappointing. There is, however, a form of the legend, which has been told to me orally and which Ashutosh Bhattacharya's statement bears out,[1] in which Cāndo is never beaten; he is merely overcome by superior forces. He is overwhelmed, but he goes down with dignity. He is forced to make an offering to Manasā, but he does so with his left hand, the unclean hand used for bodily functions, and with his face averted. Such a view of humanity is not usual, I think, in the Sanskrit tradition of Indian literature.

There are many elements, then, woven into the *maṅgal* literature. There are both Sanskritic and non-Sanskritic legends and both Sanskritic and non-Sanskritic poetic imagery. The historical implications of this are not wholly clear. Some scholars have felt that there is in the *maṅgal* poems an indication that early and indigenous mythology

[1] See Āśutoṣ Bhaṭṭācārya, *Bāiś kobir manasā-maṅgal* (Calcutta University, 1954), *bhumikā* pp. 22 ff.

and belief have been overlaid with Brahmanism.[2] Others have felt that the legend represents a decaying Śaivism being replaced by the encroaching cult of the female divinity, here represented by the serpent goddess.[3] Nor is this the only level on which complexity lies. Inconsistencies within the poems themselves—in one place, the goddess is said to have had a son named Astika, in another she is called "the virgin goddess"—and the fact of swift and seemingly random changes of scene, would lead one inevitably to the conclusion that there are within the poems several layers of myth and legend as well. And, finally, there are numbers of versions of the legend coming synchronously from various writers in various parts of Bengal. These differ from one another. There are, then, many problems of time and space, many problems in trying to get at the core myth and its meaning. Though to my knowledge no one has yet succeeded in doing this, all who know these *maṅgal* poems agree that there is much in them of importance for our understanding of a period of India's religious history about which very little is known.

The Manasā myth in broad outline (using two Manasā texts, that of Ketakā-dāsa and that of Vipra-dāsa) is as follows:

One day Śiva was sitting on the edge of a lotus-pond,

[2] T. W. Clark, "Evolution of Hinduism in Medieval Bengali Literature," *Bulletin of the School of Oriental and African Studies* (London), Vol. XVII (1955).

[3] Shashibhushan Dasgupta, *Obscure Religious Cults as a Background to Bengali Literature* (Calcutta University, 1946), p. xxxi. For a discussion of these views and of the significance of the personality of Manasā, see my article "The Goddess of Snakes in Medieval Bengali Literature," *History of Religions* (Chicago), Vol. I (1961), No. 2. (This article hereafter referred to as "*GS*.")

and, thinking about his wife, discharged his seed. The sperm fell upon a lotus leaf and ran down through the stalk until it fell on the head of Vāsuki, king of the *nāgas* or snakes, who dwelt in hell. From the seed Vāsuki's mother fashioned a beautiful girl, whom she named Manasā, and whom Vāsuki put in charge of snakes and poison. Manasā and the snakes would frequently come to play in the lotus-pond, and Śiva, afraid of the snakes, could no longer pick his lotuses there. So he asked the bird Garuḍa, enemy of snakes, to come and eat them. Manasā thereupon went to Śiva, deciding to seduce him and prevail on him to save the snakes. She won him over, and he took her home hidden in a flower-basket.

Śiva's wife Caṇḍī discovered Manasā in the basket, and when Manasā pleaded for mercy on the grounds that Śiva was her father and therefore that Caṇḍī was her stepmother, Caṇḍī began to berate her severely, accusing her of incest. The argument grew steadily more violent until Caṇḍī, enraged, put out Manasā's left eye with a needle (or, some say, with a hot coal). Manasā's remaining eye flashed death at Caṇḍī, and Caṇḍī fell down lifeless. Śiva pleaded with Manasā to restore Caṇḍī to life, which was done. Śiva and Manasā then left the house.

After walking a long way, Manasā and Śiva were tired, and sat to rest under a *sij* tree (to this day, a holy tree of Manasā), and Manasā fell asleep. Śiva, seeing this, sneaked away, but not without regret, and from one of his eyes there fell a tear, from which was created a full-grown girl called Neto. Śiva appointed Neto to be the constant companion to Manasā and went his way.

Then comes the Puranic story of the churning of the sea and the resultant poison, with some variation, interestingly giving a second version of how Manasā came to be in charge of poisonous things. When Śiva drank the sea to save the universe from being destroyed by its poison, he fell down dead. Manasā came, revived Śiva by uttering *mantras* (magical formulae) over him, and as the poison began to come out of his body she collected it, distributing half to the snakes and poisonous insects, and keeping half in her empty eye.

After one or two more stories, drawn mostly from the *Mahābhārata*, the Manasā legend proper begins.

Manasā wanted to be worshiped in the world of men. She went to Śiva, and Śiva promised her that it would be so; but despite his promise, it was not easy. Upon the advice of Neto, Manasā first disguised herself as a Brahmin woman and went among a group of cowherd boys who were grazing a herd of 1,600 cows on the bank of a river. (The interpretation might be that members of the Kṛṣṇa-cult were the first to be won to worship of Manasā. Kṛṣṇa, the cowherd god, is associated also with the number 1,600, the number of his consorts). The boys taunted her, thinking her to be a witch, which impression was not lessened when she milked a cow into a wicker basket and drank from it. The boys rushed to beat her, but she disappeared, taking with her all the cows. When they agreed to worship her, she brought back the herd, and they duly worshiped her on the tenth day of the light fortnight of the month of Jyaiṣṭha (May–June).

Near the place where the boys worshiped Manasā was

the estate of the Muslim landlords Hasan and Hosen (the names, interestingly, of two brothers, heroes and martyrs of Shia Islam). The headman of the estate, Gora Mina (Gorakṣa and Mina are the two primary figures in the legends of the Nātha cult), went to the place where the boys were worshiping and chased them away. He looked into the sacred pot of Manasā, into which she had put a deadly snake in the form of a golden bug. Gora picked up the bug and was bitten and killed. A serpent army then surrounded the city of Hasan and slaughtered all the inhabitants. Finally Hasan gave in, installed Manasā's sacred golden pot in a temple, and worshiped it.

Continuing her campaign, Manasā once again appeared as an old woman to two fishermen; when she asked to be carried across the stream, they, like the boys, insulted and reviled her. By her magic, she prevented them from catching fish. So they relented and carried her across the river, as she had asked. When they had done this, suddenly their nets were full of fish; and in the last catch was a pair of the sacred pots of Manasā, made of gold. Manasā blessed the fishermen, a shower of gold fell upon them; their house became filled with gold. They worshiped the sacred pots, and their family prospered greatly. This episode occurred in the city of Campaka, where Cāndo the Merchant, a wealthy and powerful man—some say a king—held sway. It was Cāndo who was to be the primary antagonist of Manasā, and whom she had to conquer in order that her worship might prevail.

One day, on her way to the river, Sanakā, the wife of Cāndo, passed by the house of the fishermen, who were by this time extremely wealthy. Hearing a celebration going on inside, she entered the house, and was told the story of the old woman and the golden pots. She asked for the pots, which were given her, and she took them home, where with her six daughters-in-law she worshiped them (the association of women with the worship of the serpent-goddess is interesting; see GS).

Informed of this activity, Cāndo, who was a faithful worshiper of Śiva and Caṇḍī, was enraged; he smashed the pots with his staff. At this point, Manasā resolved to turn the full power of her wrath against him. She destroyed his crops. Cāndo then consulted his friends, who advised him to employ the services of the great magician and seer Dhanvantari (an *ojhā*—one who has knowledge of occult charms, including those against snakebite).

Dhanvantari arrived in Campaka, and by his magic power restored Cāndo's fields. So Manasā consulted Neto, who advised her first to destroy Dhanvantari and thus make Cāndo easier game.

So Manasā took the guise of a beautiful flower-seller, and made garlands of poisoned flowers. These she gave to the students of *ojhā*, feeling that "if one cuts off the branches of a tree it cannot flower"; the students fell to the earth, writhing with the poison's pain. But they were saved by the great power of Dhanvantari. Again, she brought them poisoned sweets, but again they were saved by the *ojhā*. So finally Manasā, in disguise, went to make friends with Dhanvantari's wife. From his wife she found the only way in which Dhanvantari could be killed: by a certain snake entering into his nostril. It was so arranged.

Finally comes the most famous story of all, part of which is translated below. Having killed Dhanvantari, Manasā turned her full attention to her most powerful and persistent enemy, the great merchant Cāndo. His first strength lay in his six sons. So she resolved to kill them.

She first sent a snake called Dhorā, which failed in its task and as a punishment had its poison taken away. She then sent a vicious snake called Kālī, but even Kālī, vicious as she was, could not bring herself to bite the sleeping boys (a motif which recurs later in the story) and decided on another course of action. She went to the kitchen and discharged her poison into a pot of rice which the boys were to eat for their breakfast. In the morning the boys arose, ate the rice, and dropped to the ground writhing in agony. Their young wives thought they were playing, and laughed happily at their antics, but their mother Sanakā knew that they had been poisoned. She tried antidotes, but too late.

Cāndo and Sanakā were deeply grieved, and Cāndo, knowing that Manasā had brought this about, cursed her constantly. He resolved to put the bodies of his sons on rafts and float them down the river (another motif which recurs, in much more elaborate detail, later in the story). His priests advised him strongly against this, urging him to cremate his sons; but Cāndo said that the pall of smoke of the pyres would be a banner of triumph to Manasā; he refused to give her that comfort. So the bodies were floated on the river, and went to the domain of Manasā. This is the point at which our translation will pick up the story.

As can perhaps be seen from the above, and as will be seen in the translation below, the character of Manasā is a strange and paradoxical one. She is the goddess of snakes and of poison, and she strikes and kills as randomly as a snake. Her emblem is the pot, perhaps the pot of poison. But she sometimes shows a strangely merciful and often equally random compassion. She kills, but she also restores to life. The pot might also be the pot of *soma*, according to an old Vedic text the curer of poison. The Bengali scholar Sukumar Sen derives her name Biṣaharī in either of two ways. She is *viṣa-harī*, "she who destroys poison" or *viṣa-dharī*, "she who holds poison." She, like the texts which tell her story, is in many ways an enigma.

The Ketakā-dāsa *Manasā-Maṅgal*, from which the translation below is made, is one of the favorite poems of its kind in West Bengal, where it is still held in high esteem and recited frequently in the villages. The Ketakā-dāsa (who also called himself Kṣemānanda) version of the story dates from the early seventeenth century, though, as mentioned above, the core of the legend is unquestionably a great deal earlier.

Despite the fact that the author wrote an introduction to himself in the early part of his work, very little is actually known about him. His father was evidently named Śaṅkara Maṇḍal; and he lived with his family in a village called Kathaṛa under a local landlord whose name was Balabhadra. The landlord died, leaving three sons too young to assume the responsibilities of their father's holdings. Under its manager the estate gradually "became like a burning ground," and Śaṅkara Maṇḍal was forced to leave his native village. It was in the second village that Manasā revealed herself in a vision to Ketakā-dāsa and commanded him to write her poem.

The Ketakā-dāsa poem is not the earliest—the *Manasā-Vijaya* of Vipra-dāsa was written in the early fifteenth century—of the Manasā-*maṅgals*, nor, in the opinion of some, is it the best. To be sure, the ending of the Ketakā-dāsa version is not as strong as it might be. But the Ketakā-dāsa version does include some fine descriptive passages, such as those of the storm in the early part of the translated portion and the voyage of Behulā down the river with the corpse of her husband in her lap. It is for this reason that I have chosen it above others, despite its somewhat weak ending.

The translation is closer to the original than is the translation of, for example, the *Vidyā-Sundara* poem. I have omitted some of the repetitive portions, and these omissions are noted; and I have included a certain amount of material which may seem relatively meaningless to the general reader but which may be interesting to the student of Indian culture. This version of the story focuses on the merchant community, the Baṇyā caste. This in itself is of interest. I have not tried to gloss over the many inconsistencies in the text or the story itself, and in most cases the glaring non sequiturs will be accurate translations of the original. I think faithfulness adds to rather than subtracts from the flavor of this particular text. In some places, especially in such passages as the wedding scene, I have not been able to make out the Bengali, nor have those Bengalis whom I have asked about it. The customs of that time are in many cases no longer familiar, sometimes the language is completely obscure, perhaps due to a miscopying of the manuscript. Fortunately, such occurrences are rare.

The text used for translation is that edited by Jatindramohan Bhattacarya and published by Calcutta University in 1949. I have also used for reference Sukumar Sen's edition of *Manasā-Vijaya* (Calcutta: Asiatic Society, 1953). I am indebted to Mr. Samir Kumar Ghosh of the South Asian language research staff of the University of Chicago for checking the accuracy of the translation.

Manasā-Maṅgal

BEHULĀ AND LAKHINDAR

In Campakanagara lived Cāndo the Merchant, who carried on an endless feud with Manasā. That goddess, in her wrath, had killed his six sons, but even then he did not worship her or call her goddess. Though his pain and misery were very great, he did not bow his head to her, but said:

—That *ceṅgamuṛi*[1] wench—of what is she the goddess? And with staff in hand he watched both day and night, prowling from house to house, searching for Manasā, saying:

—If I could catch sight of her, I would break her head and

[1] The precise meaning of this obviously derogatory term is unclear. Sukumar Sen (*Manasā-Vijaya*, introduction) feels that it means "repulsive as a dirty shroud."

kill her. If I could rid myself of her, my misery would disappear. No more would she afflict my house. I should be released, and live in joy in all my lands.

Thus thinking he spent his days. But finally he had to go for trade to a southern city. He took the name of Śiva and set out upon his journey. He boarded his ship in gladness, and shouted:

—Cast off! Take care, and head her for the open water.

When they heard the command of Cāndo, the helmsmen steered the seven ships toward Kālīdaha.[2] But with Cāndo the Merchant went the curse of Manasā. She knew, by the power of her meditation, when he had reached Kālīdaha; she went to Neto, her companion:

—Cāndo is against me; he constantly calls me Ceṅgamuṛi Kānī.[3] Today I shall get even—I shall sink his ships. As he drowns, I know that he will worship me.

So quickly she summoned the rain-holding clouds:

—Go forth, together with the winds, O heroes great as Hanumān.[4]

And so to Kālīdaha the fierce winds went. The goddess gave them flowers and pān, and said to the clouds:

—You will sink the seven ships of Cāndo in the sea.

And at the command of the goddess, the clouds went forth.

Kṣemānanda prays: Forgive our sins, O goddess.

[2] Literally, "place of the deep black waters"—the name of a place sacred to Manasā.

[3] The term *kāṇī* means "one-eyed."

[4] Hanumān, the son of the wind, was the monkey-chief in the epic *Rāmāyaṇa* who assisted Rāma in his conquest of the demon Rāvana. Throughout the Manasā story he serves the goddess.

II

AT THE ORDER of the goddess, the rain-holders rushed forth; fierce hail-clouds went swiftly to Kālīdaha to sink the *sādhu's*[5] ship. The great hero Hanumān was with them; the winds blew fiercely; earth and sky grew dark in the roaring and tumult of the winds. The oarsmen and sailors were afraid; they saw no deliverance from the storm. From darkened shapes like elephants with trunks the rain poured down; all around the ships the thunder crashed and rumbled. Fear seized Cāndo's heart; he cried:

—I shall never reach the land again.

Flashing and crackling lightning struck and pellets of hail were driven with awful force before the wind. The helmsman said:

—We shall not escape—if our skulls are not broken, we shall surely drown.

And the merchant cried:

—I should not have set out on this voyage.

The lightning was awesome to behold, and the sun hid in the heavens. Hanumān then leapt aboard the seven ships, which whirled about like wheels. The storm blew, and the cabin roofs were carried away; the howling of the wind was like the sound of Desolation. The crocodiles and sharks and all the awful creatures of the water swam round and round the ships; the serpents of the sea swam to the whirling ships, in lust for food. The waters of Kālīdaha swelled up, full of danger. The helmsman was frozen by the icy

[5] *sādhu*—though usually a term denoting a holy man, throughout this text it is used to mean "merchant."

winds; he could not move his hands or feet, and he lay senseless in a corner of the deck. A shark seized the anchor in his jaws, and others the lines. Then Hanumān himself boarded and crushed the ships, rocking and swinging; the lightning fell, breaking, and the drums of cargo were washed away and floated on the black-waved sea. His ships were sinking, but Cāndo did not utter the name of Manasā. He said:

—He who worships Śiva's trident will surely reach the shore. And when I do, I shall wrench the breath from Manasā!

So said the Merchant. And when he heard these harsh and bitter words, Hanumān began to burn with rage. The storm raged with awful violence, and Hanumān, grown in strength, suiting his deeds to the desires of Manasā, sank the seven ships with blows of his feet. The Bangali[6] sailors all cried out:

—We are lost.

The cargo of the ships, the jars of poppy-seeds, went floating on the water. And at the last moment, on the very brink of death, the Merchant leaped from the deck of his ship. The seven ships sank, and Cāndo, drowning, choked and coughed up water. Manasā was smiling to herself.

Swift Manasā, my hope lies at your feet. So writes Ketakādāsa.

III

So WHILE the Bangali sailors wept in despair, Hanumān leapt aboard the ships and smashed them. The ships shud-

[6] *Bāṅgāli*—the term is used to indicate people from East Bengal.

dered and spun in circles, and the despairing Cāndo, terror-stricken, fell into the sea. His ships were sunk by the wrath of Manasā; his crewmen, clutching their heads with their hands, wept; and the cargo, jars of poppy-seed covered with cloth, floated on the water. The bales of cloth were also washed away.[7] The sailors cried:

—Our clothes and goods are lost! We no longer have even a cloth with which to hide our nakedness!

—We are dying, brothers! Not even by piracy, but only because of Cāndo's foolishness we are to lose our lives in this strange place, far from our homes.

And the sailors looked in vain in all the four directions. By the wrath of Manasā, Cāndo was choked with water; his eyes were red, his belly swollen; he was drowning, choking on the water, and he cried:

—The One-eyed Ceṅgamuṛi has brought this misery upon me!

In her chariot, hearing this, Manasā laughed aloud, victorious. But as she watched him drown, her heart softened. She dropped a lotus on the water.[8] Cāndo, choking, close to death, drew thickened breath. And then the lotus floated close to him. He thought:

—Manasā's birth was in a lotus. He who touches one commits great sin.

So thinking thus, Cāndo did not touch the flower, though he was close to death. Nor could he reach the shore. Then Mother Kamalā,[9] seeing his danger, cut a banana-tree and

[7] "Seven piles of quilted cloth."

[8] The lotus is a symbol of Manasā; she is born through a lotus, and in East Bengal versions of her story she is called Padmā, "lotus woman."

[9] Kamalā—"lotus."

sent it to him as a raft. To save himself, Cāndo swam quickly to the tree. Saying:
—Śiva, Śiva!
Seven times he made obeisance to that God. But because he was naked he did not pull himself out of the water.

Then Neto the washerwoman went and said to Manasā:
—Cāndo the Merchant still does not recognize your name. But though he is still opposed to you, O Devī, do not kill him. Let him live; for then only will your worship spread. Save his life.

When she heard the words of her friend, the Mother of the World took the disguise of a virtuous wife.

IV

So Manasā took the form of a beautiful woman; I cannot begin to describe her beauty. With several other women she went, the wife of Jaratkaru, Jaya Biṣaharī,[10] to bring water. She took a water-jar on her hip and went to where Cāndo the Merchant was, cast up naked on the beach. When he saw the women, Cāndo was ashamed, and hid his nakedness in the water. The women said to him:
—O mad Digambara,[11] why do you sit there like that? Put this winding-sheet around your nakedness.

And so the Merchant, in shame, put on the sheet taken from a corpse, and began to make his way from place to place, begging for food to eat. In his left hand he held a

10 "The glorious holder (or destroyer) of poison." It will be seen that Manasā has a number of names and epithets.

11 "Sky-clad," i.e., naked. Also the name of a sect of Jaina monks who wear no clothing.

staff, and on his body he wore the ragged winding-cloth. Because of the wrath of Manasā, the *sādhu* had to beg for food.

So Kṣemānanda sings, such is the great power of Manasā. Be merciful, O thou full of compassion.

V

STAFF IN HAND, the once-great merchant went from house to house to beg his food. Thinking him a madman, boys pelted him with sticks and clods of earth. Cāndo said:

—Why do you strike me? I am Cāndo the Merchant.

But no one knew him; people laughed at him. His lips were red, his body strong and healthy; but he wore a ragged winding-sheet. He wandered from place to place, a broken begging-bowl in his hand. Some, who were pious, gave to him. He begged, and got a little food and money. And finally he came to a ruined and deserted hut, and in a corner of it he made his home.

Manasā knew this. She went to the place of Ganeṣa[12] and said to him:

—O brother, lend me your rat a little while. This favor I ask of you.

Ganapati replied:

—Of course, O Jagati, I shall give you the rat. But tell me this: to whom will you now do injury?

Jagati said:

—Ganapati, even if I tell you, remember that you have

[12] The elephant-headed god, son of Śiva. He is immensely fat; his vehicle is the rat. He is also called Ganapati.

promised to give the rat to me. Cāndo the Merchant always calls me Cengamuṛi Kāṇī. What more need I say? I shall take my revenge. Now give me the rat, you glutton.

She took the rat and showed to it the grain which Cāndo had gathered by begging. The rat entered the earth; wily, it quickly chewed a tunnel through the earth. It stole the grain and came again before Ganeṣa.

Ketakā-dāsa prays for the feet of Manasā.

VI

So THE RAT stole Cāndo's grain, and when the Merchant saw that this had happened, he was much disturbed.

—I got that grain by begging alms, and now the One-eyed Ceṅgamuṛi has stolen it from me.

And so, cursing Manasā, he set forth again, wandering from forest to forest. And at the angry hands of Manasā, he suffered even greater misery.

Once Manasā took the form of a white fly, and settled near a group of hunters who were hunting birds in that same forest. For twelve years they had hunted and had not caught their prey, but on this day again were setting out on the chase. They took their nets and ropes and lures and went forth to hunt in the forest. Surrounding the forest and dropping the bait on the ground, silently and carefully they lured the birds down. The birds fed there, contented.

In this same forest Cāndo was wandering in misery, crying out in his distress. When they heard his weeping, the birds rose up in fright and flew away. Then in anger the bird-hunters surrounded the *sādhu*, and seizing him by the hair they beat him fiercely. Cāndo cried:

—Do not beat me! Why do you beat me, brothers? I am not a thief!

But they replied:

—Why did you frighten off our birds? O son of a sheep, where have you come from?

And finally they let him go. At last Cāndo, weeping, arrived at the house of a friend. The friend's name was Candraketu, son of Dharmaketu. In hope of safety and comfort, Cāndo ran toward his house, calling:

—Friend, O friend!

So goes the song of Manasā, composed by Kṣemānanda.

VII

THEN CĀNDO the Merchant said to his friend:

—O friend, how can I tell you the story of my grief? An evil fate is written on my forehead. The Ceṅgamuṛi One-eyed One has devoured my six sons and sunk my seven ships. By great good fortune and the grace of Śiva my own life was saved, and now, at last, we two friends have met. Help me now, in this time of my great danger and despair —be my friend. For friends are those who do each other service. It says in the *Rāmāyaṇa* that Rāma, giving up his kingdom, took Lakṣmaṇa and the daughter of Janakī and went into the forest; then Rāvaṇa stole Sītā, daughter of Janakī, and put her in the golden city. But the friend of Rāma, Sugrīva, king of monkeys, did service for his friend, at that time of his great anguish in the forest. Killing Bālirājā, Rāma gave Sugrīva the power of a kingdom when with a single arrow he split the seven trees. So did Sugrīva, king of monkeys, do his friend a service, and built the bridge to

Laṅka over the waters of the sea.[13] The two, then, being friends, were of service to each other to the ends of their lives. Because of the glory of Rāma and Sugrīva, the rocks and trees floated on the water, and now all the people of the world sing their praises. So it was too with the five Pāṇḍava brothers, great heroes in battle. They lost the game of dice and went to live in the forest. The five remained unknown, as friends, in the house of Birata the king.[14] So also with the king Śrīvatsa, who, performing *pūjā* to Śiva, kept that god in his mind both day and night. But evil and ill fortune tormented him, and he was forced to leave his throne and kingdom and live twelve years in the forest.[15] Like him, I have fallen on evil days; with fear and sorrow in my heart I have come to you.

But the Merchant did not know that his friend was a worshiper of Manasā, that he did daily *pūjā* to her sacred pots.

—It is good that you have come to my house. It is many days since last we met.

And he led him in, and offered him water and a seat. But in the room was the altar of Manasā: two pots were on a throne, garlanded with flowers, and on the pots vermilion and *ketakī* leaves. Then Cāndo said:

—O Ceṅgamuṛi, you have sunk my ships and all my cargo,

[13] A reference to Sugriva's and his advisor Hanumān's service to Rāma in the *Rāmāyaṇa:* they built a bridge over which Rāma passed on his way to fight with Rāvaṇa and rescue Sītā.

[14] A reference to the epic *Mahābhārata.* The Pāṇḍava princes and their joint wife Draupadī lived in disguise at the court of Birata (Virata) during their exile. In return for their help in his battles, he fought for them in the great war and was killed by Drona.

[15] A reference to a *Mahābhārata* story.

and now you come here secretly. To the house of my own friend you come to cause me grief. O stupid One-eyed One, you shall not make me bow to you. I do not know what makes my friend worship you, but I shall not!

And then, in rage, Cāndo went to break the pots of Manasā with his staff. But knowing well the danger, his friend restrained him:

—My good friend, you have lost your reason. Do no more—do not antagonize the goddess more. Had I not restrained your staff in time, you would now be in mortal peril.

But Cāndo would not be restrained. Seeing him mad, some held him, others struck him on the head; Candraketu said:

—He has come to my house to break the sacred pots. Beat him and throw him out.

So, scorned and insulted, in grief and anger, Cāndo continued his wandering from forest to forest.

Such is the song of Manasā Devī, composed by Kṣemānanda, who says: Pardon us our sins, Daughter of Iśāna.

VIII

THE SĀDHU THEN, receiving only scorn at his friend's house, went once more to wander in the forest. Alone he wandered, and in his time of peril he found no companion. But then he saw a group of woodsmen on the path. He said to them:

—Brothers, tell me, to what work do you go now, so loudly and so happily?

They answered him:

—We are going to the forest to cut wood. By selling it in the city, we shall get money.[16] This is the work of our caste, for we are woodcutters.

Cāndo replied:

—I am stronger than most of you. I shall go with you, and if I take a double load on my head, perhaps I shall get a *kāhan*[17] for it. Why do I wander thus in sadness in the forest? Take me with you, brothers, to cut wood. By your kindness I also shall cut wood and eat.

And they all said:

—Why are you so sad? Come with us. Cut wood and sell it, and live.

So the unfortunate *sādhu* went with them to cut wood. And when they had cut much wood, the woodsmen tied it into bundles. Cāndo the Ojhā[18] knew good sandalwood; he tied up great bundles of this wood, and seven or eight men hoisted them to his shoulders. Taking his great load of wood, the *sādhu* walked ahead. His body, which had matured in happiness, was racked with pain; but he was going to sell his wood and eat.

Biṣaharī saw this from her swan chariot, and said:

—Tell me now, O Neto, what I should do. Cāndo the Merchant is cutting wood, and goes to sell it. If he earns money by this and returns to his own country, he can curse me to his heart's content.

Neto replied:

—O Biṣaharī, do not be disturbed by this. Remember the

[16] "We shall get eight coins."

[17] A type of money; 1,280 cowries.

[18] *Ojhā* means a person who has occult power, especially power over snakes and snake-bite.

Son of the Wind[19]—let Hanumān mount the load of wood, and Cāndo will not be able to carry it.

When she heard the words of her friend, Manasā summoned the Son of the Wind. Immediately the hero Hanumān appeared and made *praṇām*[20] at the feet of the Devī.

—Order me, O Biṣaharī, and I shall bring you the sun or moon from the sky. I can bring you Vāsuki from hell, or the Kurma, or the Mountain itself.[21]

So saying, the great hero stood respectfully with folded hands. The Devī gave him *pān* and flowers, and said to him:

—O Hanumān, Son of the Wind, you are my cousin.[22] For Rāma's sake, because of Sītā, you made war with the Rākṣasa. Now, look there—Cāndo the Merchant is going with a load of wood. Go, mount that load and press him down. But do not put such weight on him that his back is broken and he dies; for if he dies my worship will never be established in the world.

At the Devī's command, Hanumān went and climbed up on the load of wood. Under his tremendous weight, the Merchant fell, crying out in pain. He could not lift the load again. Tears streamed down his cheeks, as in agony of mind and body he cried:

—The Ceṅgamuṛi Kāṇī has sent this misery to me.

[19] Hanumān.

[20] A gesture of homage and respect.

[21] Vāsuki: king of the *nāgas,* who live in hell; *Kurma:* the tortoise, second incarnation (*avatāra*) of Viṣṇu.

[22] Śiva, at the plea of his wife Pārvatī, had shaped the Māruts (winds) from formless lumps of flesh; Hanumān is *māruta-putra,* "Son of the Wind."

The greater was his pain, the more he cursed the Devī. And in her swan chariot, the Devī said to Neto:

—Hear—his curses increase as does his pain. He is ready to die for his pride, but not to abandon his belief.

And so again, despondent, he went from forest to forest. He walked until he could walk no more, weak, with only the fruits of the forest to eat. Luckily, a worthy Brahmin had in the forest performed a *śrāddha* ceremony for his father; when he had left the forest for his home, he had left banana skins and joints of sugar-cane behind.[23] When he saw this, Cāndo stood erect. Delighted, he took a bath in a nearby pond and worshipped Śaṅkara.[24] As he ate the banana skins and cane, his strength returned to him. Meditating on Śiva, he drank some water. He who would not have touched the best bananas now ate their skins with pleasure.

So says Ketakā-dāsa, serving the Mother of the World. Grant your blessings to your devotee, O gracious one.

IX

DESPAIRING, THE SĀDHU came to a Brahmin's house. He made *praṇām* and said:

—Hear my words, Gosāi.[25] My name is Cāndo; Campakanagara is my home. I was once a rich man, but have fallen into the condition in which you see me now. Let me stay with you for some few days. I shall carry water-jugs for

[23] *Srāddha*—a memorial ceremony for dead relatives, at which various offerings are made.

[24] Śaṅkara—i.e., Śiva. The text says "with a snapping of his fingers against his cheeks"—a manner of worshiping Śiva.

[25] Honorific title, usually applied to a Vaiṣṇava of high standing.

you—you need only give me food and water. Whatever work you ask of me, I shall do. I am Cāndo, once the greatest of merchants and ruler of Campakanagara.

Hearing this, the Brahmin said to him:

—Attend then to the work of my household. If you do so, I shall increase your wealth and honor as I would that of my own eldest son. Today, go and weed my paddy-fields.

When he had said this, the Brahmin took him out and sat him down in the paddy-fields to weed the paddy. But Biṣaharī, with her dark magic, prevented Cāndo from telling rice from weed. He weeded out all the stalks of paddy, and let the weeds remain. When he saw what Cāndo had done, the Brahmin cursed him and slapped him with his hand. Bewildered, the *sādhu* hugged the Brahmin's feet. And seeing his misery and grief, the Brahmin refrained from beating him.

So from that place too he went away, tears streaming from his eyes, saying over and over again:

—The Ceṅgamuṛi Kāṇī has sent this grief to me. What can I do? What work can I find?

He wandered aimlessly. Indeed, what could he do? Kṣemānanda says: Hear now of Lakhindar's birth.

X

As Cāndo wandered aimlessly from land to foreign land in misery, in the womb of Sanakā, his wife, his son Lakhindar grew. The days passed by, until five months were gone. Pining and grieving, the lonely Sanakā said to her maidservant:

—I am a miserable and wretched woman; my heart's lord is far away. I take no more pleasure in life; I cannot even eat. Day and night I weep in grief for my six sons; and my wise husband, who supported me in my grief, is now abroad. What has the Devī done to him? And a baby five months in my womb. Now hear me, my friend. At least feed me those things for which I long—puddings and cakes and sweets, and vegetables fried in *ghi*. I long for the smell of earthenware; I long for fermented rice-water. Give me sweet curd, which tastes like nectar, and a few *saral* and *saphari* fish fried, with *bodali* and *hiliñca* vegetables. For she whose womb is full longs for such food. Her mind is agitated and twists and tumbles in upon itself.

So Jhāuyā, her servant, satisfied her longings with these delicious dishes. But still Sanakā was indolent; her heart was restless, and drops of sweat stood out here and there upon her face.

As she came into her eighth month, the lovely woman's mind fell into deep distress, and to her darkened lips rose up deep yawns. Her ninth month passed, and in her tenth the day of her delivery came. Her servant called the midwife. Sanakā sat propped up in a corner, afraid. Bewildered by the pains of labor, she was faint; her face was broken and contorted, but from her mouth no sound escaped. Tears fell from her eyes in her agony. And on the fourteenth day of the month, the full-moon day, at an auspicious moment, she brought forth her son Lakhindar. When he was placed upon the earth, it was as if the full moon itself had descended from the sky. And when she saw the face of her son, Sanakā, smiling in great joy, took him into her lap.

To every house in that city of the Merchant the good news spread. The neighbors, when they heard of it, were full of joy:

—Sanakā has had a son!

Delighted, all came to see the new-born child; and on the fifth day after birth, according to the custom, Sanakā had a celebration. From every house throughout the city Jhāuyā summoned the people. And the barber, pleased when he heard of it, came to the house of Cāndo. Sitting down, he rubbed the baby with oil and put decorations upon his body.[26] On the sixth day the Baṇyās all made Ṣeṭera-*pūjā*, the prescribed Ṣaṣṭhī-*pūjā*.[27] Sanakā told her Brahmin servant to make the preparations, and she made Ṣaṣṭhī-*pūjā;* the sacrificial knife held in her hand, she remained awake the whole night long, the paper and ink-pot nearby. Half the night had passed when, at the appointed time, the deity came to write Lakhindar's fortune on his forehead.

Ketakā-dāsa says: At the feet of Manasā is the greatest mercy.

XI

In Lakhindar's fate Bidhātā wrote a harsh and evil thing —that on his wedding night he would die by snake-bite. He wrote:

—And then your bride, Behulā, will take your body on her lap and for six months will float upon the river. Then the

26 The text is somewhat obscure at this point.

27 Saṣṭhī—the goddess of childbirth and children. It is at this time that Bidhātā, the god of fate, comes to write the child's future on his forehead.

Mother of the World, daughter of Hara, will grant her blessing. Because of former worship, by the power of Iśvara, you will again receive the gift of life.

Then Bidhātā left the house, and Lakhindar, restless and disturbed, suddenly awoke and cried. Sanakā quickly went to him; she held him to her breast and kissed his face.

To be brief, twenty-one days passed quickly. A premonition was in Sanakā's mind; but she went to worship Ṣaṣṭhī and came home again in greatest joy. Her son was like her own heart; she held him always in her lap, and would not leave him on the ground. Her mind no longer wandered restlessly over the earth.

In this way three, and four, and five months passed, and in the sixth she gave Lakhindar his first food. On his arm she put a golden armlet, and he crawled about the house, playing and happy, showing his teeth in laughter.

Thus, his beauty increased with the passing days; so sings the poet Ketakā-dāsa.

XII

So Lakhindar was born, son of Cāndo the Merchant. And a few days after, Behulā also was born.

In the city of Nichāninagara there was a merchant, Sāya by name, whose wife was Amalā, the beauty. On a most auspicious day the goddess Uṣā, fallen to earth because of a curse, was born from the womb of Amalā. She grew, a beautiful girl with a face like the moon and the grace of the *khañjana* bird, well versed and trained in music. Her lips were the color of coral flowers, her teeth were pointed, her body had the luster of the lightning flash, her forehead was high: a lovely girl. She was born a devotee of Manasā. In her parents' house Behulā grew and danced and sang, and Amalā was charmed by her talent and her grace. From her childhood the girl was skilled in dance and song—but a husband dead and brought again to life was written on her forehead.

Behulā and Lakhindar—these two grew to maturity. But now hear more of Cāndo the Merchant.

XIII

Many miseries Cāndo endured, but finally his endless journey brought him to his own house. Under the curse of Manasā, subject to her power, his ships all sunk, the Merchant returned home. Manasā had put upon him clothes of indescribable foulness, and, having sunk his ships, had brought him home again.

To torment him more, Biṣaharī became a fortune teller, with the manuscript of an almanac in her hand. She drew a *phoṭā*[28] on her forehead, and having placed the manuscript on the ground, sat down before the *sādhu's* house. When the people of the house saw the soothsayer, they brought her a mat to sit upon. Then she drew chalk lines upon the ground and began to read the divination. —Hear, O Sanakā, lovely woman. A thief will come to your house today. There will be no hair upon his head, and he will be dressed in rags. You must remain alert, for

[28] A decorative mark.

surely such a man will come. Seize him and beat him, to the point of death.

When she had said this, the goddess went away, and once more resumed her own form. As she was doing so, Cāndo came. He came slowly through the forest—for in the daylight he was ashamed to leave the forest. He hid in the banana grove; peeping out, he watched his son Lakhāi at play in the courtyard of his house.

As evening came, the servant Ceṛī went to the banana grove. She saw hiding there a man all dressed in rags, who had the appearance of a thief. She ran at once to Sanakā; and when she heard, Sanakā ran to the banana grove. Inside the grove she heard a rustling sound, as Cāndo paced slowly through the leaves. Sanakā leapt up and ran to the house:

—A thief! There is a thief! Bring sticks and beat him!

And as the night was dark, Cāndo was not recognized. His mind was numbed, but he cried out:

—Do not beat me any more! I am Cāndo the Merchant!

When they heard this they stopped beating him, and lowered a lamp to see his face. His wife knew him then, and her heart was greatly anguished.

Kṣemānanda sings the story of the goddess Manasā.

XIV

Cāndo had come home, without his ships, without his goods. Tears streaming from her eyes, the lovely Sanakā said to him:

—The lord of my life is safe! But tell me, good and holy man, my lover, I entreat you—tell me where you have been

. . . what has happened . . . where is your ship Madhukara . . .

Then the *sādhu* said to Sanakā:

—My ships are sunk in Kālīdaha. I know not how. The Ceṅgamuṛi Kāṇī has twisted me and greyed my hair in sorrow . . . my ships were sinking, and I jumped into the water, and water came in my nose and mouth . . .

And Sanakā, in sorrow and in pity, burst into tears, and said:

—How can I go on? Our six sons dead, and now the ships all sunk and their cargo lost because of the wrath of Manasā. You have cursed her.[29] It is the failure of your wisdom which has caused all this—ah, my fate is one of misery.

When he heard these words from Sanakā, Cāndo burned in anger:

—Do not speak of her! She has killed our sons. She has taken our ships and wealth. What more can she do to me now?

Falling at his feet, Sanakā tried to make him understand:

—Hear me, my lord, O righteous man. While you were in another country, from my womb was born another son, Lakhindar. You anger and revile the goddess—do you not see what can come of this? Put my mind at ease, my husband. Do not deny your duty any longer. There is no point in anger any more.

But when he saw the face of his son, the Merchant was joyful, and he forgot his former woe. He took his little son into his lap and kissed his face.

And so Lakhindar grew, radiant as the moon, gaining

[29] The epithets are *biṣabinodinī* "charming poison-woman" or "she who is beautiful with poison," and *anantarūpinī*, "she whose beauty is infinite."

luster day by day. He was introduced to learning—chalk in his hand, he made his *pūjā* to Sarasvatī. And as his son grew strong, Cāndo grew contented in his heart. For the boy, the days passed by in wonder and in eagerness. His ears were pierced, in an auspicious moment. He played, dust on his body, the golden armlet on his arm. With other boys he played at fighting, pulling their hair, rolling with them on the ground. Parents whose sons were beaten said to Sanakā:

—Your Lakhāi is a bad boy. He fights our sons and beats them.

So Sanakā said to him:

—Hear me, Lakhindar. You are strong. You beat the sons of others; have you no fear in your own heart or mind?

Lakhindar laughed to himself at these words of his mother; but, wary, did not come too close to her.

The flute of Kṣemānanda sings: May the goddess protect Kāyasthas.[30]

XV

So DAY BY DAY Lakhindar grew, and the Merchant spoke with Sanakā. Day by day, through reading and writing, his knowledge and his wisdom grew, until Cāndo said to Sanakā:

—Our son Lakhindar is grown mature and handsome and ready for marriage. Where shall we find his bride, O Sanakā Beṇyānī?

So Cāndo sent his servant for the *purohit*.[31] When he saw

[30] A caste, traditionally originally scribes, but in the period of this text partly merchants.

[31] Family priest.

the *purohit* Cāndo gave him greeting and had a mat brought for him to sit upon. With water from a pot he rinsed the Brahmin's feet, and the two then sat together to discuss the matter. Cāndo said:

—Janārdana Dvija, for a long time you have been my own *purohit*. Whatever has had to be done, good or bad, you have taken upon yourself. First, then, I shall make a request of you. If you know any Baṇyā girls as yet unmarried, make the arrangements for my Lakhāi. The girl's family must be the equal of mine in wealth, lineage, and character. Become a match-maker, then; visit all the houses. If there is in any house an unpromised and suitable girl, I shall give her my handsome Lakhāi in marriage.

So the Brahmin Janārdana, when he heard this, set forth. In Ujānī-nagara there lived the *sādhu* Dhanapati; Janārdana went first to his house. In his house there were no unmarried girls, but Dhanapati Datta gave him some advice:

—Follow my instructions and go to Nichāninagara. In the house of Sāya the Baṇyā there is an unmarried girl.

So the Dvija went to Nichāninagara. The chief merchant of the place was Sāya Adhikari, who had an unmarried daughter, Behulā, a most beautiful girl. To the house of Sāya the matchmaker went, and when he arrived he was given a place to sit and water for washing. Then Behulā came to him, and bowed before him, and took the dust of his feet. When Janārdana saw her, with her head uncovered, he said to her father:

—O Baṇyā, hear what I say to you. I am amazed that such a lovely girl is still unmarried. You are foremost in society and head of your caste. How can you even bear to eat while such a girl remains unmarried? Find for her a worthy groom. Mark my words, for if you do not it will be to your sorrow. Cāndo the Merchant is your equal in wealth, in lineage, and in character. He has an unmarried son, Lakhindar by name. You could not find a groom to equal him in looks or qualities. Give him your daughter in marriage, O Sāya the Merchant.

Sāya replied:

—If that is the case, bring astrologers to calculate the signs of both; if they agree that it is right and proper, then it shall be done.

When he heard this, Janārdana was very happy. He quickly brought an astrologer, who made his marks with chalk upon the ground. The signs of the boy and girl came together and were favorable, and Janārdana the matchmaker said, in greatest joy:

—O Baṇyā, I say this to you: Fate has written that Behulā and Lakhindar should be together. It cannot be otherwise. Your daughter will be the daughter-in-law of Cāndo of Campakanagara.

And Sāya replied:

—So shall it be.

Thus, at the feet of Manasā, Kṣemānanda sings.

XVI

Sāya the Merchant said, his palms together:

—O Janārdana, I know of Cāndo of Campakanagara; I know that his wealth and power are very great. There is nothing else to be considered. I promise my daughter to his son in marriage.

So, with smiling face, happy at having settled the affair, the matchmaker went forth. He returned to Campakanagara and told the story.

—O Cāndo Adhikari, listen to me, and I shall tell you how it happened. According to your orders, I went to seek a bride in northern Ujānī. Dhanapati Datta there gave me this advice: there is, he said, in Nichāninagara a great merchant named Sāya, whose daughter is unmarried. Behulā is her name, a girl unmatched in beauty and in qualities. So Dhanapati said to me. So, following this advice, I went to see this Sāya. He treated me respectfully, and Behulā brought me water. Then, in the course of conversation, I said to her father, "Why do you not make arrangements for the marriage of such a worthy daughter? You are foremost among the merchants here, and yet your daughter is still unmarried. Tell me why this is." Then he replied that he had found no boy of family, wealth, and character equal to his own. I told him then that Cāndo of Campakanagara was his equal in these things. He was greatly pleased to hear your name. Then the astrologer came to make the calculations for Behulā and Lakhāi, and it was all successful. The signs of the two came together with no trouble; surely it was preordained. And there is no question of a price: he wants to give his daughter to your Lakhindar as a gift.

This much the matchmaker said, and Cāndo was delighted. Sanakā's heart was also glad; she said:

—Tell me, Dvija Janārdana. You saw this girl? How old is she? What auspicious signs has she? Describe her. Let us hear. If she is good, she will be a valuable addition to my house. Tell us, Janārdana. You observed the signs. Tell us, in all detail, what you saw.

—Hear me, then. This is the truth. I have seen her. I have seen that her beauty is greater than that of the Vidyādharīs of heaven. I have seen many people and places, but I have never seen anything to surpass her. She is like Lakṣmī, or Urvāsī, or an *apsarī.*[32] Her face is like the stainless moon, her words are a cup of nectar, the mass of her hair is fuller and darker than the thundercloud. She is a girl most chaste and devoted. Her hair hangs long, tumbling down her back . . . oh, I have nothing to compare her with. She is a lovely girl. Her walk is more graceful than that of the most graceful swaying elephant. She is more beautiful than Tilottamā.[33] Behulā Nācanī is her name. And she is religious—in each twelve months she makes twelve *vratas,*[34] once on every full-moon day; she does religious duties all the time. Your son Lakhindar is the destined groom of such a girl, and this is as it should be.

In hope of the feet of the Devī, Ketakā-dāsa sings: Biṣaharī is she who grants all boons.

XVII

Then the matchmaker said:

—Now, O Baṇyā, no more delay. Go to Nichāninagara. Take gifts appropriate for a girl, and go to meet your son's father-in-law.

[32] Heavenly nymphs, of whom Urvāsī was one. They have extraordinary beauty, and frequently entice sages from their meditations.

[33] Name of an *apsarī.*

[34] Religious vows for various kinds of observances in devotion to a particular deity.

The *sādhu* was overjoyed. He filled a pot with soft and sweet *sandeś,* and took with him clothing of great value. He took seven loads of the *sandeś,* and dressing himself in full, rich garments, he went to see the girl.

Sāya heard that Cāndo had arrived in Nichāninagara. According to custom he went forward, and, seated on seats brought out for them, he and Cāndo talked together. Cāndo said:

—When I heard the news from the mouth of the matchmaker, I came to meet you. We will be relatives by marriage, great merchant. In rank, family, and wealth, there is none greater than you. Let us then confirm relationship with one another.

Sāya the Merchant then replied:

—Your words are wise. You know of me, and I of you. I shall gladly give Behulā Nācanī to your son Lakhāi in marriage.

Janārdana was a clever matchmaker. He brought a *tulsi*[35] plant at once and placed it in the hands of the two men. And so the marriage was confirmed by interchange of *tulsi.* Sāya said:

—Then I shall give Behulā to Lakhindar.

But Cāndo then replied in these strange words:

—If your daughter is really chaste and loyal, she will be able to cook beans made of iron until they are soft. Only such a girl will be married to my son. This has been the practice of my family, down through the generations.

When he heard these words of Cāndo, Sāya laughed and said:

[35] A plant especially sacred to Vaiṣṇavas. Vows made on this plant are very strong.

—*Behāi*,[86] you have completely lost your senses. How can she boil iron beans until they are soft?

But seated on the forehead of the *sādhu*, Manasā made him speak:

—Ask your daughter. If she can cook those iron beans, she will marry my son Lakhāi.

So Sāya asked Behulā. And when they heard the question, all the people of the city laughed. Amalā said:

—O *sādhu*, you are a misery to men. How can a girl cook beans made of iron? Who sent that old Janārdana anyway, that miserable old man who made arrangements for this marriage?

So Amalā-sundarī wept in great distress.

—O Behulā, a good husband and family is not written on your forehead.

But Behulā replied:

—O mother, do not weep. I shall cook the iron beans.

When she heard this, Amalā was astonished.

—How can you cook iron beans, my daughter?

But Behulā consoled her mother:

—On the new moon day of every month I make a *vrata*, mother. Now have brought for me a brand new pot, with a brand new lid, and two and a half bunches of sweet grass. I shall fix my mind on the feet of Manasā; then I shall be able to cook the beans, no matter what the difficulty.

So Behulā Nācanī went to bathe, and the Mother of the World came to know of it. To deceive her own servant, Manasā went to the bathing place in the guise of an old Brahmin woman.

[86] Form of address for the father-in-law of one's son or daughter.

The old woman sat down on the edge of a *ghāṭ*.[37] Behulā went smiling to that *ghāṭ* and jumped into the water; and as she jumped she splashed some water on the feet of Manasā. The old woman said:
—You miserable little fool! Is your arrogance so great that you are blinded by it?

Behulā replied:
—I am the daughter of Sāya the Baṇyā. I am taking a bath in my father's tank. What is that to you? You are a nasty old woman. You tell me all about my faults, but do not see your own. You are in the way, sitting in the middle of the *ghāṭ*. I jumped into the water without realizing you were sitting there.

The old woman said:
—Perhaps then the fault is mine, due to my past actions. But come, let us both bathe peacefully here. Let us dive down, and see what comes to each one's hand.

So both dived down into the tank. Manasā came up with a conch shell and sandal in her hand; but Behulā had a golden bracelet. When she saw the bracelet, the Devī cursed her:
—In your bridal chamber I shall kill your husband, and you will gain only grief. But you will cook the beans of iron easily.

When she had spoken thus, she went away in her swan-chariot to her own place. Then Behulā knew.
—It was Manasā. She tricked me.

So she was disturbed in her heart, and wept, but went

[37] Place on the side of a river, usually with steps leading down into the water, on which one bathes and from which one draws water.

to cook the beans of iron. She had seen Mother Manasā; nothing was impossible to her now. She took a new unbaked pot and earthenware lid, and filled the pot with iron beans. She uttered prayers to Manasā, and meditated on the goddess. She lit the fire, and it burned instantly. And then the maiden cooked the beans. Manasā brought success to her—the beans became as soft as rice. She brought them out to Cāndo, and when he saw them, he was delighted.

—Surely, here is a most chaste and faithful girl! Give her to my son, O Sāya. We two are one. There can be no other way.

So when they had ascertained the entry of the sun into the proper sign, Cāndo pledged his son and went quickly home. When he arrived, he told it all to Sanakā:

—Today the arrangements for the marriage of Lakhindar have been made.

But Sanakā, weeping, replied:

—You quarrel and fight with Manasā. Due to her anger I have lost six sons. I do not know what will come of all this.

When he heard these words, Cāndo said:

—With this staff I shall smash the ribs of that One-eyed One!

Sanakā replied:

—O Baṇyā, if you abuse and curse a goddess, everything will be destroyed. An enemy of the gods does not last for long, for with a word the gods can bring everything to ruin. Listen to the story of these, who, the Purāṇas say, were ruined by the wrath of the gods. Rāvaṇa, for one, who seized the daughter of Janaka by the hair, was slaughtered with all his family. And when Śumbha and Niśumbha wanted to take Biśālakṣmī-Dūrgā in the Himālayas, their whole family of Asuras was destroyed. And Hiraṇyakṣā and Hiraṇyakaśipu of the Madhuvaṃśa, who willingly or not took fire in their hands were burned by it while still alive. Ah—he who seizes a black snake without a *mantra,* and he who is an enemy of the gods—his days are few.

So Sanakā-beṇyānī spoke, trying to convince him. But the *sādhu* replied:

—What can the Ceṅgamuṛi do? I shall have built a house of iron for Lakhindar's wedding day.

And so he summoned Viśvakarmā, the architect of the gods.

Kṣemānanda says, O Devī, grant your mercy unto me.

XVIII

Wary of Manasā, Cāndo summoned Viśvakarmā, and gave to him an *ārati.*[38] Then the *sādhu* said, with joined hands:

—On high Sātāli Mountain, O Viśvakarmā, build a house of iron. Build it high and well and tight, so that not an ant can enter. O Builder, by this house I shall save my son and my son's wife. Hear, O Viśvakarmā. Build this iron house on this great Sātāli Mountain, and then I shall be satisfied.

So he had brought a hundred thousand maunds[39] of iron, and together with the Builder climbed the mountain. They brought tools and weapons with them, and the Builder cut and scraped the iron and built the house. He built a

[38] The waving of lights and offerings before an image.
[39] A maund is about 82 pounds.

floor of iron, and iron walls in all the four directions. He made a roof, all iron, and scoured and polished the mountain's crystal slopes. And thus was built the house, tall and all of iron. He made the door frame, and on it hung a heavy door, and on the door he put a heavy iron lock. With planks of iron, shining like the thunderbolt, he made the frames, and on all four sides cut openings for windows. And then the Builder, when he had built the house, came once again to Cāndo. The Merchant gave him many gifts of cloth and jewels, and Viśvakarmā, satisfied, went home.

By the power of her meditation, Manasā knew what had occurred. She went to Viśvakarmā.

—My mind is finally at peace. My anger against Cāndo has finally passed away. Now it is all for you.

In terror at the Devī's words, the Builder bowed to her, humble before her wrath.

—Mother Biṣaharī, why are you angry with me? Do not be, for who can endure your wrath?

—Cāndo is my enemy. At his command you went and built a house for him on Sātāli Mountain. In that very house the *sādhu* will put his son and his son's new wife. I want to cause him grief. Go back again, and cut in the house a hole through which a snake might pass.

When he heard the Devī's words, Viśvakarmā was afraid and said:

—How can I do this? I have just come back from him, after accepting his gifts. How can I go to him again?

Manasā replied:

—If you do not go, I promise you that you will not escape my wrath. You know the consequences. If the Merchant asks you why you have returned, tell him that you have come to finish up some work.

So Viśvakarmā went again, and in a corner of the house he pierced a hole. He pierced the wall, and through it passed a thread.

Meanwhile Cāndo was sending messengers far and wide to summon his kinsmen. With *pān* the servants went to spread the happy news. And by the hundreds the highest people of the *Gandha-baṇik* caste[40] came to the *sādhu's* house.

In hope of the grace of Manasā sings Ketakā-dāsa, to whom the goddess told this story in a dream.

XIX

After the Builder had gone, Cāndo summoned Kājlā the garland-maker and offered *pān*. Kājlā was to make the marriage crown. With many kinds of flowers the auspicious signs were made; the garland-maker made a crown of gold on which were depicted, one by one, the symbols of many gods—the sign of the creator, four-faced, and he whose vehicle is the swan,[41] and the moon-haired one with the bull,[42] and Govinda on his mount Garuḍa, and Pavana on the deer, Indra on Airāvata, and Kuvera, Varuṇa, Yama, and the ten Dikṣapālas—these and many more did the garland-maker put upon the crown. Of all the gods, the only sign that was not made was the serpent-sign of Manasā. All

[40] *Gandha* literally means "perfumer"; here the meaning is probably more general: *gandha-baṇik*, "small tradesmen."

[41] The vehicle of Brahma.

[42] Śiva, who is depicted with the moon in his hair.

the people knew that Lakhindar had been born under the Nāga-sign and that Cāndo was grieving for his sons; that is why the serpent-sign of Manasā was not put down. But in the heart of Manasā, because of this, great fury grew.

In anger she went to the garland-maker and said:

—For this I shall bite your sons and make you childless. All the three worlds are represented on his diadem, except the serpent Kālasarpa. Why? Thinking me a mere virgin goddess, do you joke with me? Have you no fear? Do you not know the violence of the wrath of Manasā?

The garland-maker said:

—O Mother, do not wreak your vengeance upon me. I shall make your sign; I shall make the Kālasarpa, and conceal it.

Satisfied, Manasā went to her chariot, while the garland-maker made the Kālasarpa and concealed it. Manasā went to the Sijuyā Mountain, and the garland-maker to the house of Cāndo. The crown was brought to Cāndo, and in return the Merchant gave the garland-maker wealth and honor.

XX

By then all his kinsmen had heard the news and flocked to the house of Cāndo. From Burdwan and Ujānī and Saptagrām—from many places many merchants came. How can I name them all? Dhanapati, son-in-law of Lakṣapati, came, in the company of many merchants very great; the merchant Dhūsadatta came from Burdwan with many merchants, when he heard the invitation; Rām Rāya, Rāmadatta, Hari Sāu came, as did Sanātana, Śrihari, and Murāri, in anticipation; and Janārdana, Jagannāth, Jagadiṣ, Kālīdāsa, Śrīnivāsa, Bhagavān, and Nilāmbara the son of a very wealthy man; and Jādava and Mādhava, fast talkers, and the brothers Gopāla and Govinda came; Ananta and Acyuta came, when they got the invitation; the merchants Baṃśidatta, Śivasena, Śaṅkara, and Harisena came; and Saṅkhadatta, father-in-law of Cāndo, came on a palanquin, and with him many merchants—fourteen hundred merchants flocked to Campakanagara. All came to Campakanagara, where the groom Lakhindar was, dressed in a bridegroom's dress. On his body, smeared with turmeric until it shone like gold, he put a new yellow dhoti. He mounted his palanquin, like the moon rising in the dark of the evening. Lakhindar then worshiped his father and mother, and they started on their way; as they were going, a lizard made a sound above their heads—but no one heard.[43] And Sanakā kissed the bridegroom's face.

Tomorrow Lakhindar goes to his next dwelling-place. But today I do not know what the result will be, says Kṣemānanda.

XXI

Cāndo the Merchant, in great delight, went to give his son in marriage; and all the merchants of the family, great and small, went with him. Soft drums and other instruments played lightly; the people were in the highest spirits, forgetting themselves in fun.

In the distant land of Nichāninagara dwelt Sāya the Merchant; to that land went the handsome groom Lakhindar. It was evening when he went, and all the boys of the

[43] "Because of the magic power of the Devī." It is an inauspicious sign when the little house-lizard makes his ticking sound as one is leaving the house.

city played about him, throwing things. They placed Lakhindar in the bridegroom's palanquin and sang the *bekaṭa*[44] songs: the *bekaṭa* of Lakṣmaṇa was the hero Hanumān, the *bekaṭa* of Śiva was the bull; the *bekaṭa* of Kānāi, the wishing-tree of all, was the sweetness of Vṛndāvana; of Nandi, the *bekaṭa* was Mahākāla, and of Gurya, Kṣetrapāla; and the hero Kumbhakarṇa was the *bekaṭa* of Rāvaṇa; the *bekaṭa* of day was the heavenly form of the sun, and that of night, the moon; the king of birds, his *vāhana*, was the *bekaṭa* of Nārada; the *bekaṭa* of Indra, king of the gods, was Svarga, and Gaurī the *bekaṭa* of Goloka; of Ananta the *bekaṭa* was hell; of Bali the *bekaṭa* was the Ananta Vāsuki of the thousand hoods; the Bhāgirathi was *bekaṭa* to the Gaṅgā, the crossing of which cleanses sinful people; the *bekaṭa* of the north was the Himālaya mountains; of the east, the *bekaṭa* was the sun; of the west the *bekaṭa* was Vaidyanāth, who knows the beginning and the end, whose mind is fixed on the feet of Dharma; the *bekaṭa* of Yama was his powerful buffalo; and of Pavana the *bekaṭa* was his mount the deer.

To all these eighteen *bekaṭas* Cāndo the Merchant listened, happy; and when he had heard them, he said:
—Give them betel-*pān!*

So Kṣemānanda sings, meditating on the feet of Manasā.

XXII

In this way the groom's companions, with joyful hearts, arrived at night in Nichāninagara; they came all decked in

[44] Playful songs sung on the occasion of a wedding; one group sings a verse which refers to an object, here a divinity, the other group has to respond with a verse referring to the complement of that object.

festive colors, with sounding drums and instruments. As they were coming, they met a party of the bride's attendants on the road; there was scuffling and quarreling between the parties, and in the scuffle the torches were extinguished. When the groom's party had arrived, Amalā had distributed *guṛ*[45] and husked rice, and Sāya, when he saw his son-in-law, shouted aloud with joy. The young Baṇyā women, when they saw him, were completely charmed, and Amalāsundarī most of all. Sunilā, Subhadrā, and Nilā, daughters of Baṇyās, came to see, with Citrābatī, Kausalyā, and Bijayā. Rukminī, Rohinī, and the charming and chaste Satyabhamā, with Pārvatī, Tulasī, and Tilottamā; Hirā, Jasodā, and Jamunā, Līlā, Haripriyā, Sarbānī, and Madanā; and Indrānī came, and Śacī and Rupakalī, and with all these lovely and graceful women came Kamalā; and Daivakī and Draupadī, Kuntī and Ramanī, Sītā, Gaṅgā, Sulocanā, and Bhāratajananī, and with them many other lovely women came quickly. Some had put collyrium on one eye—they finished hastily, putting it on the other. Some had toe-rings on only one foot, others with armlets half-way up their arms; some had not yet hung necklaces on their throats, and others had earrings swinging from only one ear—the women of the city, in great haste, all came to dress and decorate Behulā. They rubbed her body with turmeric, and put sweet-smelling oil on her head. They combed her hair with a golden comb, and in many other ways prepared her for her groom. A string of pearls they wove into her hair, which hung upon her breast, fuller than the new cloud. The beauty of Behulā was greater than that of Lakṣmī, and the radiance of her face than the full moon. They

[45] A type of brown sugar.

decorated her with many ornaments, and put toe-rings upon her lotus-feet. At an auspicious moment two women performed the preliminary rites, presenting her with flowers and all sweet-smelling things.

Kṣemānanda says: O Devī, destroy your enemies.

XXIII

THE PUROHIT was seated, and then were brought to him a pair of earthen pots. Having purified his hands and mouth with water, he uttered the words of invocation, with folded hands, to sun and moon. He worshiped first Gaṇeṣa and then the other deities, Gaurī, Padmāvatī, Śacī, in the preliminary rite; in the *medhasāti* he worshiped with great reverence. He worshiped Vijayā and Jayā, giving gold to the Brahmins, and paid homage to Śāntibatī. With great care and in the proper way he worshiped the Dhritis and Basus[46] and Maṅgal-adhipati.[47] Worshiping the Divine Mothers also, he properly made the *dhārā*[48] offering. The Merchant, in great delight, made an offering of curd and *nandimukha* rice on leaves which he had placed upon the ground. And then the thread was tied from Behulā to Lakhindar, and there arose the sounds of rejoicing. Drums were beaten, glad sounds rang out, and Manasā was full of joy.

Behulā-sundarī, with propitious sounds and gestures, covered Lakhāi seven times, and in delight, wound the silken thread around him. And Amalā joyfully performed

[46] Classes of divinities.
[47] Name of a divinity and a planet.
[48] Name of a particular libation to Agni, god of fire.

baraṇa[49] before him with a basket of herbs, and sweet-smelling sandal, and many other things, surrounded by her women. She went to him, her son-in-law, and, worshiping, offered him *pān;* at his feet she placed her offerings of curd and, her palms together, gave him a gift of a diamond finger-ring. She annointed his forehead with myrobalan. The lamp was covered. Bringing the bridegroom's garland, the lovely bride with pleasure hung it on his neck; they looked into each other's eyes—and saw a vision of heaven. The priest had finished preparations, and at an auspicious moment the marriage was performed. With great delight in their hearts, Behulā and Lakhindar exchanged their first glance; but as they did, Manasā from her chariot felled the handsome Lakhindar with an arrow.[50]

Of the song of Ketakā-dāsa, the feet of Manasā are the highest cause.

XXIV

The companions of the bridegroom all wept inconsolably. —How can we return, with Lakhindar dead? Manasā has killed him with her arrow—she killed him as he was casting his first glance on his bride.

And so the bride's and groom's companions wept in sorrow, rolling in the dust.

—Why, O Merchant, have you defied the goddess? Have mercy on us, pardon us, O Mother of the World!

[49] Waving articles of offering before a bridegroom (or a deity).

[50] The term is *mohābān,* "arrow of enchantment," one of the arrows of Kāma.

And Behulā prayed:

—Forgive your servant, Manasā; forgive me for whatever I may have done. Why have you done this, O Śiva's daughter on your throne? I offer you a basket of bananas and curd and *khoi*—descend, O Bhagavatī, daughter of Hara. You have the form of Lakṣmī, for the pleasure of Nārāyaṇa; as Sarasvatī, you are seated on his left. As Sacī, you please great Indra; you are Śivā to great Śaṅkara. To Kandarpa you are Rati. Not born of woman, you are the infinite eternal Cause, and I have no hope or refuge other than your feet.

When she heard this supplication of Behulā, the Devī was appeased. She withdrew her arrow, and the youth again received the gift of life and rose up well. And when he saw this, Cāndo's heart was gladdened—he did not know that Lakhāi and Behulā were slaves of Manasā.

So they began the wedding feast. But the *sādhu* did not want to waste a single moment there, fearing what Manasā might do. He was anxious to enclose his son and his son's new bride in the house of iron. And so he said:

—Then let me bid farewell, *behāi.* We are going now to our own country.

Sāya the Baṇyā replied:

—Stay here the day. Rest tonight, and go tomorrow to your place.

But Cāndo said:

—Biṣaharī cherishes a bitter hate for me. She has already killed six of my sons. Who knows what she may do. I must constantly keep my mind alert, for fear of her. But I have built an iron house, upon a mountain. Today I shall take my son and his new bride to that house, and they shall stay in it. So bid me farewell, without regret.

When he heard this, Sāya said:

—I have given my daughter to your son. What I learn now—that you are fighting Manasā—strikes terror to my heart.

Cāndo replied:

—You need have no fear; bid me farewell. It is best this way.

So the two *behāis* embraced each other, and Behulā and Lakhāi mounted their palanquin.

But Amalā wept for her daughter Behulā:

—O my darling girl, you are youngest to six brothers.[51] Why did you not take a husband from nearby? How can I send my daughter into such a far country?

And all the friends of Behulā's childhood burst out weeping:

—You are going far away from us. Why must you go? How long will it be before we see your face again? How can we live without you?

But Behulā, despite the tears of all, mounted the palanquin at the auspicious moment. And the attendants moved out with the bride and groom, playing on forty-two instruments. The women of the city all ran to see. Thus did Cāndo, with his son and daughter-in-law, go to his own country. And Biṣaharī, from her swan-chariot, saw it all.

Cāndo's only thought was of what evil thing the Ceṅgamuṛi would visit on him now. A jest was in his mouth, but misery was in his heart. He said:

[51] The dearest child.

—Tomorrow, when I get up, I shall collect the wedding gifts.

XXV

CĀNDO DID NOT TAKE his son and his son's bride to his own house. Instead, he brought them quickly to the house of iron. There they lay down upon a bed of gold. Everything occurred as the magic power of the Devī had designed. Dhanvantari[52] was awake; a bright oil lamp was lit. And all around the iron house, on the mountain top, Cāndo set crows and peacocks and eagles and mongooses as guards. And in the room, in peace, Lakhindar and his wife played dice.[53]

They played with ivory dice, inset with gold and silver. At first, Lakhindar threw tens time after time, while Behulā, the servant of the Devī threw them only once or twice. But then Lakhindar began to lose the game; the dice did not fall well for him. So Behulā won the game, and was very pleased.

The night was coming on, and so the two lay down; and the Mother of the World was aware of all that happened. Again she consulted her companion Neto. Neto said:

—Do now what must be done.

So says Kṣemānanda.

XXVI

SO THE DEVĪ Biṣabinodinī summoned many snakes to go and bite Lakhindar. At the command of Vāsuki, the king

[52] Perhaps here a kind of generic name for *ojhā*, a magician with power over snakes.

[53] A following passage is filled with technical dice terms which I have been unable to identify, and have omitted.

of snakes, they all came forth; snakes from the depths of hell came to the Devī, when they heard her call: Puṇḍarika in great delight came forth, with five heads upon a single neck, whose sight was blurred, who had dark fangs beyond description; and with his vermilion-colored body the serpent Mahijaṅga, equal to his enemy Mahākāla—these and all the snakes of hell advanced, and the *kulukulu*[54] sounds were heard, destroying the meditations of the yogis. Quickly the hooded snakes came forth, and with them the crystal-eyed Talajaṅga.

And, Ketakā-dāsa says, when she saw them, the Devī was delighted.

XXVII

In the three worlds there are many snakes of Manasā. She called them all:

—Hear me, O great serpents! Who will relieve my troubled mind? On Sātāli Mountain there is a house of iron, and in that house Behulā and Lakhāi lie sleeping. The house is all of iron, even its door. And all around the house are guards, awake and watchful. Who then will go to bite Lakhindar? Who among you can do this?

When they heard the Devī, those serpents whose hoods were expanded like great lakes bowed down; none among the tough-skinned ones agreed to go. But then the serpent Baṅkarāja said:

—Give *ārati* to me, and I shall do the job.

So the Devī gave him flowers and *pān* and sent him forth. Baṅkarāja went swiftly in the first watch of the night

[54] Sound to herald a portentous event.

and peeped into the room. Behulā was awake, and when she saw the awful snake she rose up startled. She began to cajole the snake in sweet and charming words:

—Where have you been, O uncle?[55] I have not seen you for a long time, and have been lonesome for you. My heartless father pays no heed to me. How can I tell you how lonely I have been, that you have not come to look for me. But whatever anger you might have had with me, now put away; come, drink some fresh milk from this golden bowl.

When he heard this, the serpent went to drink the milk, his hood hung down. Behulā was not afraid, and as he drank she clamped a pair of golden tongs around the serpent's neck.

—You have drunk the milk. Now lie down and sleep in peace in this snake-basket!

Thus Baṅkarāja was captured. Waiting, the Devī finally said:

—Tell me, O my wise companion Neto, why doesn't he return?

Neto replied:

—Behulā may have made the snake a prisoner.

So in the second watch of the night Manasā sent a second serpent, and in the third watch a third. [And these Behulā captured in the same way, with honied words and milk]. So in the first three watches of the night, three snakes were captured. And then Lakhindar woke. Behulā said to him:

—My lord, I do not know what is happening. By great

[55] Father's younger brother, with whom the warmth and closeness of relationship is proverbial.

good luck your life has been saved three times from the wrath of Manasā. Three snakes have climbed the mountain and have come to this house to bite you. But when I saw them, I captured them with these golden tongs.

When he heard this, Lakhindar was distressed, and said:

—Beloved, hear me. I am very hungry; I am weak from lack of food. I am dry with thirst, and the breath in my mouth is like dust. O Behulā, if you want to save my life again, then give me food. I do not know what the Devī will do to me, but I know that I need food.

But Behulā replied:

—Hear me, lord of my life. I too am a prisoner in this room. Where can I get food? Ah, fate has written truly that I shall lose my husband on my wedding night—our only hope is at the feet of Manasā.

But then her eye fell on the rice and pot, auspicious things which had been placed nearby, and on the three hearths three coconuts used for offering. She took milk from the coconuts to use in cooking rice, and within the iron room she began to prepare the food. She tore a piece from the border of her sari to kindle the fire—and as the fire burned, the anger of the Devī burned twice as fiercely. Three serpents she had sent, and none had yet returned.

—The night is drawing to an end, and my defeat draws closer. Tell me, wise Neto, what I should do. Whom shall I now send to kill Lakhindar?

Neto replied:

—Let the Kālanāginī go to bite Lakhindar.

So Manasā called the Kālanāginī and said:

—The room is all of iron, as is the door; the guards are

watchful. So listen to me carefully, O Kālī. In the north-east corner of the house there is a hole, which Viśvakarmā made, just big enough to pass a thread. You can enter by that hole. O Kālinī, save me from disgrace! If you succeed, I shall give you all the wealth I have.

In the last watch of the night the Kālinī went quickly to the Sātāli Mountain. Who can interpret the enigmatic words of fate—the dead can come alive, if it is so written on their foreheads.

Within the room, Behulā was serving the food which she had cooked:

—Get up and eat, my lord.

But by the goddess' power, he had fallen fast asleep. She tried to rouse him, as he lay nodding drowsily, but she could not. And soon not only he, but snake-charmers, mongooses—all the guards, and finally Behulā herself, were overcome by sleep. And then the Kālinī, her breath raising the ashes of the dead fire in little clouds, entered the room through the thread-broad hole.

When she entered, she saw the beauty of Behulā and Lakhindar, Lakhindar lying in Behulā's lap as the fallen moon upon the earth; she said:

—Where should I bite that beautiful body? How can I kill him? But the Devī has commanded me. How can I deny her? I do not like this work that she has given me. I myself am the mother of six scores of snakes, and my heart is pained by this task of killing him.

Tears ran down from the eyes of the Kālinī; when she looked at Lakhāi, her heart was torn. Instead of biting him, she went to curl up at his feet. But just as she was doing so,

Lakhindar turned abruptly on his side, and his foot struck her fang. At this the Kālinī rose up:

—O sun, O moon, and all the gods! You are witnesses to this—it was not my fault. He kicked my tooth! It was not my fault!

Lakhindar woke, burning with the poison from the bite on his foot, and cried:

—Wake up! Wake up, Behulā, Sāya's daughter! Something has bitten me while you slept.

Then Behulā, in the waning of the night, woke suddenly and saw the snake. She seized the golden tongs and threw them; they struck and severed the snake's tail,[56] and Kālinī in anguish fled. Behulā wrapped the severed tail in the border of her sari, and then, bewildered, took her husband in her lap.

—My father-in-law fought with Manasā . . . this is the result . . . I am a cursed woman! What shall I do now? The whole night long I lay awake, but now . . .

And so, her dying husband on her lap, she wept there in the iron house.

So Ketakā-dāsa writes, with the blessing of Manasā.

XXVIII

The Kālinī had killed her lord, and Behulā held him in her lap:

—What has happened? What has happened to me? Why should my husband lie like this? His face, which was radi-

[56] In a version of the story told to me orally, the missile was a box of vermilion powder, which spattered on the snake; this is why the snake has red spots on its back to this day.

ant with the radiance of the moon, is turning ashen gray. His lips are closed . . . Ah, as I look upon his face, my heart is torn. What has fate inscribed upon my forehead? On this auspicious night, on this, my wedding night, my husband is dead. What shall I say to people? On this night of blessedness and beauty the daughter of Sāya has become the murderer of her husband. Who will call me "faithful wife," when they hear of this?

She put her face to his, her eyes to his; holding his feet, the young girl wept. She whispered into his ear:
—Take me with you . . . without you, my life will only be a stain upon the earth. She who is a widow might just as well drink poison. How can I bear it . . . rise up, lord of my life! Without you I have nothing, either now or afterwards.

So the unhappy woman wept, and found no solace in her grief.

The poet Kṣemānanda sings: the Devī will conquer, the Devī will protect.

XXIX

So, HER DEAD HUSBAND in her arms, Behulā wept.[57] Sanakābeṇyānī heard her weeping in the room, and when she heard, her heart dried up within her. She ran to see her son; she saw Behulā sobbing, and the dead Lakhindar on her lap. When she saw this her heart was torn, and tears fell from her eyes. She embraced her dead son, and wept:

[57] A repetitive section of Behulā's lamentation has been left untranslated.

—O Behulā, have you come here to bring me sorrow? What have you done to my Lakhāi? My son, my son, my baby Lakhindar, O son of a childless woman! This iron house was made for you . . . she has sent her snake to bite you . . . she has cursed me. There is no one left to give me *tilāñjali* . . .[58]

And then, mad with grief, she turned to Behulā with curses:

—Why doesn't the new vermilion in the part of your hair fade away?[59] Why are your wedding clothes not soiled? Why has the dust not gathered on the lac on your feet? O Behulā, miserable girl, your husband is dead, before his wedding night has reached its end!

Then Sanakā ran and said to Cāndo:

—O Merchant, the boy has been killed within the iron house!

And Cāndo, as if in pleasure, raised his staff and shouted:

—Good! It is good that she has killed him! What more misery can she bring upon us now? The Ceṅgamuṛi Kāṇī has finished the dispute.

Then he turned to his weeping wife in anger:

—She has killed him! Throw away her leavings! Go cut a banana leaf for me; I will eat baked fish and rice.[60] Manasā in her vicious anger has now taken seven sons. Is there no mercy in her cruel and spiteful heart?

[58] An offering of water and sesamum to the dead, which should be done by a son.

[59] This and the following remarks are insults; widowhood is scorned in older Indian society. Vermilion in the part of the hair is a mark of a married woman in Bengal.

[60] A non-Brahmin custom in Bengal is for fish to be eaten on the thirtieth day after a death, signifying the end of the period of mourning.

Kṣemananda says: Such is the mercy of Manasā. Give mercy to your worshipers, O Devī.

XXX

So LAKHINDAR DIED within the house of iron, and when Cāndo got the news his heart dried up; he trembled in his grief for his lost son. On that glad day he got the news and trembled, leaning on his staff. Lakhindar was dead. He said:

—Let there be no more fear. My feud with Manasā, which has lasted so long, is ended. There is nothing more which she can do to me.

But Sanakā cried:

—There was none as dear to me as my son! No one as lively and beautiful . . . but in your foul and violent anger you broke the goddess' pots and cursed her . . . Six sons are dead, and now my beautiful Lakhāi. By the anger of the goddess, seven sons were killed by snakes; *I* am the victim of her anger. How much did I oppose your quarreling with her; I did not look to her with sinful eyes. And now my heart dries up; how can I show my face to people in my shame? And when I look at your face, my breast is torn; the earth is covered with darkness.

The people of the city, hearing her wails, began to shout:

—Because of the *sādhu's* madness, what will happen to us? He has done an evil thing!

And the women, when they heard the story of Behulā, covered their ears with their hands. Her body was burning with grief for her lord. The people said to her:

—You are a most wretched woman. The god of fate has brought you great affliction; but you say impious words.[61] Why would you go floating on the water?

XXXI

For Behulā had said, in tears:

—I shall take my husband's body on my lap and float upon the river for six months. I shall, by the power of my former worship, make Manasā restore my lord to life. I shall fulfil my *dharma;* this I wish to do—let no one stop me. When I have done what I set out to do, I shall return. My debt to the Devī, which was written on my forehead, has been fulfilled. Build me then a raft of banana-wood, and make it ready for the trip. Lash the logs together, and hammer in bamboo pegs. Prepare the raft and float it on the water.

So writes Ketakā-dāsa, at the feet of Manasā.

XXXII

So they prepared the raft and floated it on the waters of the Gaṅgura, and brought it to Behulā. She got aboard it and took her husband's body in her arms. But Sanakā came weeping and said:

—O miserable girl, I have never heard of such behavior. A young widow should stay closed up in her house. Why will you take Lakhindar on the river? How do you know that Manasā will bring him back to life?

[61] Ketakā-dāsa or the MS seems to have transposed the sequence of events here; Behulā has not yet said the "impious words"; the impiety was in suggesting that the body not be burned. I have added the "had said" in the next line.

Behula humbly replied:

—My mother-in-law, you will have your son again alive in your house. Have a woman fill a lamp with a cowrie's worth of oil and light and guard it. That cowrie's worth of oil will burn six months. If in six months' time the lamp still burns, you will know that Lakhindar is alive. Or if a sprout comes out from boiled rice, you will know that your son lives. So take some rice, and put it in Lakhindar's golden dish, and plant it beneath the pomegranate tree.

And then she took a piece of charcoal and drew a peacock on the wall:

—And if in six months time this peacock spreads his tail, you will know your son is alive.

Then she bowed to all the people:

—Give me your blessings, that my husband may live again.

The people were grieved in their minds, their garments wet with the tears of their eyes. They fell at Behulā's feet and praised her, saying:

—Return home soon.

And so Behulā, upon her raft, drifted out upon the river.[62]

XXXIII

I SHALL RETURN home when my husband is again alive.

She drifted past Navakhaṇḍa and in three days' time passed Dubrājpur, her lifeless husband in her lap; she drifted with the twisting Damodār, past Jajhati and Govin-

[62] A section describing how Amalā, Behulā's mother, got the news of Behulā's decision, has been omitted.

dapur, past Gaṅgapur and Burdwan. The bamboo pins which held the raft together began to rot, and all around the raft the crocodiles, their backs like saws, and sharks and other creatures of the water rose to the surface and then sank down again. Behulā wept in terror when she saw them and clung closely to the corpse. So the rotting raft drifted, falling slowly into pieces. And Behulā uttered constant prayers to Manasā:

—Why, O goddess, do you bring such misery to her who is your servant? You can bring to bear your power where you will . . . be merciful—at least let this raft be whole again.

And so the raft was whole, and drifted slowly. Lakhindar's swollen body smelled with foul odors, but Behulā in increased love and dedication, said:

—This is better to me than the perfume of flowers.

The raft reached the Kejuya *ghāṭ*, at which there was a shrine of Manasā. Behulā went ashore and bathed and made her *pūjā*; for three days she worshiped before the earthen image of Manasā Biṣaharī, and fasted at the Devī's shrine, before the image. And then she heard a voice speak to her from the sky:

—At Surpur your husband will surely gain the gift of life.

At this she smelled again the putrid odor of the corpse; she finished her *pūjā* there and drifted on to Amadipur.

As she drifted on the river, she passed a man with elephantiasis sitting on a *ghāṭ* and catching fish. His legs were swollen horribly. He had four women in his house. And since he could not eat plain rice, he was always fishing at the *ghāṭ*. A wooden necklace hung on his neck, and from his ear there hung an earring made of a cowrie shell. He sat there, casting his hook from side to side and pulling in big fish.

The raft drifted close to where the man was sitting. When he saw the great beauty of Behulā he was astonished; he desired her.

—What country do you live in, lovely woman? Whose daughter are you? Have they found no one suitable for you, despite your youth and beauty? Why are you floating in the river on that raft? Come to my house. I shall make you chief among my women.

When she heard this, Behulā laughed:

—Vile man! You are so filled with foul disease that you can barely move. Why this desire for women? You fish all day and catch a little for your rice. You are like a dwarf, standing on a mountain to reach the moon. Should I go with you, to put on old torn clothes and rags, and live a wealthy woman? You lecherous old man—you think because you wear an earring in your ear that you seem handsome to me? Tell me why I should come to live with you.

The man replied:

—Hear me, woman. You have contempt for my disease—this shows you to be a woman of little knowledge. I keep four women in my house, and we sport together constantly. They eat the best of betel in their *pān,* they wear vermilion in their hair, and live together happily. The only problem with this disease is its odor. Come, be the fifth woman in my house. I shall make you happy, and shall sleep with you only with your permission. Come. You shall be the chief among my wives. I hear your sweet voice, and my heart will not be stilled—my heart is pounding, and my whole body is aflame. Come, steer your raft this way, I pray you.

Then Behulā, very angry, said:
—You see me and lust for my body. But before you cause me trouble, know that I am a faithful wife, and the power of my vow's truth can turn you into ashes.

The man replied:
—All right, then. As you float, I shall swim after you, and I shall finally catch you. You boast of chastity; you are beautiful, and a whore so proud a man with elephantiasis seems despicable to you. You float there on your raft, so righteous and respectable—I command you now. Steer here to the shore. I tell you, you will not regret it. Come with me to my house. I am not deceiving you. Why are you so hostile to me?

But Behulā went floating by. The man, anxious lest she escape, leapt into the water after her. But, his legs heavy with his disease, he could not swim. Behulā cursed him, as he drowned and cried:
—Save me! I cannot swim!

His nose and mouth filling with water, he cried out:
—Help me, beautiful woman! I know now that you are a true wife.

But at his plea Behulā only laughed, and took her husband's body closer in her lap. And so, with neither food nor water, Behulā floated many days.

Thus is the song of Manasā, sung by Kṣemānanda. Be merciful, O daughter of Śiva.

XXXIV

So SHE DRIFTED day and night, and travelers passing on the shore looked back again, so beautiful was she. She drifted on the raft upon the waves, the corpse upon her lap. Past impenetrable jungles and forests, across bottomless depths, the corpse upon her lap, her lips murmuring prayers to Manasā.

—At your feet, O Devī, is my only refuge and my hope.

The corpse smelled foully, but Behulā was firm. Her love increased as her husband's body decomposed. She beat away incessant flies which swarmed around the corpse; the worms and fishes swarmed night and day, and flies settled thickly on the body. However much she beat at them she could not keep them off; flies and mosquitoes entered the openings of the body; the bones became exposed, and how can I describe the sores and spots appearing on the rotten flesh? As many flies as she would beat away, as many more would come to take their place. They left their eggs and young on the body of her lord, and Behulā wept.

—His beautiful body, putrid and melting—how can I ever bring him back to life? My mind despairs.

The raft floated by a *ghāṭ* where dogs came down to drink. To the *ghāṭ* had come a huge black dog, wearily, his ears hanging down, extending his long tongue, to drink. Easily do dogs smell rotten flesh—it seems to them as the sweet smell of flowers does to us—and as the raft came near to him, he began to tremble. He raised his head and looked in all the four directions. He barked and ran about, sniffing the earth, and finally he saw. His heart began to pound with greed and lust at the corpse's smell, and he leaped into the water. Behulā, when she saw the dog, began to hiss "chi! chi!" to frighten him away. She screamed:

—Foul dog! May you be eaten by a crocodile!

Her curse was not in vain. For the raft had drifted such a distance from the dog that he, exhausted, had no strength to turn around and reach the shore. A crocodile seized him. And smiling in relief, Behulā drifted past the *ghāṭ*.

So writes Ketakā-dāsa, serving Jagatī.

XXXV

She came to a ghāṭ at which were men who levied toll; the guards, when they saw her youth and beauty, began to smile and joke:

—Stop here, woman. Why are you riding on this raft? Perhaps you are whore, eh? Are you going to sell your wares today at Jagatighāṭ?

As Behulā floated toward them on the shore, they laughed and called:

—What is that you carry in your lap?

Behulā replied:

—Hear me, toll-takers. Do not stop me. Rather, hear my prayer. My body is a woman's. But I am a wretched and humble girl. What do you want of me?

—You are very beautiful. Why do you try to trick us? Give us that great pile of jewels you carry in your lap.

And others said:

—Jump into the water! Catch her and bring her here!

When she heard this, Behulā replied:

—Would you jump into the water for no reason? This is the body of my husband, five months dead and rotting, which is in my lap. I am carrying him in hopes of restoring him to life. Another month I have to travel, before this can be accomplished. It will be done by the grace of the goddess, as is written in my fate.

When they heard this, and saw that what she said was true, they called her "true, chaste woman" and let her go. Behulā blessed them all.

XXXVI

She took her husband on her lap and drifted, in despair. The flies swarmed ceaselessly on her dead lord's face; as ceaselessly she brushed them off with the border of her fine silk sari. But with her husband's rotten flesh upon her lap, her heart could not be still. Day and night she drifted, carried by the current of the channel water. The jungles by the river were haunted by the forest-dwellers, tigers and lions; and hares and deer also grazed and wandered. By the mercy of the Devī, the beasts did not catch sight of her; they smelled the corpse and became restless, but nothing else.

But there were two brother jackals, Hukāi and Makāi, goat-stealers, who were standing on the riverbank with a pack of other jackals. They also smelled the corpse, and called out in their language:

—Throw the corpse overboard, O lovely girl! Do so, and give us life. For we have fasted seven days and nights. Give us the corpse and go home; your name will be forever famous if you do. Give us food—give us flesh to eat. You should be at home, fulfilling your family duties.

Behulā replied:

—O jackals, this corpse is all the wealth I have. He whom

you see, the odor of whose rotting corpse you smell, he whom you want to eat—he is my very life.

—But what do you hope for? Why do you carry the body on your lap?

—O jackals—and especially you female jackals—listen. My lord will again be restored to life. This is not too much to hope.

But when they heard this the female jackals said:

—Incredible! Never have we heard anything like this. A corpse cannot be brought to life. Hear us, girl. Draw near to the bank. Give us the corpse to eat. Go back home, and we shall return to the forest. Youthful and lovely girl, return home while you still have your youth and beauty. O shameless girl, to float like that upon the water!

In Behulā's mind there was anger at the jackals' words. She said:

—Let this talk go. No matter what you say, my lord will regain the gift of life!

The jackals went back into the forest, and Behulā drifted with the corpse past Usamanpur; through all these months, the vermilion in her hair did not fade at all. She drifted toward the deeps, the lair of the *bodālyā* fish.[63] Beneath the dark waters moved great schools of fish, and sharks, and alligators like floating *tāla* trees, and porpoises rising suddenly from the water, and beneath the waves great turtles and leeches. In that water the *bodālyā* fish all lived, great fish with heads and gills like blacksmith's bellows. The movement of their bodies churned the water, when they smelled the corpse. Then from out of the depths came the

[63] A large fresh-water fish, possibly the sheat-fish *silurus glanis.*

great fish, rising, swimming to the raft, and the greatest of them snapped and tore the knee-cap off the corpse. Behulā, with a scream, saw the fish and tried to beat it off. But, lusting for the corpse, it would not be driven away. So Behulā hid her husband's bones in the border of her sari, her mind in anguish; and all around her in the water swam the fierce *bodālyā* fish.

—You have eaten my lord's bones—how shall I bring him back to life again? But I shall utter *mantras* to Manasā with singleness of mind; I shall find you again, wherever you may go.

So she turned her endless miseries over in her mind, and the great fish swam around the little raft.

Behulā passed the *ghāṭ* of Hāsānhāṭi, and was carried by an adverse current to Narikeladaṅga. There she worshiped Biṣaharī's image. Floating off again, she came to Vaidyapur; and at the *ghāṭ* of Vaidyapur there was a Vaidya bathing. As the raft came close to him, the Kavirāja[64] said:

—Girl, turn your raft this way. I shall revivify that corpse for you. Why go further? I shall bring it back to life if you will spend three days and nights with me.

Behulā replied:

—Vaidya, those foul words be ashes in your mouth. I pray to Manasā, and doing so shall keep on drifting on this water.

So saying, Behulā drifted past Vaidyapur into the Ganges. She washed the corpse in pure Ganges water; but even that pure water did not destroy the poison of the snake.

[64] An epithet for practitioners of Ayyur-vedic medicine; the Vaidyas are traditionally physicians.

And so to where the three streams flowed in three directions went Behulā. So says Ketakā-dāsa.

XXXVII

At the Triveṇi, where three rivers come together, Neto came each day to wash the gods' clothes in a golden vessel. And now, as fate had written it, after six long months Behulā drifted to that very *ghāṭ*, close to the place where Neto came to wash the clothes. She tied her raft to an *okṛa* tree and went to bathe in the waters of the Jāhnavī, first muttering the *mantras* of Manasā a hundred times.

To the *ghāṭ* that morning Neto came to wash the clothes, and her little son came with her. Even though she begged him to go home, he paid her no attention. So he was bitten by a snake. His mother placed the writhing child dying on the *ghāṭ* and went on undisturbed to wash the clothes. When she had finished, she made ready to return to the eternal city of the gods. She bent and slapped the dead child on the back and muttered a *mantra* over him. At once the child rose up alive. So Neto gathered up the clothes in a golden basket. This same thing she did each day. And this day Behulā, hidden in the forest, observed it all. She said to herself:

—If she can raise the dead to life, she must surely be a treasure-house of power and of goodness. I shall fall at her feet and beg her; if she will say that special *mantra* for my sake, my hopes will be fulfilled.

And so, next day when Neto came, Behulā ran and clutched her feet. Neto said:

—O lovely girl, why do you fall thus at my feet?

And disturbed, she withdrew from her. As Behulā tried to tie the tresses of her hair to Neto's feet, Neto drew back saying:

—Do not weep so, do not weep . . .

Neto took her by the arms and drew her up. Behulā sobbed:

—True woman, hear my story, as far as I can tell it . . . Sāya Sadagara is my father . . . my name is Behulā . . . on my wedding night my husband was bitten by a snake . . . and for six long months I have drifted with his corpse upon the rivers . . . but now, how great is my good fortune! Raise him up again . . . you must be a great goddess . . . and I shall serve your feet forever. From today you are as dear to me as any aunt. You will see—you sit and watch, and I shall wash your clothes. Behulā is your slave.

But Neto said:

—Girl, you will not be able to wash them well enough.

So at the feet of Brahmanī sings Ketakā-dāsa, to whom she has been merciful in a dream.

XXXVIII

So Behulā clutched and held the feet of Neto, and in humility and supplication said words of praise.

—O Neto, you are as my aunt. For six months I have floated on the water, and now, due to former merit, I have met you. Hear my prayer—raise up my husband.

But Neto said:

—Do not fall thus at my feet, O lovely girl. I am a low-caste washerwoman—why do you fall thus at my feet?

Behulā replied:

—O aunt, I am saluting you as one should salute a benefactress. I shall wash your clothes for you, for I am your slave.

Neto said:

—But I wash the garments of the gods. If you do not wash them perfectly, the gods will curse you.

Behulā replied:

—Aunt, I know it well. Give me one piece to wash.

And again she fell at Neto's feet; so Neto gave her a piece to wash, and together at the Triveṇi *ghāṭ* they washed clothes in the golden vessel. The washerwoman washed them with soap, but Behulā rinsed them in pure Ganges water; the washerwoman washed them with *kiñcra* flowers, but Behulā washed them until they became as bright as the sun. The two washed clothes and spread them out to dry, and those which Behulā had washed were best.

When the day was drawing to a close, Neto took Behulā back to the city of the gods. She hid Behulā and went alone to court to bring the gods their clothes. The gods were sitting there—Brahmā, Viṣṇu, Maheśvara, Kuvera, Varuṇa, Yama, and the gods of the ten directions, and Ravi and Śaśi and the others, when Neto brought the clothes into the court. And when they saw the clothes, Śiva the Three-eyed One said to Neto:

—You have washed our clothes for many years. Why today are they especially beautiful?

Neto replied:

—O Hara, what shall I say to you? The daughter of my sister has come to my house to visit me. Today she helped me wash the clothes.

Thus said the washerwoman of the gods. Maheśa said:

—I have not met her. But your sister's daughter would be my granddaughter. Bring her here, that we might see her.

Hearing this, the washerwoman went quickly out to where Behulā waited, and she said:

—I know you are a dancer. I will take you now to the court of the gods. In the evening you will dance and enchant them.

So said Neto. Behulā replied:

—Aunt, when I go into the court of the gods, I shall sing most sweetly. I shall take with me a drum of *khayera* wood and a pair of cymbals. And I shall also take this snake-basket in my hands, and this pair of golden tongs.

With this the beautiful girl hung jeweled *nupur*[65] upon her feet and *kiṅkiṇī*[66] upon her hips, and went into the court of the gods. She wore vermilion in the part of her hair and collyrium around her eyes. A seven-stringed necklace was on her throat and earrings in her ears; on her wrists she wore conch bangles, and on her fingers rings: she was dressed as a dancer, a heavenly *vidyādharī*.[67] She took up her husband's dead and six months rotten corpse and went with the washerwoman to the court. She danced, and with her drum and cymbals sang most sweetly: the gods were charmed.

So says Kṣemānanda, at the lotus-feet of Manasā.

[65] Heavy anklets worn by dancers to give a rhythmic sound.
[66] A string of musical bells, worn by dancers around the waist and hips.
[67] A class of heavenly musicians.

XXXIX

THE GODS WATCHED her dance, enchanted. Her grace was that of the proud peacock, her song like that of the nightingale. Dancing, she kept the insistent rhythm. Now she hid her face with her sari's border, now she showed it, smiling. She danced to the rhythm of the drum, graceful as a floating cloud, bending the three parts of her body, twisting; and on her ankles jingled the jeweled *nupur*. She danced, and then she stopped, and sang as sweetly as the nightingale.

On one side stood Neto, watching the dance and playing the brass cymbals. Now she bent down with the rhythm, now she stood up straight and said to Behulā:

—Good, good, O lovely girl!

And on Behulā's hips sounded the rhythmic *kiṅkiṇī*. Behulā danced close to Hara; she danced to bring her husband back to life. Lifting and placing her feet, slow and gracefully she danced, moving with the grace of a swan. Her dancing and her sweet voice charmed the heaven-dwellers; they cried out:

—Good! Well done!

She did not miss a step in the rhythm of her dancing, and the minds of the gods were transported with pleasure, like that of the peacock at the return of rain. Her body and her hands moved gracefully, and in the *tribhaṅga* posture she sang sweet words. The gods all said:

—She dances well!

Then Śiva summoned Behulā and asked:

—Who are you, dancer? In what country is your home? Tell me truly; have no fear.

When she heard this, the lovely girl stopped her dance and spoke, in the court of the gods.

This song of the Devī, sung by Kṣemānanda, will grant all boons to those who are her worshipers.

XL

SHE SAID:

—As you ask me, O Three-eyed One, hear, O gods, a story of misery and sadness. My father-in-law is Cāndo the Merchant. Sanakā is his wife, and Lakhindar, their son, is my husband. I was married to Lakhindar on a full-moon night. But my husband's father was carrying on a feud with Manasā. On my wedding day that goddess sent a snake, which bit my husband. He died then, the poison of the *kālinī* in his body. So, drifting on the river, I have brought him here to bring him back to life. O gods, be gracious. Give him back the gift of life. Grant me this boon, great gods.

When he heard Behulā's words, Maheśa smiled.

—Who has the power to bring to life one who has been killed by Manasā? Only if Biṣaharī herself is graciously disposed toward you can your husband be restored to life. Who can grant this boon to one to whom she is opposed? Only Biṣaharī knows the remedy for this; therefore in your mind meditate constantly on her.

At the words of Hara, the other gods all said:

—Go, Neto. Bring Manasā here. Tell her that her desires will be fulfilled, that there will be established on the earth *pūjā* to her as Mother of the World.

So Neto went to the Sijuyā Mountain, that eternal place, refuge of Jagati.

—Praise be to Manasā. Neto the washerwoman holds her fan. At the feet of Manasā, Neto bows. Come, O Mother, come. The gods are calling you to court.

The mother of Astika said:

—For what reason do they summon me?

The washerwoman replied:

—Devī, I do not know. Come to the court and hear for yourself.

But Manasā remembered the affair of Behulā, and said:

—No, I shall not go.

But the washerwoman fell and clutched the feet of the Devī, saying:

—Surely, you must go, O Devī. Please come to the court of the gods. You cannot ignore the entreaty of a friend. Go to the court, O Biṣaharī . . .

When Manasā saw and heard these things, she was moved. She went to the court of the gods and took her place upon her throne. Behulā ran to her and clutched her feet.

—After six long months I have finally reached your feet.

Seeing Behulā, the goddess hung her head in shame. And when they saw this, all the gods began to smile. Maheśa asked:

—Why, O Manasā, did you cause Lakhindar to be killed?

Why were you so angry with Cāndo? To kill his son on his wedding night was a terrible thing to do—there was no reason for you to do such a thing to him. And now, if you are still opposed to him, who else can show him mercy? Give Lakhindar back his life again. This will cause your worship to be established on the earth.

While Hara was saying this, deceitful thoughts crossed Biṣaharī's mind. She said:

—Why do you say all this to me? Who is Cāndo? Who is Behulā? Who is Lakhindar? For a long time I have had no antagonism in my heart toward anyone.

But Behulā replied:

—O Mother, leave these tricks of yours. On the blessed night of my marriage, a black snake bit my lord Lakhindar. With a snake-basket and a pair of golden tongs I caught three snakes in the first three watches of the night. But when the Kālinī came—upon your order, Devī—toward the end of the night my lord was bitten. The serpent fled, but I struck it with these golden tongs and cut off its tail. The severed piece I gathered up.

Then, there in the court of the gods, Behulā removed the cover from the basket and showed the snakes—Baṅkarāj, Udāykāl, and Kāladanta, three most poisonous snakes. Seeing them, the gods said:

—Most certainly it was Manasā who caused Lakhindar's death.

Manasā replied:

—I know nothing about all this. What snake would bite the handsome Lakhindar?

Then Behulā, weeping, seized the feet of Manasā:

—Call the snakes into the court of the gods. The one whose severed bit of tail this is is the one which killed my husband.

So Biṣaharī summoned all the snakes, and great joy arose in the mind of Behulā. All the snakes, except the Kālinī, came. Behulā, when she saw this, wept and said:

—O Devī, I am an unhappy woman who has lost her husband. Why do you play these tricks on me? Be merciful to me. Summon the Kālinī.

Finally Manasā consented. Behulā fitted the bit of severed tail to the body of the snake and said:

—Hear, O gods! This is the one which bit my lord.

Caṇḍī saw in this her chance to shame Manasā before all the gods. She said:

—Lord of the Universe, this my daughter Manasā is indeed most good and true, having caused a snake to bite the husband of Behulā on their wedding night. Cāndo the Merchant is your servant. He put his son in a house of iron to protect him from Manasā's wrath. But into it there crept a snake of Manasā to bite him. You see what she is. Dhanapati Datta did not honor me, but I did not take his life because of that. He whose son was killed in that iron house will curse you, Manasā, while breath is in his body.

Then the Devī, thus chastened in the court of the gods, began to speak to Behulā honestly.

—Hear me, Baṇyā girl, Behulā Nācinī. Your father-in-law always calls me Ceṅgamuṛi Kāṇī. He has opposed me always. With his staff he has insulted me; with it, in his wrath, he has smashed my sacred pots. He does not worship me on my holy days, and he prohibits my worship in the houses of his people. Within his own court he speaks ill of me and insults me. For this I had his six sons killed and their wives made widows. For this I sank his seven ships in Kālīdaha. Even then he did not worship me. Finally I took his son Lakhindar, and because of this you have come here to the court of the gods and shamed me.

All the gods then said:

—Biṣaharī, Mother, you have been deceitful for no cause. We do not kill those who oppose us. The gods are angry, and request you to grant Behulā her boon, and save her husband.

Behulā also said:

—Do not be angry any more, O Mother. I shall make my father-in-law worship you. My husband and I will be your slaves. I have come to you after six months drifting on the water, and now, if you raise up my beloved, I shall honor your desire. O Manasā, grant this my dearest wish.

Thus, in the court of the gods, the Devī was disgraced.

—Forgive her sins, and raise Lakhāi again!

XLI

The gods sat looking on from all four sides, and Manasā sat amidst them, preparing to bring Lakhāi to life. She raised a screen of cloth around him and within it put the pile of bones. The Devī herself, with her lotus-hands, joined those bones which were scattered and loose. In six months' time Lakhindar's moon-like face, his eyes and ears, his hands and feet, his well-formed body, all had rotted away. For in him was the poison of the Kālinī snake. In his body

there was no breath; he was like a figure in a picture. But Manasā cleaned the bones and uttered a *mantra* over them:
—What do you do on the branch of the *simul* tree, O crow? O powerful Yama-crow, my son is bitten by the serpent's tooth. Seize the snake and eat!

As Biṣaharī said these things, meditating on Yama, slowly the poison began to descend.
—Make bones and flesh, O poison living in these bones; let the poison be drawn out from the body, O peacock!

Thus Manasā called to the deadly poison, and in response the poison began to descend.
—O black snake, the mongoose bites you. O blue poison, come to me. Let the poison be dissipated; let these bones join together once again.

So she spoke to the poison. And at the *mantra* the poison turned to water and left Lakhindar. Then she uttered the life-giving *mantra* to herself, and the breath stirred in him. As if awakening from sleep, Lakhāi arose. He gained the gift of life, and lay in the arms of Manasā. And then the Devī, having cast the screen of cloth away, showed the gods the live Lakhindar, and they, in joy and praise, showered flowers upon her.

When she saw her lord restored to life, Behulā, taking up the drum and cymbals, began to dance and play. But the *bodālyā* fish had eaten the kneecap of Lakhāi; he could not stand. Biṣaharī said to Behulā:
—Where is that fish? In what waters does he live?

And when she heard, she summoned Jālu and Mālu, and said to them:
—Jālu and Mālu, you two brothers, go and catch the *bo-*

dalyā fish and bring him here to me. Go quickly to the forest and prepare a net of hemp. Catch the fish and bring him here to me.

So Jālu and Mālu went and cut the hemp, and seasoned it in water, and wove the strands into a net. By the goddess' grace they soon caught the fish and took it to the heavenly city, to the joy of both Behulā and Biṣaharī. The goddess slit the fish's belly with a golden knife and took from it the kneecap of Lakhāi. She joined the kneecap to the leg, and once again alive and whole the handsome Lakhāi rose to his feet and stood. Then Behulā gave to him a cup of palm toddy and bowed low to the feet of the goddess.

Kṣemānanda says: Take away my sins, O Bhagavatī.

XLII

When her lord had been restored to life, with palms together Behulā stood before the goddess. At the feet of Manasā, in the presence of all the immortal beings, she humbly said:

—How shall I praise you? The land and the water, the heaven and the earth are your creation. You are the heart within all creatures. You are creator, upholder, and destroyer. You are the great god Indra, your truth is infinite. Giriśa was meditating on the beauty of your form when he destroyed the Disembodied One.[68] You are Nārīpurusha, the companion of Kāma, Sanātanī the mother of all. You are she whom the thousand-headed Phaṇīndra praises; you

[68] The god Kāma, god of love, who was burnt by Śiva for disturbing that ascetic's meditation.

are she under whose control is Bidhātā himself. O mother of Astikamūnī, Vāsuki is your brother, on whose head is the earth. You are the creator and protector of heaven, earth, and hell; the worlds all tremble for your mercy. Even the gods do not know how to praise you—how then should I, a lowly woman? What praises should I offer to your feet? In many lives I have worshiped you. And now has come that blessed day when I am granted my living lord again![69]

So Behulā spoke like this, praising Manasā, and then Lakhindar played the drum while Behulā danced. Close to Manasā, playfully, she danced and sang, and Manasā was enchanted. Behulā saw that she was pleased to grant another boon. She said:

—O Mother, put away your anger. Give me again alive my six brothers-in-law.

The Devī assented to her wish. She went to the house of Yama, and when he saw her Yama asked:

—Why do you come to my city, Manasā?

Manasā replied:

—Hear me, Yama. I had a quarrel with Cāndo the Baṇyā, and so I killed his six sons with poison. They are now in your city. But today, in the court of the gods, I was merciful: let them go again to their parents' house, having gained the gift of life.

Yama said:

—When you have bestowed your favor, Biṣaharī, who has the power to gainsay it? Take the sons of the *sādhu*. I shall not object.

Yama spoke, and Manasā bestowed her blessing on the

[69] A repetitive passage of praise to Manasā is omitted.

six sons of Cāndo who were in the city of Yama, and they came back to life. And again Behulā danced for joy, and said to Manasā:

—Grant me one last boon, Ṭhākurāṇī. In your great wrath, you took his seven ships with all their goods at Kālīdaha. This last petition I lay now at your feet. Raise them up again; let them be fourteen ships, by your blessing.

Manasā replied:

—Your wish is granted, and the seven ships are now fourteen, all laden with wealthy cargo.

Behulā said:

—My father-in-law is very stubborn, if when he gets all these returned to him he does not worship you. If he does not, we shall not enter the world of men; we shall return to you. Of this be sure.

Manasā said:

—Good! Good! Good! You hear, O gods, these words of Behulā. Cāndo will worship me!

Then a tumult rose in the city of the gods, and praise for Manasā. The joy of Behulā was very great—her husband, his six brothers, and fourteen ships were all restored. The captains and the helmsmen and sailors of the ships were also raised—this boon also Biṣaharī gave. They said farewell to the gods in the court, and the eight bowed low to the feet of Manasā. The fourteen helmsmen took their places in the ships; Behulā and Lakhindar boarded one, and the six brothers six other ships, and they set sail.

Ketakā-dāsa sings: Cāndo the Merchant is indeed fortunate.

XLIII

Floating down the waterways of heaven, the ships again came to the Triveṇi. Sailing all together, they came to Gāerpur, and sailed from there to Vaidyapur. The blessings of the goddess were in their minds as they sailed past all the places which Behulā had seen from the raft. They stopped at Narikeladaṅga, where Behulā worshiped the earthen image of the goddess, daughter of Hara. Putting cloth upon her head before the goddess, she prayed:

—May my father-in-law have proper inclination toward you, O Devī.

And the heart of Manasā softened toward her. The ships sailed past the place where the fish had eaten Lakhindar's kneecap, and they named it Bodālyā-*ghāṭ*. They sailed past the *ghāt* of the dogs; at the place where the eruptions had arisen on Lakhindar's body, Behulā told her husband of these things. They named the place Machiśvara. They sailed past the *ghāṭ* where she had seen the man with elephantiasis, and they named it Goda-*ghāṭ*. They sailed on constantly, past Gaṅgapur, and finally they reached Burdwan. The helmsmen steered the ships into the winding Dāmodār. Behulā's heart was glad—she had gained her dearest wish, her husband had been restored to life. Sailing through the night, the ships reached Navakhaṇḍa, and in the second watch Dubrājpur, and finally reached the *ghāṭ* of Campakanagara.

So writes Ketakā-dāsa, serving Kamalā.

XLIV

So at last they came to the city of their own country,[70] Behulā Sāvitrī,[71] as beautiful as a nymph of heaven, and Lakhāi, restored and twice as handsome as before, by the goddess' grace. They came to the Campatola *ghāṭ*, when it was night. On the ships, Behulā and Lakhindar talked of how to make their entry and make themselves known to Cāndo. Then Behulā, servant of the Devī, ocean of wisdom, summoned Viśvakarmā; she gave him *pān* and said to him: —Make for us a fan of great value and beauty, and paint on it the story of my father-in-law Cāndo and Sanakā-beṇyānī; then draw Behulā and Lakhāi. And draw pictures also of all the residents of the city.

Then she gave an *arati* and flowers and *pān* to Viśvakarmā.

Kṣemānanda says: O Devī, bless your worshiper.

XLV

At Behulā's request, Viśvakarmā gladly made a fan of highest value. Very carefully and beautifully he prepared it, lovely as the moon. He made a shaft of purest gold. It was so lovely that when one saw the fan and felt its breeze, his heart could not be still. The wonderful shimmering gold touched the heart with beauty; on the fan glittered a

[70] First they went to the place of Behulā's parents; that long section has been omitted.

[71] Sāvitrī by her deep devotion to her husband persuaded Yama, the god of Death, to restore him to life.

golden lotus, which shone and beautified everything around it. It was as if made from bits of the full moon and golden *kusuma* blossoms. How can I describe it—there is nothing to compare it to; it was as the brightness of the sun, which cannot be compared. To the brilliant gold, all eyes were drawn, as if by a rope of beauty. It was as if the moon had wept a teardrop on the earth. And on the fan were pictures most wonderful to see. By pictures, Viśvakarmā told in a special way the story of their past adventures. There were pictures of Cāndo and Sanakā, and in a room of their house the six widows of their sons. And there were pictures of all the inhabitants of the city, neighbors, and a picture of the iron house on Sātāli Mountain, with Behulā and Lakhindar. There were the scenes of grief when Behulā had departed on her raft. All these Viśvakarmā painted on the fan, and pictures of Cāndo's servants also. Then Viśvakarmā, with great pleasure, made the handle all of gold. He said to Lakhāi:

—Listen carefully. I have made the fan for you. From it you will get all that you desire.

Having said this, Viśvakarmā went to his own place. Then pondering, Behulā Nācanī said to her husband secretly:

—Lord of my life, hear what I am going to do—you will understand the reason for it afterwards.

Lakhindar replied:

—Whatever you have in mind, that is also my desire.

With these words of her husband in her heart, Behulā became a Ḍomnī.[72]

[72] A female member of the Ḍom caste.

At the feet of Manasā, Kṣemānanda describes those to whom Manasā was merciful.

XLVI

So taking the fan, Behulā donned the dress of a Ḍom woman, silver earrings in her ears shaking and jingling, heavy pieces of silver strung together around her neck. Lakhāi became a Ḍom and Behulā a Ḍomnī, and she constantly waved the fan. But hear now what was happening at the house of Cāndo.

Since the month in which his son had died, Cāndo had performed six times the monthly rites. It was on the day of the sixth month's rite that Behulā and Lakhāi returned. The daughters-in-law of Cāndo had gone to fetch water, six widows, water-pitchers on their hips. When they reached the Campatola *ghāṭ* they saw the ships at anchor in the water, and on one of them a woman. They said to one another:

—Perhaps she is selling something.

So they went to her and said:

—Ḍomnī, how much do you want for that fan?

The Ḍomnī said:

—If I get a hundred thousand coins I shall sell this fan. I shall not sell it for less.

She knew them all, but they did not know her; they could not guess who she was. They said:

—This playful Ḍomnī wants a lakh of rupees for it! Do you think we can earn that much by the breeze it blows?

Behulā replied:

—Your taste is common. Perhaps that is why you have become widows. But she who knows real pleasure, she who is really a lover of fine things would pay far more for it.

The six replied:

—Come, then, let us go to our house. We will show the fan to our mother-in-law.

Behulā said:

—All right, then, let us go. But first tell me for whom you draw this water.

Cāndo's daughters-in-law laughed and said:

—Today is the sixth monthly rite for the dead Lakhindar. We are daughters-in-law of Cāndo the Merchant, whom everyone knows.

When she heard this, Behulā smiled to herself. The six put their water-pitchers on their hips and left, the Ḍomnī walking behind them. When they had reached the house they placed their pitchers on the ground and went to tell their mother-in-law Sanakā of the Ḍomnī.

—O Sanakā Śaśurī, listen—a Ḍom girl has come with a marvelous fan to sell. And the most wonderful thing—she looks very much like Behulā. But she spoke sly words to us . . . she is outside now, Ṭhākurāṇī. Come, see for yourself. Please give her the price which she asks and get the fan.

So Sanakā went out to see the fan. Like the other six women, she could not recognize Behulā. She said:

—Tell me, Ḍomnī, what is your name? In what village do you live?

The Ḍomnī replied to her in these false words:

—My name is Behulā Ḍomnī; my father is Sāya Ḍom. My

husband's father's name is Cāndo Ḍom, and Lakhai Ḍom is my husband, living in my house. My birth was in a lowly family of Ḍom caste. We make baskets of all kinds, and winnows, and fans, and sell them in the city. By this, by following the custom of our caste, we stay alive. The price of this most lovely fan is a lakh of coins. See—it sparkles like the cool moon; its decorations are of purest gold; in every sandal-bearing breeze it makes, Spring seems to come. In time of scorching heat, it touches the body with a wonderful coolness. She who is a true lover of fine things will give me a lakh and more of coins for it.

These things Behulā said to Sanakā, and hearing the names, all Sanakā's former grief awoke. She began to weep before the Ḍomnī, saying:

—O *sati,* true woman, what does this mean? Is it possible that Behulā and Lakhāi have become Ḍoms? Yama has given me much sorrow. Ḍomnī, bring the fan to me, that I may seę it.

Hearing this the Ḍomnī, with face averted, placed the fan in Sanakā's hand. And when Sanakā looked at the fan, she saw her family.

So Kṣemānanda writes the Manasā-*maṅgal.*

XLVII

Sanakā-beṇyānī, when she saw the fan, saw that much was drawn on it. She saw her family. Behulā and Lakhindar were there, and all six sons, and fourteen ships. When she saw all this she said, in tears:

—I shall buy the fan. But first, tell me—who is it who knows how to make such things?

When she saw the fan, her heart was full, and grief welled up and burnt deep in her heart. Weeping, she said:

—O Ḍomnī, raise your face and tell me this. Ah, when I look at you, all my former grief and sorrow rises up to fill my heart. I cannot be sure . . . but tell me, are you Behulā? Tell me, tell me—relieve your heart and mine. If you are Behulā, I am your mother-in-law.

But the Ḍomnī said:

—But you are a Brahmin woman.[73] My caste is that of the lowly Ḍom. Because I resemble your daughter-in-law does not mean that I am she. I sell baskets from house to house. Why do you weep so?

Sanakā looked again closely at the Ḍomnī's face:

—On seeing you, grief for Behulā tears my breast, and my heart weeps. Your words do not satisfy me. I have never seen, nor have I heard of, such a fan as this. Who gave it to you? My son and all my family are upon it—Why?

The Ḍomnī only said:

—We know how to make such things.

Kṣemānanda says: Now hear the description of the true meeting.

XLVIII

So Sanakā asked for the story which was pictured on the fan, and Behulā said:

[73] It has been clear up to this point that Sanakā was a member of the Baṇyā or merchant caste; perhaps the term "Brahmin" is not used literally here.

—Hear me, and I shall tell it all. That girl, floating on the river there, a corpse held in her lap, is I. So weep no more —that indeed is I. I have brought my husband back to life, according to the promise I had made.

Sanakā said:

—Behulā, is it really you? Where have you come from? What has happened to Lakhāi?

Behulā said:

—Do not be distressed. Open the door, and look within the iron house. The lamp, filled with a mere cowrie's worth of oil, still burns. It was said that if that happened, you would find your dead son once more living, in your arms.

When she heard this Sanakā, anxious, opened the door of the iron room and saw the lamp was burning brightly. She saw too that a stalk was growing from the boiled rice. When she saw these things, her heart was gladdened, and she raised her arms as if she would touch the sky. She took Behulā in her arms and wept.

—O Sati Sāvitrī, tell me of this wonderful thing. Where have you come from? How have you brought your husband back to life again? Your birth was indeed blessed. You are the truest wife in all three worlds.

Behulā said:

—Do not be troubled more. But where is my father-in-law? Though he has carried on a feud with Manasā, he is now freed from his former curse. Make him worship Manasā—if he does I shall bring him back his seven sons and fourteen ships.

Sanakā said:

—What more could he want? Falling at his feet, I shall

make him understand. Nara, run and tell the Merchant that Lakhāi has returned, alive, and with him his other six sons, and fourteen ships!

When he heard this, Cāndo was beside himself with joy; weeping in his joy, he began to dance around his *hental* staff.

—Where is Behulā? Where is Lakhāi? If I could see in this city my dead sons once more alive, then I could worship Manasā!

At this the people of the city were delighted; to her father-in-law Behulā said excitedly:

—The fourteen ships are floating on the water at the *ghāṭ*. Come and see—on them are your six sons and Lakhāi. If you come quickly you will see them!

But not trusting the words of Behulā, Cāndo jumped up upon the wall, and from there he saw the fourteen ships floating in the river. When he saw this, his heart leapt with joy, and he raised his hands to touch the sky. All the people shouted praises of Behulā:

—Because of your goodness you have brought your husband back to life. Cāndo fought the goddess, but when he sees these things, he will surely worship her. By the goddess' mercy he has gained that which was lost—we also shall worship her in this and every birth!

But Cāndo, unrelenting, said:

—Only if those fourteen ships sail to this house across dry land will I bow to her. Only then shall I worship her. For only then will I know that Biṣaharī has brought all this to be.

The people said:

—*Sadhu*, you are mad. Ships cannot sail where there is no water.

But Behulā prayed:

—Mother Biṣaharī, I am your avowed slave. My father-in-law is stubborn and is still opposed to you. Though he has regained all his wealth, he still will not bow down to you. For my sake do this for him—by your serpents bring the ships across the land.

And Manasā felt this prayer of Behulā in her heart.

Kṣemānanda sings: Forgive our sins, O Bhagavatī.

XLIX

MANASĀ KNEW that to be accepted in the world of men, Cāndo must worship her. So with special joy she gave this order:

—Listen, powerful snakes, Cāndo, that most wicked-hearted man, still does not praise or meditate upon me. Hear me. Go and carry the fourteen ships.

So Jagati spoke, and gave *ārati*. And four hundred serpents went and took the ships upon their backs and carried them to the house of the *sādhu*. Seeing this, with joyful heart, Sanakā took her sons from the ships and with her daughters-in-law, went into the house. Incense was lit, the conch-shells sounded as the ships were worshiped. The Devī had been gracious to them, and all the people said:

—The merit of Behulā must be very great. Never has anything like this been seen. But even though all has been restored to him the *sādhu* does not worship the Devī's feet.

Sanakā herself then said to Cāndo:

—Hear, O Merchant. Now worship Biṣaharī, toward whom

you have had such hostility. It is by her blessing that our sons have been brought back to life, and that our ships have been restored. O you who are chief of merchants, I beg you, let your anger pass away, and ask her blessing; worship her sacred pots. There is nothing to be gained by further anger and bitterness. Give me peace of mind. Now worship her; do not ignore my prayer.

Thus, falling at his feet, Sanakā implored him and disturbed his mind.

So writes Ketakā-dāsa.

L

BUT THE SĀDHU paid no heed to Sanakā's words; though he had regained all that he had lost, he still refused to worship Manasā. Instead, he turned over in his mind the insult and disgrace which she had brought upon him.

—How shall I force my mind to meditate on Manasā? Shall I now worship her whom I have always fought? Shall I now fall at her feet? This is madness! I have cursed her, and called her Ceṅgamuṛi Kāṇī. Shall I now in repentance and shame bow my head and clasp my hands before her? To shave my head for her would be worse than death for me. I cannot find it in my heart to worship her. Shall I make offerings to Biṣaharī with this hand, with which I have worshiped my golden Gandheśvarī? Yet, my son's wife is a new Sāvitrī. I have my sons and fourteen ships. If I do not worship her, I shall surely lose all that I have regained.

The *sādhu* remained sunk in thought:

—Should I now abandon my quarrel and worship Jagati?

Meanwhile, Viśvakarmā made a pot of gold and decorated it with vermilion, and fashioned a *puṣpajhāra.*[74] On it was placed an unbroken *sij* branch, with bananas and unboiled rice and other things, and all within the house began *pūjā* to Manasā. In Campakanagara were nine lakhs of Baṇyās; they all came to the *pūjā* for Manasā. Faith in their hearts, they meditated on her.

—Appear to us, O Devī Biṣaharī!

To receive the *pūjā,* Biṣaharī with nine crores[75] of snakes descended to the earth. The Devī knew in her heart of Cāndo's hesitation, and was wary.

—I do not understand his actions; at any time he may strike me with his *hental* staff.

And so she said aloud:

—Hear me, Merchant. I have been against you for a long time. But now I would show you my mercy. Cast your staff away, O Merchant.

When he heard this, Cāndo smiled to himself.

—Do not fear my staff any more. It is by your blessing that I have gained what was lost to me. I shall worship your feet as should be done.

The Devī said:

—Throw away your staff.

Cāndo replied:

—Then I shall throw my staff away.

And Manasā granted him the highest blessing, and, descending to receive the *pūjā,* forgave all sins. In all the *sādhu*'s lands a glad outcry arose, and Cāndo worshiped her with many offerings.

So writes Kṣemānanda, the servant of the goddess.

[74] A vessel with a perforated bottom, from which a stream of water flows over a sacred object during religious ceremony.

[75] A crore = ten million.

Glossary

Airāvata Indra's favorite elephant and the prototype of elephants.
Ananta Śeśa, the serpent on whom Vishnu sleeps.
anna 16 annas = one rupee.
anusvāra a symbol indicating nasalization, employed more frequently in Sanskrit than in Bengali.
aparājita the name of a creeper or flower (*clitoria*).
Aparājitā "unvanquished, unrivaled"; an epithet of Kālī.
ārati the waving of lights and offerings before an image; an offering.
āśram a hermitage or monastery.
Astikamuni the son of Manasā by the sage Jaratkāru.
asuras demons, enemies of the gods (*devas*). There is a constant struggle in process between *devas* and *asuras*.
Aśvins twin gods who were the husbands of the Vedic sun god's daughter. They were believed to do good deeds for men.
Bābu 1) a form of address to a Bengali gentleman; 2) in indirect reference, a fop or dandy.

Bali overruler of the lower regions, including the Kingdom of the Nāgas, of which Vāsuki is the ruler.

Bālirājā son of Indra, the brother of Hanumān and Sugriva. In the *Rāmāyaṇa* Bālirājā attempts to usurp the throne from Sugriva and is killed by Rāma.

Baṇyā a member of the merchant community.

bandhuli a kind of flower.

behāi father-in-law.

Bhāgavatī "divine one"; "goddess."

Bhagirathi a tributary of the Ganges, or *Gaṅgā*.

bhaṅg hemp, hemp-leaves.

bhaṇitā the "signature line," in which the poet addresses his characters or comments on the situation. The word may also mean "prologue or introduction."

bhāṭs panegyrist-soldiers, whose job it was to sing the glories of the king, and in battle to stir the soldiers on to acts of valor. They also served as messengers.

Bidhātā the god of Destiny.

Biṣaharī a name of Manasā. Sukumar Sen suggests the meanings "she who destroys poison" or "she who holds poison."

bodālyā a large fresh-water fish, possibly the sheat-fish *seluris glanis.*

Brahmā a later form of the Vedic high god Prajāpati and the most important god of early Buddhist times. In later Hinduism he remains the creator of the world but is of secondary importance only. He is often depicted with four arms and four faces.

Burdwan a city in West Bengal, of long-standing importance as an administrative center.

cakora bird a fabled bird said to subsist on moonbeams.

campa a campaka flower.

campaka a sweet-smelling yellow flower.

Caṇḍāla an individual whose caste was not associated with one of the 4 theoretical divisions (*varṇa*) of society and who was therefore "outcaste" or "untouchable." In theory his occupation was usually the carrying and cremation of corpses or the execution of criminals.

Caṇḍī a fierce, blood-thirsty mother-goddess of Bengal; like Durgā and Kālī she has become identified with the consort of Shiva (Śiva).

caryā-padas ninth- or tenth-century Buddhist esoteric texts.
ceṅgamuṛi a derogatory term, the precise meaning of which is unclear. Sukumar Sen suggests "repulsive as a dirty shroud."
Damodar River a tributary of the Ganges, flowing past Burdwan in West Bengal.
devas gods. See *asuras.*
dharma "duty" or the obligation to live one's life according to the role allotted to one in the societal and cosmic schemes. See p. 171 ff.
Dharma the personification of *dharma.*
dhobi a washerman.
dhoti a long piece of cloth worn by men wrapped around the lower half of the body.
Dikṣapālas 1) guardians of initiation ceremonies; 2) guardians of the directions, i.e. the lokapālas.
Ḍom a low caste with many subcastes of different occupations. The Ḍoms in the *Manasā-maṅgal* appear to be basket-makers, but the term is also applicable to certain groups of wandering musicians, executioners, and burning-ground attendants.
Dvija "Twice-born," one who has undergone the ceremony entitling him to wear the sacred thread, i.e. a Brahmin, Kshatriya, or Vaishya.
Gaṇeśa the elephant-headed god, son of Shiva (Śiva). He is immensely fat; his symbol, and his vehicle, is the rat. He is also called Gaṇapati.
Gandharvas the heavenly musicians, who have a partiality for and a power over women. Their female counterparts were the *Apsarīs,* who enjoyed tempting meditating sages.
Gaurā, Gaurī "fair one," a name of Parvatī, the wife of Shiva (Śiva); also an epithet of Rādhā, Krishna's (Kṛṣṇa) favorite lover.
ghāṭ a passage or steps leading down to a river; a landing-place.
ghi clarified butter.
Giriśa "Lord of the Mountain," a name of Shiva (Śiva).
Goloka "the place of cows"; Krishna's (Kṛṣṇa) heaven.
guṛ a particular kind of brown sugar.
guru preceptor, teacher, spiritual guide.
Hanumān son of the wind and monkey-chief who helps Rāma conquer the demon Rāvaṇa in the epic *Rāmāyaṇa.*

Hara a name of Shiva (Śiva).
hāsya-rasa the humorous rasa.
hental a kind of date tree.
Indra storm-god and war-god of the early Aryans, who destroyed his enemies with the thunderbolt; under the name Śakra he remained one of the chief gods of early Buddhism; in Hinduism, mounted on an elephant, he became the guardian of the eastern portion of the universe and the ruler of one of the lower heavens.
Indrānī the wife of Indra; Sachi.
Iśāna a name of Shiva (Śiva).
Jagati "mother."
jāmādār a police officer.
Janaka pre-Buddhist King of Videha and traditionally Rāma's father-in-law.
Jaya jaya "victory, victory."
kadamba a kind of tree with golden blossoms.
kāhan a type of money; one *kāhan* = 16 *paṇas* or 1280 cowries; a rupee.
Kālasarpa "black snake"; the symbol of Manasā.
Mount Kailāsa a mountain in the Central Himālayas believed to be the home of Shiva (Śiva).
Kālī a mother-goddess, often portrayed as a terrible hag. She is felt to be a ferocious form of Durgā or Caṇḍī, aspects of the wife of Shiva (Śiva).
Kālidaha "place of the deep black waters," a place sacred to Manasā.
Kālidāsa court poet to Vikramāditya (probably Chandra Gupta II, late fourth and early fifth century A.D.) and usually considered the greatest of Sanskrit dramatists. Of his three plays which are still extant, the "Recognition of Sakuntalā" is the best known.
Kāma, Kāmadev the god of love, who shoots flower-arrows from a bow of sugar-cane strung with a row of bees.
kamalā "lotus."
Kānāi a name of Krishna (Kṛṣṇa).
Kāñci (Conjeeveram) a city in South India and center of the powerful Pallava and Cola kingdoms. In the early centuries A.D. it also had the reputation of a fine center of learning.

Kandarpa a name of Kāma.
Kāṇī "one-eyed."
kapināsa, kapilāsa (according to Rajyeswar Mitra) a stringed instrument mentioned only in the *Manasā-maṅgal* and in the *Chaitanya-maṅgal* texts.
kāvya classical Sanskrit court poetry.
Kāyastha a caste or cluster of high castes.
khayera a variety of Bengal *acacia.*
khoi dried paddy.
kiñcra, kiñjal a flower of the *nagakeshar* tree.
kiṅkani a string of musical bells, worn by dancers around the waist and hips.
Krishna, Kṛṣṇa "black"; the most important incarnation of Vishnu (Viṣṇu). He is perhaps most frequently worshiped in his pastoral and erotic aspect as the flute-playing lover (Krishna Govinda) of the cow-girls.
Kshatriya a member of the warrior or ruling class.
Kshetrapāla a name of Shiva (Śiva).
Kubera the god of wealth.
Kumbhakarṇa the brother of Rāvaṇa; he sleeps six months and gorges himself during the other six.
Kūrma the tortoise, second incarnation of Vishnu (Viṣṇu).
kusuma "flower"; safflower.
Kuvera the god of wealth.
lākh one hundred thousand.
Lakshmaṇa loyal brother of Rāma.
Lakshmi wife of Vishnu (Viṣṇu) and goddess of good fortune, usually depicted seated on a lotus and attended by two elephants. She was believed to incarnate herself as the wife of each of her husband's incarnations.
Lokapālas the guardians of the universe: *Yama* (the post-Vedic judge of the dead and ruler of purgatory) in the South; *Indra* in the East; *Varuna* (the Vedic guardian of the cosmic order but later the god of waters in Hinduism) in the West; *Kubera* (the god of wealth) in the North; *Soma* (the moon-god) in the North-East; *Vāyu* (the wind-god) in the North-West; *Surya* (the sun-god) in the South-West; *Agni* (the fire-god) in the South-East.

Mahākāla a form of Shiva (Śiva) in his character of destroyer.

Maheśa, Maheśvara a name of Shiva (Śiva).

mahut an elephant driver.

Mallik a title used by military officers given land and lower administrative positions under the Moghuls.

Manasā the snake goddess. Although she is sometimes vaguely identified with Durgā, her existence is autonomous.

maṅgal kāvya Bengali poems describing activities of particular gods and goddesses. Although dating from the fifteenth century and later, the *maṅgal* poems draw upon much older legends from both folk and Sanskritic traditions. See p. 247 ff.

mantra incantation, spell, charm, hymn in praise of a deity, sacred text or utterance.

Māruts in the Ṛg Veda, chariot-driving storm-spirits who accompanied Indra across the sky.

medhasāti the receiving or offering of an oblation.

Mogul a Muslim of Moghul origin; a non-Bengali Muslim.

Mount Meru the theoretical center of the world, of which the Himālayas were the foothills. The gods lived in mountains around Meru.

nagakeshar a kind of flowering tree which provides material from which dye is made.

Nāgas snake-spirits who were half-human with serpents' tails, believed to live in an underground city and to occasionally bestow wealth on mortals.

Nandi the bull on which Shiva (Śiva) rides.

Nārada a riśi, traditional author of the Ṛg Veda; in later mythology, a friend of Krishna (Kṛṣṇa); the traditional inventor of the *vīṇā*.

Nātha a yogic cult.

Nawab a Muslim ruler.

nim a kind of tree, the leaves and branches of which have a bitter taste.

nupur heavy anklets worn by dancers to give a rhythmic jingling sound.

ojhā a person who has knowledge of occult charms, especially those against snakebite.

pada 1) In Bengali poetry, a stanza or a couplet; 2) A Vaiṣṇava poem.

pāda in Sanskrit prosody, a "quarter" or line of a four-line stanza, varying in syllable length.

Padmāvatī a name of Lakshmi; the goddess Durgā.

pān a betel roll.

paṇa a kind of money; 1/16 of a kāhan.

paṇḍit a scholar.

Pāṇini a Sanskrit grammarian of the fourth century B.C.

Pāṭhāns tribesmen of the mountains of the Northwest frontier, famous as fierce raiders of the plains.

Pavana the god of the wind in the *Mahābhārata.*

Prabāsi "an emigrant"; the name of a Bengali literary magazine.

Phaṇīndra "serpent-king," a name of the cosmic serpent Śeśa in the *Mahābhārata.*

Prajāpati the creator god of the Vedas; the universe was created from the sacrifice of his body (by the gods, who appear to have been his children).

praṇāma homage; a form of salutation which involves bowing and touching the feet of the person addressed.

pūjā worship, homage; reverence.

Purāṇas texts containing a mixture of legend and religious instruction, dating in their present form from about the fourth century A.D. though much of the legendary material upon which they draw is far older.

purohit the chief priest in the performance of Vedic-period sacrifices; in later times a court chaplain; also, a priest performing rituals for a family or group of families.

rahāb the Muslim name for an ancient stringed instrument of the vina type, related to the European rebec.

Rāhu a demon who is said to be trying to eat the moon when there is an eclipse.

Rājput a ruling caste whose members were theoretically fierce and noble warriors *par excellence.*

Rākshasa a class of several kinds of demons. The term most commonly refers to those particularly evil beings haunting burning grounds, disturbing sacrifices and devouring human beings. Their chief abode was Laṅkā, in Ceylon.

Rāma hero of the *Rāmāyaṇa,* destroyer of the demon Rāvaṇa. He is also considered one of the incarnations of Vishnu (Viṣṇu).

rasa "flavor," a mood or esthetically refined emotion, dissociated from its counterpart in personal experience, conveyed to the audience by a poem or play. Classical esthetic theory felt that each work should have a dominant *rasa*. See pp. 10–11. The basic *rasas* were love, courage, loathing, anger, mirth, terror, pity, and surprise.

rati passion, sexual pleasure.

Rati the consort of Kāma, the god of love.

Rāvaṇa the demon-abductor of Sītā.

Ravi the Sun.

Rudra in the Ṛg Veda the unpredictable god of storms, of disease, and of healing, later identified with Shiva (Śiva).

Rudras beings supposed to have sprung from Rudra's body, regarded as lower manifestations of Shiva (Śiva).

Rukmiṇī Krishna's (Kṛṣṇa) first queen; see Śīsupāla.

Śachī a name of the wife of Indra.

sādhu "honest, pious, virtuous"; "a saint, a merchant, a usurer."

Sādhyas a class of semi-divine beings, variously twelve to seventeen in number, inhabiting a region between heaven and earth; in some texts they are identified with the *Siddhas*.

Sāhitya literature.

Sanātarū "the eternal"; a name of Durgā, or of Lakshmī, or of Sarāsvatī.

sandeś a sweet made from milk.

sannyāsi an ascetic, a man who has abandoned the life of a householder to become a mendicant.

Sarasvati the wife of Brahmā, patron of letters, music, and art, and the traditional inventor of Sanskrit and the Devanagari script. She is depicted with a *vīṇā* and a book, accompanied by a swan.

Śaśi the moon.

śāstras 1) later versions of the sūtras in verse; 2) any books of laws or maxims.

satī a chaste or virtuous woman, a woman who thinks, feels, and acts as a true wife should.

Sāyed a Muslim title, used theoretically for the direct descendants of Ali.

Shaikh, shekh one of a dissenting sect of Muslims; also a general term for Hindu converts to Islam; also a title applied to a particularly brave soldier.

Siddhas semi-divine beings inhabiting one of the spaces between earth and heaven (*Bhuvaraloka*); sages who have achieved semi-divine status through meditation.

sij a kind of tree sacred to Manasā.

simul the silk-cotton tree.

Śisupāla Krishna's (Kṛṣṇa) cousin and rival for the hand of Rukmiṇī, Krishna's first queen. In the *Bhāgavata Purāṇa* Rukmiṇī's evil brother Rukma persuades her father to marry her (against her will) to Śisupāla, from whose custody, however, Krishna abducts her on the morning of the wedding.

Sītā wife of Rāma and the epitome of the virtuous wife. Rāma won her hand in marriage at an archery contest.

sitar an instrument similar to and derived from the *vīṇā*. It has two layers of strings and a sound box made from a large gourd or from wood.

Śiva "the Propitious"; a name first given to the Vedic god Rudra, who may have gradually been identified with a pre-Aryan fertility god. His character is ambivalent; on the one hand he is associated with horror and destruction, and on the other, he symbolizes peace and asceticism. He is the lord of snakes and the patron deity of ascetics. He is most often worshiped in the form of a phallic emblem (*liṅga*). His mount is a bull (Nandi).

śloka 1) a couplet; 2) the meter of most of the Sanskrit epics, consisting of eight syllables to the line or quarter.

smṛti "remembered"; non-*śruti* religious texts, such as the *sūtras* and *śāstras*.

soma an intoxicating drink of the Veda, considered sacred and personified as a god.

śrāddh a memorial ceremony for dead relatives at which various offerings are made.

sṛṅgāra rasa the erotic rasa.

śruti, "heard" a term applied to religious literature which is believed to be literal, divine revelation, e.g. to the Vedas.

Sugriva the King of the monkeys and brother of Hanumān.

Sumeru Mount Meru.

Sundara "beautiful."

Surapati a name of Indra.

sutras prose texts of instruction, usually on the scriptures (*Śrauta sūtras*), on household religious ceremonies (*Gṛhya Sūtras*), or on human behavior (*Dharma Sūtras*).

Svarga one of the heavens.

svayamvara a ceremony at which a girl selects her husband from a number of suitors.

syāmarāya an epithet of Krishna (Kṛṣṇa).

tāla a palm tree.

Taltola a section of Calcutta.

tambura a stringed instrument which provides the drone of the tonic as a background in a musical performance.

tīla sesamum, sesame, jinjili; mole, freckle, spot.

tilaka A mark of sandal-paste worn on the forehead or on the bridge of the nose, sometimes as a mark of membership in a particular religious sect.

tribhaṅga a stylized dance pose, associated with Krishna, in which the body is bent in three places.

Umā a name of Parvatī, wife of Shiva (Śiva).

vāhana vehicle and symbol (e.g. Nandi is the *vāhana* of Shiva).

Vaidya a caste, the members of which are traditionally physicians.

Vaidyanāth "Lord of physicians"; a form of Shiva (Śiva).

Varuna the Vedic guardian of the cosmic order; in Hinduism the god of waters.

Vāsuki king of the Nagas.

Vasumatī the personification of the earth.

Vidyādharas heavenly magicians who could fly through the air and take whatever shapes they wished.

Vijaya legendary conqueror of Ceylon; also a name of Durgā in the *Mahābhārata*.

vīṇā a stringed instrument with a long fingerboard and two sound-boxes.

Viṣṇu, Vishnu to his devotees, the Universal God, of whom all other gods are but manifestations. He is usually depicted as blue in color, with four arms, holding conch, discus, mace, and lotus, seated on a throne, and wearing a crown and a holy jewel. His mount is an eagle with half-human face. At various times he has incarnated himself to save the world from destruction. His main incarnations or *avatārs* ("descents") are ten: the

Fish (*Mātsya*); the Tortoise (*Kūrma*); the Boar (*Varāha*); the Man-Lion (*Narasimha*); the Dwarf (*Vāmana*); Paraśu-rāma; Rāma; Krishna; Buddha; and Kalkin, the incarnation yet to come.

Viśvakarmā the Vedic architect identified with Prajapati; later the patron deity of manual labor and the mechanical arts.

Vrindāban a place sacred to Krishna (Kṛṣṇa).

Yakshas, Yakshasas a sort of gnome or fairy; supernatural beings who guard treasures.

Yama the god of death.